Secrets Among the Cedars

Intertwined Series

Book Two

By

SHERRI WILSON JOHNSON

Secrets Among the Cedars, First Edition
Text copyright © Sherri Wilson Johnson, 2015. All Rights
Reserved.
Cover design by Lynnette Bonner at
http://indiecoverdesign.blogspot.com
Cover images: Rachel by Kayla Johnson Photography
Nature photo: Cedar Key by Sheri Marsh McLeroy
ISBN-13: 978-1518601729
ISBN-10: 1518601723

SECRETS AMONG THE CEDARS

DEDICATION

To all the people longing to find their purpose in life, may God show you your calling and may it light a fire in you.

ACKNOWLEDGEMENTS

To my Lord and Savior, Jesus Christ—thank you for giving your life for me and for answering the Prayer of Jabez (1 Chronicles 4:9-10) I've been praying regularly.

To my husband, Dan, who keeps on believing that I can write more stories.

To Kayla, Seth and Thea, I couldn't be more proud to be your mom (and mother-in-law). Keep walking in the Lord. He'll never fail you.

To Phil, Katie, Andy and Fred for letting me use you in my book.

To Christy, Kellie, Jill and Jen: Thank you ladies so much for all your input!!

To Rachel Hendrix for letting me use her as the face of one of my favorite characters ever!

To all of my family and friends, for your love and support.

To my writing friends, for talking shop with me.

CHAPTER 1

Cedar Key, Florida

Kathryn Bellamy leaned against the steel pier railing and took a generous bite of her salted caramel ice cream which teetered over the edge of the waffle cone enveloping it. The creamy coolness slid down her throat as dolphins slipped through the water out to her right. The Gulf of Mexico's balmy salt-infused breeze whipped her hair away from her face and flapped her bohemian skirt and blouse against her road-weary body. It felt good to wear such freeing attire, so different from her normal suits she wore in the courtroom. After working at the courthouse for two solid years, seldom leaving the office before sunset, her hair and skin needed this kiss from the sun. Too bad she wasn't in Cedar Key for pleasure. This tiny fishing village below the Suwannee River would be the perfect place for her to relax and regain her focus on life.

Pelicans and sea gulls soared across the early evening orange and pink sky, and fishermen pulled their boats in beneath billowing clouds. A pelican balanced on the railing and waited for something to eat in the lapping water. Day's end was almost at hand. The six-hour trip from home northwest of Atlanta made Kathryn ache to stretch out on the king-sized bed at her rental condo. She might be here to research the Ezzo murder case, a make-it-or-break-it case for her career, but something about this sparsely populated island on the scrubby nature coast of Florida pushed her woes off the edge of the pier and out into the bayou.

She took another bite of her ice cream and licked her lips, but when whoops and hollers escaped from the people at the end of the pier, her enchantment ended. She squinted in the glare of the sunlight. A scrawny gray-haired man in a T-shirt and cut-off jeans whacked a well-toned and well-tanned young man on the back. What was all the fuss about?

Ice cream dripped down Kathryn's arm, and she took another bite of melting paradise. She wiped her arm and then tossed her soggy napkin in a nearby trashcan, filled with remnants of sunbaked squid and shrimp. Another roar of victory came from the crowd, and she couldn't help but direct her attention to the racket. Her curiosity ran away with her like a runaway buggy in the Wal-mart parking lot back home. Well, she'd have to meet the locals anyway if she was going to figure out the connection between the biggest murder case in her county and this dreamy spot, so she might as well start with this commotion at the end of the pier.

Kathryn marched toward the excitement, her new leather sandals clacking against her heels and then on the concrete. She ate the last bite of cone and rubbed her fingers together, the sticky ice cream coating her hand and arm. She should've gotten more napkins at the ice cream shop. She laughed and stepped around someone's cooler. Look where she was. The end of a pier with a bunch of fishermen and tourists in a place that felt like it was 5:00 p.m. twenty-four hours a day, seven days a week. Her stickiness didn't matter.

She stood on her tiptoes and looked over the crowd. Mr. Center-of-attention held a fishing rod, bigger around than any she'd ever seen before, with a shark, four-feet long at least, attached to its end. He wiped his sweat-dampened brow with a red bandana as the onlookers huddled around him. Kathryn's mouth fell open and alarm inched its way down her spine. There were sharks in the shallow waters of Daughtry Bayou? No way was she going to dip so much as her pinky toe in there. She'd stick to business while she was here and swim in the pool at her condo.

The buzzing crowd dissipated, but her curiosity carried her right up to the lucky fisherman to get a closer look at the shark before he released it back into its natural habitat.

"Hey! Don't throw it over yet. I want to see it." Kathryn examined the leather-like body and the ominous teeth of this notorious creature. "Oh, that gives me the heebie-jeebies." She shuddered and backed away.

When he laughed, a pair of smooth and creamy eyes, the color of her caramel ice cream and at least six inches above her own, knocked all thoughts of his big catch out of Kathryn's mind. His chestnut-brown closely cut hair, side-parted to the left, gave him the look of a schoolboy, but his well-trimmed beard detracted from the boyish guise. What was a polished man like this doing on a grimy fishing pier in this remote place? He fit into this scene as poorly as Daddy did at the bowling alley.

"Did I scare you?" This man, with an upper East Coast accent thicker than molasses on one of Aunt Anne's biscuits, gripped his fishing rod and held the shark's head down with his foot.

Kathryn gulped down the bulge in her throat and attempted to pull her attention away from his eyes—oddly familiar eyes. Did she know him? She stammered for the right words. "No…no, you didn't scare me." She swept her gaze across the shark, now flopping chaotically on the pier. "But he sure did." She pointed out to the water and shook her head. "To think I was considering going swimming in there!"

"Nobody swims in there." He laughed again and cut the hook out of the shark's mouth. Then he grabbed its tail with his left hand and squeezed its body against his chest with his right arm. He started to hoist it over the railing and back into the water, muscles bulging beneath his soiled tank top.

"Wait! Can I take a picture of it before you throw it back?" No one would believe the shark story if she didn't have proof of it.

"Sure. But hurry." The shark thrashed against his chest.

Kathryn yanked her phone out of her purse, clicked on the camera icon, and snapped his picture. "Thanks!"

He tossed the monster back into the sea. "No problem." He wiped his hands on the back of his shorts and extended his right one to her. "I'm Phillip. How ya doin'?"

Her cheeks burned. It had to be from the sun. At least that's what she'd blame it on. She reached out and accepted his hand, the waves crashing against the concrete pillars. "I'm Kathryn. Nice to meet you."

"Same here." Phillip pulled his hand away and looked at his palm. He raised his right eyebrow and tugged back the left corner of his mouth.

Kathryn gasped. "I'm so sorry! My hand is sticky from the ice cream I was eating a few minutes ago—before you distracted me with your catch." She captured the back of her skirt as a gust of wind threatened to rip it from her body.

"Oh, so it's my fault your hand's sticky?" He winked

and commandeered a hook out of his tackle box.

"Maybe not entirely." She giggled. "Someone on the sidewalk told me Island Trading Post had the best ice cream, so I had to try it. I picked the wrong time of day to eat it outside, I suppose, because it started melting before I made it to the pier." She held her right hand up, palm facing Phillip. "Anyway, your shark blood and fishiness trump my stickiness any day."

He tied a hook the size of her cell phone on the end of his line, placed on it a chunk of something that looked and smelled rotten, and released his line out into the brackish water. He lifted his sunglasses from where they hung on the front of his shirt and eased them onto his face then glanced over his bronzed shoulder. "Yeah, sorry about that. I've got some hand wipes in my tackle box there, if you need one."

"Thanks." Kathryn accepted his offer. Ice cream and bait were a disgusting combination.

"If you'd like, we could get an ice cream together this evening when it cools down. They don't close till 8:00 p.m."

A melted chocolate sensation flowed throughout her at this stranger's boldness. He was braver than most men she knew. "Oh, well, thank you for asking. I'm actually only here for a few days to work and don't have a lot of time on my hands."

He nodded and cranked his reel a few turns. "No problem. Just thought I'd offer."

She crossed her arms and encircled her elbows with her index fingers, something she'd done since childhood when she had a decision to make. Daddy had always warned her against doing it in the courtroom because he said it made her look indecisive. Right now, she was indecisive. She swayed and tapped her right foot on the pier's concrete deck.

What would be the harm in a little old ice cream? This guy seemed nice.

She dropped her hands to her sides and balled her fists. No! What was she thinking? This whimsical place had already caused her to loosen up a bit too much. She'd better get back to the condo where she wouldn't be tempted to fritter away any more of her time. "Thanks, but I really can't."

"The offer comes with a rain check. If you change your mind, I'll be here a while."

* * *

Kathryn tucked her left foot underneath her on the sofa and rubbed her right foot across Sadie's back, calming her woofing. The taupe-and-chestnut brindled Silken Windhound slept on the shag rug between the sofa and the coffee table, her silken, white legs twitching as if she were chasing a rabbit. They'd both slept through the entire night without stirring, the bed in the master bedroom like a marshmallow cloud. Kathryn sunk deeper into the over-stuffed sofa, which she'd be tempted to take home with her if the design wasn't seashells and sand dunes.

She'd never before seen an evening like last night. The sunset's pinks and purples majestically swept across her heart and freed her like an ensnared animal set free from a trap. The sea breeze, a welcome intruder, had rocked her and Sadie to sleep. After the drive down, which had tied her back and neck into knots, and the hours of research she'd done after dinner, a night like last night was the perfect ending to her week. Now she must get her mind off relaxation and back on the case. A win would guarantee her promotion to Senior Assistant District Attorney, and she'd be one step closer to her goals.

Kathryn walked Sadie, tossed her leash on the island's granite top, and opened the treat jar, white with black puppy paws on it. "Here you go, girl." Sadie swallowed the biscuit whole. Goodness, she acted as if she were starving. "Sadie! Shame on you. You couldn't have tasted that." Sadie whimpered and ran to her bed beside the sliding glass door.

Kathryn changed into her white Bermuda shorts, coral camisole, and floral-printed mesh shirt. Back in the kitchen, painted turquoise-and-yellow with starfish and crabs everywhere, she reached for her keys and purse. "I'll be back in a bit." Sadie's white ears drooped, and she whimpered again. "I'm sorry. I won't be gone long. I want to get a good meal in me and get a few things from the grocery store before I start digging further into this case."

She needed to nose around town to see if anyone knew about the pistol used in the murders. She groaned, stepped out on the covered porch, and locked the door. She'd walk to town, but since she'd have groceries when she returned, she'd drive.

She turned on to 8th Street at the end of the long crushed-shell path, then right onto G Street. Small bushes and flowering shrubs decorating the yards of cottages and condos led the way to town. She rounded the bend where G Street became 1st Street and inched her way along, studying a ramshackle building on stilts out in the water. It hadn't fared well against the storms and harsh sea winds.

That's how she felt these days. Life as an Assistant D.A. was often like trying to survive a hurricane without a storm shelter. Was the promotion really worth all this?

On Dock Street, where she'd gotten her ice cream and dinner yesterday, she parallel-parked in the only remaining spot in front of a sandwich shop, next to the pier entrance. She climbed the flight of stairs and entered the restaurant. Utensils clinked on dishes and the thirty plus patrons' voices hummed, while island music serenaded everyone from the overhead speakers.

"Welcome," the waitress wiping down a table in the corner called out and waved. "Feel free to seat yourself. The porch is open out back if you'd like to watch the fishing on the pier."

"Thank you." Kathryn adjusted her purse strap on her shoulder and tucked her hair behind her right ear. Her cheeks had to be as pink as a flamingo. She could stand in front of a courtroom full of people all day, but hated looking like a newcomer in a local spot.

"Thanks for joining us today!" The cook yelled through an open window behind the bar.

Kathryn waved and smiled, then scooted toward the porch door. Maybe out there she could sit alone without bringing too much attention to herself. She found a seat at a table with a side view of the pier. An older couple in bike shorts with helmets sat at the table facing the windows, but no one else occupied the porch.

The menu wasn't anything fancy, just biscuits and sandwiches. At least coffee shared a spot on the menu. She needed a lot of it today to get motivated to work. It might've been a bad idea coming to Cedar Key alone. Without pressure from her co-workers, she wasn't inspired to do anything but relax.

After she ordered a patty melt and fries from a waitress with a smile brighter than the sun, she slid the menu into its holder and yawned. Regardless of her good night's sleep, she'd stayed up too late reviewing the Ezzo file. They'd had enough suspicion to arrest Ezzo on murder charges, but would the charges stick? Ezzo knew the dead men from Long Island but that didn't mean he was responsible in any way for those deaths. But he had to be. The problem was: without a murder weapon, everything they had was circumstantial.

However, Louie Ezzo was a high-profile man who didn't seem to be the type of crime lord to waste his time or his freedom on his lackeys, Bobby Esposito and Manny La Duca, and he certainly wouldn't waste it on small town men from Perkins County like Stephen Diggs and Tommy Jones. It just didn't fit. Maybe she'd watched too many mobster movies, but a man like Louie Ezzo was powerful enough to hire someone to do his dirty work for him.

The weapon was missing, so that narrowed Kathryn's chances of nailing Ezzo with these charges. Witnesses had overheard Ezzo in jail talking to someone about Cedar Key and the gun. That's the only lead she had. Her investigators had come up empty-handed when they'd been here. Maybe she'd find a witness somewhere and figure out how Cedar Key factored into these murders. This community wasn't that large. She'd search out the Chief of Police after lunch and see if he could help her make some headway on this case.

The waitress brought a glass of water and silverware to the table, then hovered over the couple, who must have been regulars judging by their conversation with the waitress about their grandchildren. Kathryn sipped her water through a straw and let her gaze follow the pier walkway out to the end where she'd seen the shark and the terrific-looking guy from New York. Phillip, was it?

She pulled out her phone and opened her gallery of photos. She studied the picture of this handsome man with his shark. She sighed. They didn't make them like that back home. Something about him was familiar, but he was no homegrown country boy. Not with that accent. There was no way she'd seen him before.

The patio door opened with a squeak, and Kathryn turned her attention to the intruder of her peace and quiet. A giggle escaped her throat when Phillip shut the door behind him and nodded. She shoved her phone into her purse, heat rushing to her face.

Dressed in blue-and-white plaid shorts, a deep blue graphic T, and sandals, he surveyed the porch through eyes hidden behind black horn-rimmed frames. He made his way to her table, and her heart threatened to leap out of her chest, jump through the screened window, and flop into the water below as Phillip's shark had done yesterday.

CHAPTER 2

Girl, it's been too long since a man smiled at you. Remain in control!
She couldn't afford a distraction from this case right now no
matter how handsome that distraction was.

He shoved his hands into his pockets. "I see you
found the best seat in the house. How ya doin'?"

She wrung her normally composed hands in her lap.
"I'm less sticky than I was yesterday."

"And I'm less bloody." He raised his eyebrows and
chuckled. "Care if I join ya?"

"Well, I—well, sure." She motioned to the seat across
from her. She let her eyes lock with his, and the familiarity
registered with her again. Did she know him?

"Have you ordered yet?"

"I just did. The waitress should be back in a few
minutes to get your order."

He tapped his fingers on the table. "Oh, they know
what I usually order. But I'll eat whatever they bring me."

"So you're a regular?"

He scratched his beard. "You could say that."

She puckered her lips. "But your accent? You're not from around here."

"No, not originally."

"Let me guess. New York?"

"Upper East Side Manhattan." He shrugged his eyebrows.

"Oh..." What was a guy like that doing here?

He raised his index finger and smiled, dimples in his cheeks peeking out from underneath his beard. "Now before you go thinking I'm something I'm not..." He laughed.

So he had to prove he wasn't a rich kid. Whatever. "I wasn't." She made an X across her heart.

"I grew up in Long Island, then studied law and practiced in New York City for a while. I earned my own way. I didn't have everything handed to me, if you know what I mean."

Like a train slamming into a car across an intersection, her imagination collided with reality. "You're—you're an attorney?"

"Formerly." He cocked his head. "I'm in real estate now, with a side order of P.I. work on occasion. But I guess once you're an attorney, you're always an attorney. Right?"

Kathryn held out her right hand, and he accepted it with a lifted eyebrow. "Nice to meet you officially, Phillip, the attorney from Manhattan. I'm Kathryn, Assistant D.A. from Perkins County, Georgia, northwest of Atlanta."

"Perkins County. I don't think I've ever heard of it."

"You wouldn't have. It's a sleepy county, and my town is even sleepier."

"Sleepier than Cedar Key?"

She curled her upper lip. "No, not that sleepy."

"What's the name of your town?"

"Mitchell's Crossing."

"Sounds sleepy for sure."

"Compared to Manhattan, anything would sound sleepy."

Phillip chuckled. "True. So you're a lawyer?"

"Yes, when I have to be a grown up."

"Law must be treating you right. You don't look as beat up as I did when I was practicing."

"Is that why you quit?"

Phillip pursed his lips. "Uh, I got sick of having to defend people that I knew were guilty."

"Having to?"

"Yeah, my New York family is a bit unruly. Somebody's always getting into some kind of trouble, and I was obligated to defend every crook and thug they knew." He drummed his fingers on the table.

"Seems like they couldn't force you to defend them."

"Yeah, well, you'd have to meet them to understand. Anyway, I wanted freedom. So I moved to Savannah, but the same thing happened there. When my grandma moved back to New York, Ma recommended that I come take care of her rental properties. That's how I ended up here."

The waitress opened the door to the porch carrying two plates of food, and they pulled back their hands. She placed the plates on the table in front of them, grabbed the ketchup off the table next to them, and pulled two straws out of her apron. The older couple left their tip on the table and exited, waving goodbye.

Was Kathryn in a dream? What were the chances this guy would be an attorney? She never met attorneys outside of court. Of course, she rarely got out socially because her case load demanded too much of her time. What would it be like to walk away and never look back like Phillip?

"Kathryn?" He chomped off the end of one of his fries, revealing straight but not perfect teeth.

So there was something flawed about him after all. What a relief, considering Kathryn was a tangled mess of cobwebs. "Oh, I'm sorry. I guess I was distracted by the—the food." Yeah, that was it.

"Ms. Susan wanted to know if you needed anything else."

Kathryn scrutinized her plate and smiled at the waitress. "No, ma'am. Everything looks great. Thank you."

After Susan left them alone, Kathryn seasoned her fries with salt and pepper. "What'd you get?"

"Deep-fried Pollock on a hoagie bun. Wanna bite?" He held up half of his sandwich.

She protested with her hand. "Thanks, but no. You order that all the time?"

"Not all the time. A guy's got to think about his figure." He laughed and squirted ketchup on his fries.

"Yeah, right." She exploded with laughter.

After Phillip swallowed a mouthful of his sandwich, he pointed at her with a fry. "So what's your last name and what's your story?"

"Bellamy. And yours?" She'd spare him the details of her story. He'd get up and run if she told him.

"My last name? It's a mouthful. You sure you want to know?"

"Of course."

"Tagliaferro. It means ferocious warrior or something like that." He balled up his fists and shook them in the air. "A good, strong Italian name."

Kathryn's mouth flew open. Did he say Tagliaferro?

Phil Tagliaferro. As in Maria's ex-fiancé? No wonder he seemed familiar. She hadn't recognized him before because of the beard. The last time she'd seen him was at the wedding that didn't take place between him and her college roommate. Her spot as the maid-of-honor had disintegrated as soon as Phil discovered Maria in the groom's dressing room with the best man. She'd never understood why Maria favored what's-his-name over Phil.

"Imagine the teasing—"

Kathryn's face must have turned as pale as her legs in the wintertime because Phil stopped mid-sentence and placed his hand on her wrist. A fry lodged itself in her throat, and no amount of water would wash it down.

"Kathryn?"

She scratched her eyebrow with her thumb and cleared her throat. "Do you not recognize me?"

He knotted his brow. "I'm afraid I don't. Should I?"

She should reroute the conversation before their friendly bantering came to a grinding halt, but something compelled her to confess their connection. "I was...Maria's maid-of-honor." She squeezed her eyes tight then reopened them one at a time.

His face drained of its color. "You were?"

Kathryn eyed him, the table shaking from the tapping of his foot on the floor underneath.

A crease formed between his eyebrows, and with an eagle's stare, he studied her. "Yes, yes, you were."

A nervous giggle flew out of her like a caged bird upon release. Why did she sound like a Billy goat?

He pointed his long, slender finger at her. "Ah, Kathryn—I don't know why I didn't put the name with the face before now. I should've remembered. I'm sorry."

She waved her hands in dismissal. "No problem. How would you have remembered me?"

"How could I have forgotten you?" He winked. His glasses did nothing to disguise the spark in his eyes.

Kathryn took a generous bite of her patty melt and tried to ignore the heat that trembled throughout her. She'd have to dig deep to resist her curiosity about Phil. She needed to get away from her friend's ex-fiancé posthaste.

* * *

Phil took another bite of his sandwich and wiped his mouth with his fingers. How could he have forgotten Kathryn? Her Southern voice was like sweet tea and a Sunday afternoon on a porch all rolled up into one. She smelled like peaches and cinnamon, and she epitomized the Southern belle. Except for the fact that she was an Assistant D.A. He couldn't imagine this dainty lady, a hair taller than five feet, fighting her way to victory in a courtroom. Instead, he pictured her in a hooped skirt with a parasol tossed over one of her slender shoulders.

Kathryn's cheeks were rosy from his comment, and her eyes glimmered in the early afternoon light. Framed by her silky brunette hair, they looked like onyx stones set into her heart-shaped face, magnificent. Her wispy blouse of coral and green made them glow like a beacon from the lighthouse on Seahorse Key.

He dipped a fry in ketchup and popped it into his mouth. "Now that we know we've met before, you can call me Phil, and you can tell me what brings you to Cedar Key."

Kathryn brushed her hair out of her face. Her pistachio-colored bridesmaid dress from the wedding must have accentuated her glow on that day, especially with those eyes. Too bad he hadn't noticed. Judging by the way things had turned out, it was a shame he hadn't had the opportunity to meet her before she'd become the maid-of-honor and he'd become the groom-to-be.

Get a hold on yourself, man!

She finished her bite of the patty melt and wiped her mouth with her napkin. "I'm working on a case, and there's supposedly evidence down here that'll point us to the murder weapon."

"A murder case? Shouldn't your investigators do that for you?"

"They've already been down here. Everybody has been down here. No luck. I thought I might find a detail they missed or overlooked that would lead me to the weapon. Not because I'm a control freak or anything like that."

"Of course not." Phil snickered.

"I'm not. I promise. But evidence points to the fact that there's a connection between Cedar Key and that missing weapon, and I intend to find it."

"If you need a P.I., let me know."

"I just might do that."

"I'm heading back to Savannah Monday for a week, but I'll be around all weekend."

"I'm going back Monday too."

"Can I have your number? Just in case."

She made a clicking noise with her tongue against her teeth as if she was calling a dog. "How about you give me yours instead?"

Cautious and beautiful. A deadly combination. Phil wiped his hands on his napkin, reached into his shorts pocket, and pulled out his gold-plated business card holder. He opened it and retrieved a pristine card, extending it between his forefinger and middle finger, to the most cautious woman he'd ever met.

She accepted the card. "Sorry if I seem awkward. It takes me a while to unwind. I rarely get out of the office or take a vacation. This isn't even a vacation. I wish I were here for leisure. I—"

Her ponderings didn't distract him from mulling over their former connection. Was this brunette, electric-eyed classy lady still in contact with Maria? Better yet, was she a *Miss* Bellamy or a *Mrs.* Bellamy? Her right hand held no wedding or engagement ring, but Phil had learned that women didn't always wear their rings when they abandoned home for this Gulf coast escape. He shook his head at his ridiculousness. What did it matter? A friend of Maria's couldn't be a friend of his. Besides, she'd go back to Georgia, and he'd never see her again.

She snickered. "Sorry, I didn't mean to ramble." Her eyes sparkled like the dark marsh at high tide but were distant. Was the distraction caused by her duty or by her disinterest in him because he was Maria's ex?

"You weren't rambling." A school of dolphins slipped through the water beyond the pier, where black cormorants perched on weather-beaten posts, stretching their wings and puffing out their white chests. He pointed, his mouth full, and Kathryn squealed.

"I love dolphins." She clapped her hands like a young girl and smiled.

A sweet smile from a Southern girl. Enough to buckle his knees if he weren't seated. "I do too. I never tire of watching them."

"How could anyone?" She sipped her water and watched the dolphins go on their way.

Susan brought their tickets and a to-go box for Kathryn. Something dipped inside of Phil. He didn't want to say goodbye to this delightful woman. "I can't get over the fact that we've met before. How crazy is that?"

"Yeah, crazy." She grabbed her to-go box, reached for her ticket, and stood. "Well, I've got to get back to work. Thanks for the company."

"Here, let me get that for you." He tried to slide the ticket from her fingers. She had a death grip on it.

She tugged it away from his grasp. "No, that's okay. I've got it."

"Please, let me treat you to lunch as a welcome to Cedar Key and an open invitation to come back when you have more time to stay."

"Thanks, really. But I can't."

He could take a hint. He must have *QUARANTINE* or *PLAGUE* written across his forehead because she obviously couldn't wait to get away from him. Had he said something wrong? He shouldn't have brought up Maria again. Or maybe Kathryn was a Mrs. after all.

Then she tossed her sable hair over her shoulder with a swing of her head and pulled the porch door open. She turned to face him with a smirk. "It was really nice seeing you. I hope I run into you again."

He smiled, and a strange exhilaration shot through him from her sudden change of attitude. Something he hadn't felt in a long time.

CHAPTER 3

Had Kathryn really told Phil she hoped to see him again? She'd lost her senses. She should step out into the water and call for all the sharks to come bite her legs off. That was the equivalent of flirting with Maria's ex.

She needed another ice cream to cool her down from her time with Phil and to get her mind back on the case. Had he seen her sweating? It'd taken every bit of control she had not to take him up on the offer to pay for her lunch. What a sweet gesture. No one had done that for her in years.

She was not here to meet men though. She had to focus on this case and not let a man distract her. A handsome man. A friendly man. Maria's ex-man. *Ugh!*

She walked the short distance to the Island Trading Post and ordered a double scoop of chocolate chip cookie dough ice cream in a waffle cone. One bite and her mind forgot all about Phil. She'd been so busy over the last few years, she'd forgotten the pleasure of such simple things.

Kathryn reached for a napkin from the dispenser on the counter. "Excuse me. I'm an attorney from Georgia, and I'm investigating a murder case. Have you seen any suspicious activity lately?"

The young man with shaggy brown hair in a red Panama Jack T-shirt scratched his head. "No, ma'am, I sure haven't. Not much of that in Cedar Key. You could talk to the Chief of Police. You'll see him riding around on his golf cart."

Golf cart? "Okay, thanks. Great ice cream, by the way!"

She stepped out of the store, scanning the strip for a golf cart. There were at least ten. How would she be able to spot the Chief? Her ice cream dripped down her hand. Again. She'd focus on the case later. Right now, she was going to enjoy every bite of her treat.

She unlocked her car as her cell phone rang. She dropped her shoulders, set her to-go box on the roof of her car, and dug the phone out of her purse. If only she could ignore whoever was on the other end, but it might be D.A. Schwartz or the public defender's office.

Before she could speak, a piercing whistle sounded through the earpiece. She yanked the phone away from her ear, dropped her ice cream on the pavement, and flung her hand over the phone to muffle the noise. When the whistling stopped, she brought the phone back to her ear. Her ice cream rested in a puddle at her feet. "Hell-lo?"

"I'm watching you. Be careful, little lady," a distorted voice blared then dead silence.

Kathryn gasped and pulled the phone away from her face again. The call log popped up on her screen, but the number was blocked. Who could it have been? Although the voice sounded harmless enough, like someone's great-grandmother speaking through a handkerchief, her arms and legs tingled with adrenaline.

She tugged her car door open, but a white envelope

the size of a greeting card wedged beneath her windshield wiper distracted her. She grabbed it and her leftover food, and plopped down into her seat. She cranked the car, turned the air on high, then studied the chicken scratches on the front of the envelope. She ran her finger underneath the flap and slid out a sympathy card. A lock of white and brown fur fell to her lap. Fur that looked like it came from Sadie. She snatched it up and read the words scrawled on the inside of the card.

It would be a shame if something happened to your dog. Watch your step, Kathryn Bellamy!

Her heart hammered, and the knot in her throat prevented her from swallowing. Had something happened to Sadie? Had someone followed her here to Cedar Key? Tears slid down her cheeks, and she swiped them away with the side of her hand.

She wiped the beads of sweat off her upper lip, and her gaze landed on one of her crumpled business cards stuffed in the console—her name and title etched in thin black ink. What was it that put her on the verge of throwing that card and all her other ones in the trash and slamming her office door forever? Whose life and dream was she living anyway?

She'd do anything to make Daddy proud. It was Daddy that wanted her to be the first female judge in "good old boy" county and then ultimately Supreme Court Justice one day. Was that what had pushed her to where she was now? Or had she really wanted the position she held? Whichever it was, it was what had put her life in danger and had given her reason to doubt her dog's safety too.

She squeezed her eyes shut and shook her head. "You just need to solve this case and take a real vacation. That's all.

You've come too far to turn back now." Kathryn tucked the note in her glove compartment in case she needed it for evidence later and then put her car into drive and headed back to the condo. The grocery store would have to wait.

* * *

Sadie scurried to meet Kathryn when she returned to the condo after lunch with Phil. Kathryn's heart skipped a beat like an amateur drummer as relief flooded her to see the dog alive and well. She ran her hands along her coat searching for a missing lock of fur. Everything looked fine. Who'd have left such a disturbing note on her car? Was it someone connected to the Ezzo case?

After two hours of working on the case, pacing the ceramic tile floor, and talking to herself about the unlikelihood of Louie Ezzo's guilt, Kathryn needed a break. Her mind screamed for the missing piece of this puzzle. The Ezzo family was famed for crimes of all kinds, but rarely was a family member found guilty, especially of murder. Someone always took the fall while the suspected Ezzo went free. Four men were dead because of a botched drug deal, though, and Kathryn couldn't let him walk this time if Louie was guilty. She'd make sure he and anyone else involved went away for life.

Kathryn slipped her feet into her flip-flops and grabbed Sadie's leash. "Come on, girl. Let's go for a ride to town." Sadie abandoned her spot on her bed, where she watched the sea gulls and pelicans, and ran to Kathryn. Her bushy tail beat out a rhythm on the bar.

In the entryway, Kathryn caught her reflection in the mirrored clock, shaped like a ship's wheel, and gasped. Why did she look like the victim in a domestic abuse case instead of an Assistant D.A.? Couldn't she at least look good on the outside even if she felt like wet Georgia clay on the inside? If she'd known she looked this ghastly, she wouldn't have eaten lunch with Phil.

Phil? What did it matter? No matter how attractive he was, he was Maria's ex, and she was here to work.

She pulled her compact out of her purse and powdered her nose then smoothed on a bit of Dusty Rose lip balm. She smacked her lips and ran her fingers through her hair. "This will have to do, Sadie. I do believe you look prettier than me." Sadie woofed.

After Kathryn stopped for an iced cappuccino, she pointed her midnight blue Honda toward the city park next to the yacht club. She didn't need a heavy drink like this if she intended to keep the figure she'd worked so hard for, but she craved it because of the heat. Besides, ice cream had proven to be the wrong choice. The cappuccino would do the job. She needed the sugar surge if she was going to muddle her way through the details of this case.

The sky looked like ashes and billowy cotton. Hopefully, an evening storm wouldn't crop up before she got back to the condo. But storms had been brewing all week out in the Gulf, so there was no guarantee.

She pulled her car under the massive palm trees beside the picnic area, then hooked Sadie up to her leash and followed the paved path to the nearest table underneath a pavilion. The ocean lapped on the beach area, the only one in Cedar Key, and the palm fronds danced in the hot, salty breeze. Children laughed and played in the playground, and tourists bustled around the storefront area, filtering in and out of establishments with bags of goodies in their hands.

Kathryn breathed in and closed her eyes. She might form an addiction to this place.

"Let me drink this, Sadie, and then we'll go back to the condo. I don't want to miss one single sunset on the dock. How 'bout you?" She tugged Sadie's right ear; Sadie barked, drool sliding out of her mouth.

"Yeah, I hate missing sunsets too."

At the sound of the deep voice coming from behind her, Kathryn jumped and almost dropped her drink. The hair stood up on the back of her neck, and her back stiffened. Some watchdog Sadie was.

Sadie darted away from her toward the stranger, and she had no choice but to turn around. She locked her gaze with Phil's, as he squatted to meet her baby. Her breath caught in her throat, causing a hiccough to erupt from deep within, and she covered her mouth with her hand. What was he doing here? Had he followed her? Maybe he was the one behind the threats. Kathryn reached for her keys and positioned them between her fingers in case she needed to defend herself. Sadie certainly wasn't going to do it.

Not seeming to notice the strange reaction he'd caused, Phil complimented, "Your dog is amazing! What kind is she?"

"She's a Silken Windhound."

"She's beautiful."

"Thanks. I wish everyone around here felt that way."

"What do you mean?"

After Kathryn explained to Phil about the threatening note, he responded with obvious concern stamped across his face. "I can't believe anyone would threaten her." He ruffled Sadie's ears and stood, pulling his white V-neck T-shirt down over the low-slung waistband of his faded jeans.

"I agree." Kathryn sighed and arched her right eyebrow. She tried to ignore the toned muscles bulging from beneath his shirt. He looked great in white. He'd probably look good in any color though. Why had her mouth suddenly gone dry? It had been too long since she'd been this close to a handsome man in a conversation outside of the topic of law. "She's supposed to protect me from strangers." She tugged at the leash and rolled her eyes.

Phil crinkled his brow. "But I'm not a stranger."

"To her you are. I suppose I should've gotten a Rottweiler." Sadie wagged her tail and whimpered for Phil to play with her. Kathryn tightened her hold on the leash and dragged her back, shoving her keys into her pocket.

"Am I bothering you?"

She felt a pang in her chest. She shouldn't have been so rude. "No, of course not. But you are following me, right?"

"No way! I live here. Remember?" He shrugged his eyebrows. "I always stop at my favorite spot to watch the clamming boats come in before heading back home." He directed his attention toward the dock adjacent to the shops.

Was there no escaping this man? She smiled but groaned and returned to her seat. "Favorite spot?"

"Yep. You can't beat the ambiance."

"Is that what you call it?" She giggled.

"Of course." He held up a sack he'd held underneath his arm. "Care if I join?"

She held up a finger. "On one condition."

"Okay, shoot."

"Don't feed Sadie any of whatever's in that bag…"

Phil tucked his legs underneath the table and sat on the bench opposite Kathryn. "Deal."

"…no matter how hard she begs." Kathryn laughed and sucked on her straw. Then she grabbed her forehead and scrunched up her face.

"What's the matter?"

"Brain freeze!" She stomped her foot on the ground. Like that would help.

"Put your tongue on the roof of your mouth and hold it there."

She squeezed her forehead again. "What?"

"Just do it. Trust me."

Kathryn pressed her tongue hard up onto the roof of her mouth and within seconds, the brain freeze disappeared. "Thanks. Where'd you learn how to do that?"

"Oh, we Italians know all sorts of useless things."

"We Southerners know a lot of useless things too." She laughed. "But that wasn't so useless. You saved me a lot of pain."

Phil bowed his head and folded his hands. He whispered words Kathryn couldn't discern and nodded several times. He was praying? She wouldn't have guessed he was a man of faith. Since he was, he must be trustworthy.

Phil looked up, opened the bag, and pulled out a colossal cinnamon roll.

Kathryn burst into laughter. "You're going to get so fat eating like that."

"They're good!"

"I know they are. But they'd be the death of my waistline."

"No, you're so thin; it'd take a lot to kill your figure."

Kathryn froze mid-slurp. Had her heart stopped beating? This guy was slicker than her driveway on an icy winter morning. She had better proceed with caution, or she'd be metaphorically hydroplaning in no time.

He wiped icing away from the corner of his mouth with his thumb, his cheeks a touch rosier than before he'd made that comment. So the big New Yorker could blush after all. His beard couldn't disguise his embarrassment. "Did you figure out anything more on your case?"

Kathryn shook her head. "I studied the files for hours. I think the weapon, a .22 caliber pistol, is hidden somewhere out there." She pointed to the Gulf.

"What?"

"Witnesses say it was transported here, and the evidence was washed away. So far, we've found no connection between the suspect and Cedar Key."

"I'm glad to help, if you'd like me to look over your file."

Her gaze traced his face, landed on his lips, and then returned to his eyes. Was he trustworthy? It didn't matter. She couldn't ask for help from such a new acquaintance. "Thanks, it's classified. I hope you understand."

"Absolutely." He smiled and shoved the last bite of his cinnamon roll into his mouth. "How long have you been practicing law?"

"About five years, not counting law school internships."

He licked his fingers. "What's been your most interesting or memorable case to date?"

"Besides the one I'm working on now?" Kathryn sipped on her drink and followed a boat from the yacht club pier until it disappeared behind the buildings on Dock Street. "I guess I'd have to say the Clark Buchanan case out of South Carolina. He was in exports but made most of his money exporting drugs. He was arrested in Georgia and let out on bail until his trial. He went home to his wife, Cora, but took off one night and was never seen again. Until he turned up dead, that is."

Phil's eyes widened. "Dead?"

"Yes, someone he owed a chunk of money to came after him and shot him down."

"How long ago was this?"

"Just last year. I spoke with his wife, and she'd left town just before he was killed. I was afraid that whoever killed him would come after her."

"Did they?"

"No, she ended up at a ranch in South Georgia and later married the owner's son. They own a B&B. I've often thought about stopping by sometime and meeting her. In fact, I might do that on my way home."

"Sounds like an interesting case." Phil tossed his sack in a nearby trash can. "So do you talk to Maria much?"

Kathryn choked on her drink. This man was going to be the death of her. If he wanted to know about Maria, why didn't he just call her himself? "No, I haven't spoken with her since she moved back to New York. She sort of erased Georgia from her mind."

"I guess it's easy to do when there are bigger and better things waiting on you. I'm glad I missed that train wreck. Lucky for me, I moved to Savannah right before she returned to New York."

"I'm sorry she did that to you."

He removed the cap from his water bottle and gulped the drink down. "Don't be. I dodged a big bullet."

"Really?"

"Yes, definitely! If we'd married, we'd probably be divorced by now. Or she'd still be cheating on me."

"I wish I'd known it was going on. I would've said something. You didn't deserve that."

"Water under the bridge. Life goes on. And all those other clichés people say. Right?"

Kathryn shrugged. "I suppose so. It still had to hurt a lot. Rejection stinks."

"Yeah." He steepled his fingers on top of the table and drummed their tips against each other. "If I remember correctly, forgive me if I'm wrong, you had a boyfriend at the time."

Kathryn didn't want to talk about Zeke. Not with Phil anyway. It had taken her a year to recover from their break-up. She blew out a big breath. "Yes, I did. That was a long time ago though." She stood. "So…I need to let Sadie take a walk before I head back to the condo."

"I'll walk with you, if you'd like. There's a path along the water's edge."

Kathryn pulled her keys out of her front pocket as they approached her car parked in front of the city park. "Well, I had better get back before the sun goes down."

"Oh yeah, you want to see the sunset." Phil cut his eyes sideways at her.

"Right. And I don't want to be out after dark." She brushed a stray strand of hair away from her face.

"Maybe you should give me your number."

"In case you need me to come rescue you?"

"Ha!" He stepped back.

"I'll call you if I need anything. Thanks." After Sadie jumped into the car, Kathryn climbed in after her and shut her car door. She looked up into those caramel eyes for what she hoped was the last time. Her heart couldn't handle all the fluttering this man caused. What did it matter though? He was Maria's ex, which made him off limits.

So why couldn't she stop thinking about him now?

CHAPTER 4

Kathryn parked in the side lot of the grocery store and left Sadie in the car. A grilled steak for dinner and a swim in the pool afterward might cheer her up since she hadn't solved the case yet. She walked along the mural-covered wall of the store, stepping around the front of a beat up yellow pickup truck.

Kathryn tugged the glass door open and stepped up into what looked more like a convenience store instead of a full-fledged grocery store. The prices were probably sky high. She grabbed a battered blue plastic basket and found the produce section to her right. She chose a large potato to bake and a bagged salad then headed for the meat department all the way in the back. After she picked out a t-bone the size of Texas, she strolled up and down the rest of the aisles and let her thoughts drift back to the case.

How would the charges against Louie Ezzo stick if his gun couldn't be located? Maybe she could stay here a few more days. She'd be cutting it close if she remained any longer since the trial was in two weeks, but she needed more time here to find the gun. If only Ezzo's defense attorney hadn't asked for an immediate trial based off the fact that the weapon hadn't been found and Ezzo was sure there'd be no conviction, she'd have years to work on this case. But everyone was entitled to a speedy trial, and that clock had already begun to tick.

Kathryn found her way to the front of the store to check out. Three men stood near the register, encircled by the odor of cigarettes, and stalked her with their eyes. The one with greasy brown hair lifted his chin and gave her an arrogant smile. Another winked at her with beady dark eyes. The third man studied the floor. Could one of these suspicious looking guys be behind the threats?

Kathryn hurried to the register and placed her basket on the counter. "Hi. How are you?"

"Good." The skinny man behind the counter with tattoo sleeves running down both arms took her items out of the basket and scanned them with the barcode wand. He didn't seem too eager to make her feel welcome at all.

"This seems to be a place a lot of people in town would visit. And I'm guessing a lot of vacationers come here too. Have you heard anyone talking around town about a Cedar Key connection to a murder in Georgia?"

He shook his head and placed her salad and potato in a bag.

"How about anyone trying to unload a gun?"

"No." His voice sounded like sandpaper scratching across glass.

"What about a man by the name of Ezzo?"

He stopped with the steak in his hand, half in the grocery bag and half out, and looked at her with bloodshot amber eyes. The three men, now huddled in the corner by the bread, scurried out of the store like cockroaches when the lights come on in the middle of the night.

"Did I say something wrong?"

"No." He shifted his attention from her face to outside the store and back. "Look lady, you don't want to go sticking your nose in places it don't belong."

She put her hand high on her hip. "What do you mean?"

"You're new here, right?"

Kathryn nodded. He didn't have to know she was only here for the weekend.

"There're a lot of things you don't know about the way things are done in this town."

"Like what?" She challenged him with an arched eyebrow.

"We're kind of like the edge of the world. Ya know? If the world was flat. People come here with their secrets, and they leave 'em here. Those secrets are better left buried."

"If you know something, you had better tell me."

The man placed the steak in the plastic bag with trembling hands and glared at her. "Mind your business." Obvious fear hid behind his boldness.

"What would you think if I subpoenaed you for the Superior Court in Georgia?"

He gulped and his Adam's apple bulged. "You're a lawyer?"

"You bet I am. Now what do you know?"

"You'll have to subpoena me." He shoved the bag of groceries at Kathryn. "It's on the house."

"Oh no, it's not!" She tossed thirty dollars at him. "Keep the change. And consider yourself subpoenaed." He didn't have to know that she couldn't subpoena him without having his name. Kathryn flung open the door and rushed out onto the sidewalk. She bolted around the side of the building to the parking lot, and the three suspicious men darted behind the building. She unlocked her car and found Sadie awaiting her return unharmed. Kathryn pressed the pedal to the floorboard. She had to get to the condo without someone following her.

* * *

Fifty feet out in the water at the end of the covered dock, Kathryn sat with Sadie by her side basking in the orange sunset. Katydids chirped in the grasses and fish splashed to the surface of the water feeding on bugs. Kathryn sipped coffee from a seashell-adorned mug, her mind drifting back to her run-in with the store clerk. He knew something. That gun was here in Cedar Key, and she had to find it. But what if she didn't?

She needed to call the D.A. and let him know she'd had no success yet. Why had she thought she could find the gun? Her investigators and the detectives hadn't been able to. *Way to go, Kathryn.*

She'd made it look like the people who worked so hard for her didn't know what they were doing, and here she'd failed too. Daddy would be ashamed of her. But then again dear old Dad might not be. Hadn't he always told her that the way to get to the top was to use others as steppingstones? Taking others down for your own gain was always okay in Daddy's eyes.

That's what he'd done to Mom. She'd paid his way through medical school by working every job she could find. And what did he do to thank her? He cheated on her. Now he was married with a new family. The only way Kathryn felt she could get his attention and make Daddy happy would be to push her way to D.A. then to judge and then onto Supreme Court Justice. Then maybe he'd be proud of her? Maybe he might love her?

Could she do it? There had to be something else she could do with her life. Something that really mattered. Putting away criminals mattered, yes, but there was so much hard work and no time for Kathryn to enjoy anything else. That's one of the reasons Zeke left her. Her job wasn't family-friendly. So he moved on.

Kathryn brought her cup to her lips again with care and played with Sadie's ears. Dolphins glided across Daughtry Bayou. If only she could go with them. They seemed so carefree. Would she ever do something with her life that would bring joy?

The fishing line pulled inside her reel, and the end of her rod bent toward the water. Kathryn set her mug on the dock and grabbed her rod. Something big had to be on the other end. As long as it wasn't a shark, she'd be okay. The last thing she needed was to go over the edge of the dock into the dark brine.

She pulled back on the rod, and it bent nearly in half. She reeled until her wrist felt like it would break. What was on the other end of that line?

When she finally got her line reeled in, a small ray flipped and flopped at the end of it. A beautiful creature, but not anything to brag about. Kathryn stepped on the barbed tail, removed the hook with her pliers, careful not to get nailed with the barb, and flipped the ray back into the water. She put a fresh piece of squid on the end of her line and sent it out as far as she could. She reeled in the slack and returned her thoughts to the case.

In the file, a statement from a witness continued to

badger her. Something about a honeymooning couple? What would a honeymooning couple have to do with a murder weapon? If the gun was out there, where was it? Phil wanted to help her find it, but could she put aside her attraction to him and work to solve this case?

Kathryn's hands ached from holding the rod, and her shoulders begged for a respite from reeling, so she reeled in the line. She cleaned up her fishing supplies, scooped up her mug, and grabbed Sadie's leash. "Come on, girl. We're not going to solve this case sitting out here on the dock."

As they stepped with care down the narrow walkway in need of repair, the hairs on the back of her neck and on her arms stood to attention. The Gulf breeze blew the palm trees and the bushes surrounding the condo. Could someone be hiding in them? She ran across the patio around the swimming pool and shoved the back door open. Sadie followed her inside. Kathryn locked the door.

Although no one pursued her and she had once again let her imagination take over all sanity, a scene from a horror film played in her mind. Why was it that the girl always ran upstairs to get away from the bad guy leaving her only option for freedom the bedroom window, where she'd have to jump to her death to escape? Or worse, lay on the ground with broken ankles unable to get away from the perp, who always ended up back outside by the time she jumped? Kathryn was smarter than that.

Or was she? Hadn't she just locked the back door, making it more difficult for her to escape if someone was inside with her? She scurried throughout the condo checking for an intruder. Sadie stayed right at her feet but didn't seem to be on alert. After a thorough check in every closet, underneath every bed, and in each shower, Kathryn relaxed her shoulders.

Mom always said that God watched out for her. It didn't often feel like He cared about her life or protected her, but if anybody could protect her, He could. Or He'd send someone to do it. Kathryn refused to be intimidated or let the Ezzo case ruin the splendor of Cedar Key.

* * *

At 7:00 a.m., beams of sunlight streamed in through the skylight and peeled Kathryn's eyes open one by one. She stretched and yawned then her hand landed on Sadie's head. Sadie was sprawled out on the other side of the bed with her head on the pillow next to hers. Kathryn slipped out of the covers, careful not to wake her companion. Maybe she could have a cup of coffee before Sadie's morning walk.

She glided through the hallway, feeling as carefree as a feather, toward the kitchen and started a cup of coffee. She pulled up her email on her phone and composed a message to D.A. Schwartz.

I need to run a few things by you before I leave Cedar Key. Give me a call at your earliest convenience. I'm checking out at 11:00 a.m. Thanks.

She poured her coffee into the seashell mug she'd used last night, and Sadie clicked into the living room. Kathryn grabbed the leash off the bar. "How about you do a quick walk out here in the back this morning?"

While in the backyard, Kathryn's phone rang. "Hello."

"Good morning."

"You didn't have to call me so early, Mr. Schwartz. I know you're getting ready for church."

"It's okay. What's up? Any new evidence?"

Kathryn told the D.A. about the note, the call, and the grocery store incident. She straightened her shoulders, gathering the courage to ask for more time. She couldn't fail at this case. If she were ever going to meet Daddy's expectations, she'd have to win against Ezzo. "Would it be all right if I stayed a few more days?"

"Why?"

"There are a lot of tourists here. Most of them should head home today. With mostly locals here tomorrow, I should be able to get some answers. I haven't even been able to talk to the police yet."

"Okay, I'll get someone to handle your cases. Be back Wednesday morning."

"Thanks, I will."

"Be careful."

Kathryn walked Sadie, then called the property management company and worked it out to stay until Wednesday. That would give her three full days to do her investigating. Surely she could find that murder weapon in that amount of time.

While she ate breakfast, she reviewed the evidence. Again. All four victims were shot in their hands and feet with a gunshot wound to the center of their foreheads at close range. What victim would stand still long enough to be shot in four separate places before allowing someone to get close enough to shoot him in the head? The killer was sending a message. But was that message sent before or after their murders?

What if the victims were killed first and then shot in their hands and feet afterward to drive a point home? What better way to say that they'd failed at their jobs than to take their hands and feet away from them? What better way to send all future drug traffickers who worked for them a message that if their hands tainted the goods in anyway, they'd be lost, and if their feet wandered too far off track, they'd never walk again?

Kathryn wasn't here to ponder motive though. She was here to find the gun, a gun which hopefully held the fingerprints of the killer. It seemed unlikely that Ezzo pulled the trigger on those four men. He wouldn't waste his time killing two guys who cheated him out of some cocaine and two who were too ignorant to know they'd been cheated.

After thirty minutes, she was about as close to finding the weapon as she was when she arrived on Friday evening. Just like everything else in her life, this case was going nowhere fast. There had to be a way to find out where that gun was. Somebody had to know something.

If history had told her anything, the place to find out the juicy details and secrets of a town was church. Cedar Key had to be no different. There was little she could do this morning anyway. She might as well head toward town and find a place to go. She searched the Internet for churches, and the first one that popped up was the Baptist church. That'd be as good a place as any to go. Maybe she could find some answers there.

* * *

Kathryn parked on the street and inched her way up the sidewalk to the entrance of the charming white church packed into the corner of 2nd and E Street. People stood on the lawn shaking hands, patting backs, smiling at each other. Stained-glass windows above paned windows glinted in the morning sunlight. Freshly stained rails on the handicap ramps on both sides of the building sent the message that people who the world would consider imperfect were welcome and loved here. The church was built in 1922 and had probably seen a lot of people come and go through its doors who weren't sure if church was the place for them, and it looked like it had survived. Openhearted and full of charm. That's what this place was. It could obviously handle a woman like Kathryn who hadn't stepped foot inside of a church for years.

Several people greeted her before she headed up the red brick steps and through the double wooden doors into the foyer, so she must be welcome. She straightened her blue pencil skirt and adjusted her purse strap on her shoulder. Why had she dressed as if she were going to court? And why hadn't she thought to search for a Bible at the condo? Now everyone would know she wasn't a regular churchgoer.

As she strolled into the sanctuary, she stepped back into her past. This was like Grandmother's church. There weren't many people here, but those who were, nodded and smiled. She'd sit on the back row and slip out at the end of the service undetected. No, that wouldn't work. In order to find out the town's gossip and uncover any evidence about the case, she'd have to stay and meet some folks afterward.

She scanned the sanctuary then a hand waving in the air invaded her nostalgia. This was not a simple casual wave, this was a "come over here and sit with me" kind of wave. The hand was attached to Phil, who sat by himself on the third row. This man was everywhere she went. But she couldn't accuse him of following her this time. He motioned for her to come and sit with him. He didn't have to ask her more than once.

CHAPTER 5

Somehow, Phil had managed to focus on Pastor Todd's words and not let the professionally dressed beauty next to him distract him from the message. "Where your treasure is, there your heart will be also." Pastor's words were Jesus' words, and their truth rang out into the congregation, echoed off the walls, and penetrated Phil's heart. He chewed on his thumbnail and bounced his right leg on the ball of his foot.

Where was his treasure? It used to be in his career in New York and his future with Maria, earning the big bucks and gaining popularity. But he'd left that behind. Even when he'd practiced law in Savannah, his heart hadn't been content. So he'd given all of that up to live here in Cedar Key, and he still felt empty most of the time.

What was he running from? Why did he have to hide here in this out-of-the-way, almost-forgotten place? Was he wasting his life here?

Kathryn reached into her purse and pulled out a tissue. She wiped her eyes and sniffled. Was she running from something too? Maybe she was as dissatisfied with her career in law as he'd been. Being a defense attorney wasn't easy. There's no way being a prosecutor could be any easier. If only he could reach out to her, but what she needed wasn't comfort from him. She needed the comfort that only God could give her. Did she know that though?

Phil shouldn't judge her. He didn't know her heart. But something in her eyes said she was lonely and wondering about her purpose in life. He stretched his arm across the back of the pew and patted her shoulder three times. He had to take the chance that she wouldn't run from him. Kathryn faced him and smiled with a glimmer in her eyes. She'd accepted his gesture of kindness.

After church, several people introduced themselves to Kathryn. This was Phil's opportunity to ask her to lunch before she got away from him. And before Tom Smith, who looked like an arrow headed for a bull's eye, invited her first.

"Would you like to go to lunch?"

She crossed her arms and encircled her elbows with her fingers. A cute habit she'd probably done since she was a child. "I'm not sure."

"Aren't you hungry?"

"Yes, I am."

"But you're leaving?"

"No, I'm staying a few more days. I have to find that weapon." She looked at the ceiling and groaned and then nodded at Mrs. Edison, who gave Phil a smile and winked. That old lady was determined to find him a wife.

"Well, you've got time for lunch then. I won't take no for an answer." *Come on, Kathryn. Join me.*

She twisted her leg and bit her lip. "Okay, I'll follow you."

He scooted her out the door before Tom could get to her. Victory! "Is it all right if I ride with you? I walked this morning."

She twisted her mouth into a pucker and squinted. "You're sly."

"Why am I sly? I didn't plan this. I didn't know you'd be here."

"Oh, yeah. You're right." She laughed and led him to her car. A very practical charcoal gray Honda.

Phil would've guessed her to be a fancy car kind of lady. So she was sensible and not frivolous. This was a good thing. He climbed into the passenger's seat.

"Please excuse the mess." She threw a plastic bag to the back seat.

"You should see my SUV."

"So where are we headed?" She cranked the car and the twang of country music came through the speakers.

Phil didn't like country music, but he didn't mind it so much while in the company of this country girl. "How about the sandwich shop again?"

"Sounds perfect." Kathryn eased out onto E Street.

"So you're still coming up with zero?"

She growled. "Yes! And it's driving me crazy." She squeezed the steering wheel until her knuckles turned white.

"What have you found out since I saw you yesterday?"

"Without divulging too much information, the man who runs the grocery store is a little bit threatened by my presence here."

"How so?" He turned sideways in his seat to get a better look at this serious-minded woman whose looks and allure distracted him from the matter at hand.

"I asked him if he knew anything about the murder or the weapon when I was at the store yesterday, and he told me I should mind my business. He said there were secrets here that were better left buried."

"What? So he does know something."

She nodded.

"Do you want my help?"

She sighed and halted the car at a stop sign. "I didn't think I was going to need any extra help, but now I think I do. My investigators came up empty and so did the detectives. I think it's time for a local to step in. But I have to know I can trust you."

Finally. She was letting her guard down. "You can trust me."

"Of course you say that, but I have to know for sure. Do you mind if I run a background check on you when I get back to my condo?" She raised her eyebrows in obvious hopefulness.

"Nope, I don't mind at all."

"How much do you charge?"

"I'm not charging you anything. You've got me so curious about this, I want to do it for free."

"No, I'm going to pay you."

"I'm not going to charge you. I want to help you put this guy away."

"I want to put him away too." They got out of the car and climbed the stairs to the restaurant. "Well, I want to put the killer away."

"Is there a difference?"

She nodded. "I'm not convinced that he is the killer."

"You're not?"

"Not entirely. It doesn't make sense that a man with his power and connections would dirty his hands on the murders of four seemingly insignificant men."

Phil held open the door for her. "The porch again?"

"Sure." They found a table with a clear view of the Gulf.

"So you've got to find the weapon and pray there are fingerprints on it to prove whether your guy is the killer or not?"

"That sums it up. He'll go free if I can't find the gun. He might still go free once I find it if his fingerprints aren't on it and if there are no witnesses to come forward. For his sake, I hope that happens if he's innocent. It makes me very angry that he won't talk. I may not be sure he actually pulled the trigger, but I know he knows who did. You'd think he'd want to clear his name."

"Not if he ordered the hits."

"But would a man go down for something he didn't do when he could pin it on the guy who did?"

"In my experience, yes. If he ordered the hits and then turned the guy in, he'd be killed in prison. He'd take his chances with the prosecution not being able to prove their case over ratting someone out. Anyone who would accept the job of knocking off four men would have no qualms about taking out the boss man."

Kathryn cleared out the corners of her eyes and ran her fingers underneath her lower lid, smoothing out her eyeliner which had smudged in church. This case could possibly be unsolvable, and the stress was apparent in her eyes. "It's very likely that four men died, and their murders won't ever be avenged."

"I'm sorry."

They ordered when the waitress came. "Enough talk about the case. It's depressing. Cedar Key is much more interesting to talk about."

"Cedar Key? There's not much excitement happening

here."

"Exactly. I love it here and hope to come back once this case is finished when I can enjoy myself and stop being so bogged down with investigating and so paranoid."

"Paranoid?" Phil took a bite of his burger and wiped his chin with a napkin.

Kathryn scrunched her face. "You'll laugh."

"Never."

Kathryn studied his eyes, obviously measuring his trustworthiness. "When I left the condo this morning, I noticed a note taped to the front door. I broke out into a sweat. I got the salad tongs and a gallon-sized plastic bag and turned into a forensics investigator. I didn't want to damage any of the potential DNA that could be on the note." She scowled. "You're laughing!"

"No, I'm not." But he was. "Please, continue. I just have a funny feeling about where this story is headed."

"I must've looked like a regular Sherlock Holmes or something when I pulled the note away from the glass with the tongs and stuck it into the baggie. I used another baggie as gloves to open the note."

"What did it say? Who was it from?" He leaned closer in. She weaved a fascinating tale. Or was it the glow in her cheeks and the sparkle in her eyes that captivated him?

Kathryn chewed on her bottom lip for a few moments and then laughed. "It was from the rental company letting me know they'd added chlorine to the pool and to wait an hour before swimming."

Phil roared with laughter and nearly fell out of his chair. This woman was a breath of fresh air, and she didn't even know it. She wasn't as intense as he'd thought she was when he first met her. She was a delight. He had to find a way to see her after she left Cedar Key.

Kathryn threw one of her fries at him. "You said you wouldn't laugh."

"Sorry!" He covered his mouth and snickered. She was adorable when she played at being angry.

"Now you see why I'm anxious to get this case solved? I'm utterly paranoid."

Maybe she was a bit paranoid, but she was the cutest paranoid he'd ever seen. Maybe he could be the hero she needed. "I want to help you, but I have to know the details. All right?"

"I already told you the main points."

"Vaguely."

She took a sip of her water, wiping water droplets from her lips, and conceded. "I live out in the country off Highway 278 where nothing too violent ever happens. 278 runs east to west and dumps into the airport in Atlanta. It has become a popular route for running drugs. Everything from cocaine to meth to marijuana. You name it, we've got it. Occasionally, the big drug lords come into our area instead of sending their goons, and incidents of crime always go up when they're there."

"I know all about that, being from New York." He winked.

She nodded and swirled a fry in her ketchup. "About two months ago, a drug deal went bad. A couple of guys decided to mix sugar in the bags with the cocaine."

"Ouch. Not smart." He'd seen that before and it never ended well.

"Nope. When the transporters got back with the goods, my guy—or one of his thugs—killed them for not testing it first. He and two of his associates then came to my county and killed the guys who sold the cocaine-sugar mixture to them."

"You gotta be kidding."

"I wish. The police arrested all of them and charged the two associates with accessory to murder. They bonded out and no one has seen them since. The main suspect is sitting in our jail without bail because he's a flight risk since he's charged with murder, but we can't convict him without the weapon. We're not really sure who pulled the trigger. It could have been one of his accomplices."

"That's insane."

"Tell me about it. As you probably know, weapons are usually disposed of before anyone can find them. When the accomplices were in jail, someone overheard them talking about the gun being hidden somewhere in Cedar Key, so investigators came down here and tried to find it. When they failed, I decided to try to find it myself."

"Why Cedar Key?"

"I don't know, but this is where we're concentrating our efforts because of what those two men said in jail. Where my team *was* concentrating its efforts. Everybody gave up but me. This guy is going to go free if I don't find the gun."

"Providing he's guilty."

"Right, providing he's guilty. If he's not guilty, then I don't want to convict him of murder. He's going to be charged with accessory to murder though. He's going to go down for something. I'm just not one hundred percent sure what yet."

"I'm in. I know you can't tell me anything else until you check me out, so you go back and do that."

"Thank you. I only have until Tuesday night to find it. My D.A. says I have to be back in court on Wednesday morning."

"For the trial?"

"For jury selection and then the trial, yes."

Phil cocked his neck. "That quick? It normally takes years on something like this."

Kathryn raised both palms in the air admitting her confusion regarding this turn of events. "Since the D.A. refused to offer a plea, the defendant has decided that a speedy trial would be in his best interest over a fair trial because he knows we don't have a weapon, and he knows without it, we'll have no choice but to drop the charges."

"Interesting. Sounds like he's got you where he wants you."

"He thinks he does, and that's why I'm determined not to let this case go to trial without the gun."

"Okay, I'm hooked. I'm going to Savannah tomorrow to check on my house, but I'll cut my trip short and be back by late afternoon."

"How will you get there and back so fast?"

"I'll fly. We've got an airstrip."

Kathryn rubbed her hands together and smiled. "Thanks again for your help. I've got to find the evidence to put Louie Ezzo and his thugs away for good."

* * *

How was it possible that the first pleasant woman Phil had met in years was Maria's friend and also Uncle Louie's prosecutor? The woman he'd just committed to help solve her case. He should win an award for his bad luck.

Phil leaned against his silver Range Rover Sport, too distressed to go inside his house after Kathryn dropped him off. "Come on, pick up the phone." He ran his fingers through his hair and waited for the ringing to stop.

Sweat trickled down his face and back; a lump the size of Staten Island grew in his throat. He had better not get Pops' voicemail. Of course, it wouldn't surprise him if he did. They hadn't spoken in over two months except through Ma.

"Hey, son. Whatcha calling me on a Sunday for? You know I'm golfing. Or maybe you don't know. How long's it been since you had time to check in with your old man?"

"Sorry, about that Pops. And sorry to disturb you while you're golfing. This is important. Tell me what you know about Uncle Louie being in jail." Phil paced the path from his porch to his mailbox on Whiddon Avenue and back again. He kicked a rock, and it pinged off the street sign.

"What's it to ya, Phillip? You don't practice law anymore. Remember?"

"I know, I know. But tell me anyway." He shoved his left hand into his pocket and jingled his change.

"You wanting to defend him?"

Phil halted. "No."

"Then why ya askin'?"

"Pops, please. I've been hearing some talk down here, and I've got to know."

"Talk down there in Cedar Key?"

"Yes, sir."

"All I know is he's sittin' in the Perkins County jail. He couldn't get bonded out because they said he was a flight risk. Where's he gonna go? Everybody he knows is in New York."

"Why did they arrest him?"

"They say he murdered two guys there and two here in New York. So maybe they have enough evidence to hold him. I doubt they have enough to convict him."

"Why?"

"Would your uncle let himself get one drop of someone else's blood on him?"

"Okay, so say he didn't do it, but maybe he had someone else do it. Is that possible?"

Pops roared with laughter. "You're not as sharp as you used to be when you was practicing law. Anything is possible with Louie."

The rest of the conversation soured Phil's stomach even more than it already was. He had a lot to think about after talking to Pops.

* * *

Kathryn drove away from Phil's white-and-turquoise beach house on stilts, the events of the day swirling in her head like a hurricane. Lunch with Phil was probably the best time she'd had with a man in ages—if ever. The appeal went beyond his physical appearance. Kindness bubbled out of him and poured all over her. A genuine kindness. He didn't merely flirt with her or seem out to get something from her like so many of the men she encountered daily at work. He laughed, and the room lit up. Kathryn felt lighter when with him. He made her believe that life didn't have to be complicated. He'd taken a genuine interest in her case and showed a true desire to help her succeed.

And church—what had happened to her in there? Maybe tiredness and worry had overtaken her, but it felt like something else. She hadn't let her guard down like that in years. She should've gone into that building as armored as she went to court. But she hadn't, and what resulted was a chink in her armor and new questions about her purpose.

The reality that she'd placed her treasure in her career had seeped into her heart during the pastor's message. She'd never wanted it to be that way, but Daddy had pushed her, and she wanted to prove to him that she was tougher than Mom. To make him proud of her so he'd never replace her. Now she was sitting in a puddle of success and loneliness. Mediocre success, at that, and it had resulted in her failure at love and her dissatisfaction with everything.

If career and love weren't where her treasure needed it to be, then where? The pastor and everyone she met at church seemed to have something she didn't have. Was it joy maybe? Their treasure was in a relationship with God and their friends. Was that the secret? Was that Phil's secret? He'd walked away from law and from a family that manipulated him, and he was obviously happy. The glimmer in his eyes said that.

Kathryn opened the door to the condo, and Sadie greeted her with a wagging tail and overzealous tongue. "Hey girl. Did you miss me?" Kathryn kicked off her shoes and deposited her purse and keys on the bar. A swim was what she needed to shed her unrest—to clear her mind of everything that bombarded it.

* * *

Phil slammed his front door and yelled until his throat burned and his chest threatened to explode. He tossed his phone on the table and flipped himself over the back of his brown leather couch. "Why, Lord? Why did Uncle Louie commit murder? Why does Kathryn have to be the prosecutor?" He tossed his glasses on the coffee table and closed his eyes. He plopped his forearm over his eyes to starve out the light.

Pops had all but commanded him to represent Uncle Louie. Said he owed him the favor for allowing him to escape New York. The shame in Pop's voice crushed him, shame over Phil leaving the family. Not shame over Louie's crime. Pops would defend his brother-in-law over defending his own son? What a backward way of thinking.

Phil pushed himself up and rested his elbows on his knees. He ran his fingers through his hair and scratched his beard. "What am I going to do?" He needed to talk to Kathryn but didn't have a way to get in touch with her. He opened his laptop on the coffee table. "There's got to be a number or an email address for her somewhere." He pulled up Perkins County's website and searched for her by name. "Bingo!" There was her email address.

Hey Kathryn, I enjoyed lunch today. And I'm glad you were able to attend church. I'm contacting you via email because you didn't give me your number. We'll talk about that next time, by the way. I need to let you know something I found out about the case. Please call me as soon as you get this. Phil

Phil hit send and then shut his laptop. Going to Savannah tomorrow was not an option. He'd have to reschedule the appointment with the potential buyer of his house. Where was his number?

He jumped up from the couch to retrieve the file from the glass table in the foyer when his phone rang. Even though he tried to stop it, a smile spread wide across his face. Case or no case, he was about to talk to Kathryn again. He hit the answer button. "Well, hello. That was fast!"

"Hello, Cuz." The raspy voice boomed into Phil's ear. "You expecting a call from someone?"

He stepped back, disappointment streaming into his

body like the sunlight coming in through the backdoor window. "Drew, what do you want?"

"I think you know. I talked to Uncle Marco, and he told me you asked him about Uncle Louie."

Great. Pops had turned around and called Drew as soon as they'd hung up the phone. His own father would turn against him like this? Phil imagined Drew's club-fisted hand wrapped around his phone as it used to wrap around his neck when Drew would hold him under the water at Cayuga Lake during summer vacations near Taughannock Gorge. "Yeah, I did. What's it to ya?"

"If you're asking about him, then you're interested in helping."

Phil pounded his fist into his temple three times. Why had he inquired about Uncle Louie? He might as well have poked a hornet's nest. "No, I'm not."

"Louie's not going down for murder, and you're going to make sure of that."

"No, I'm not. I'm not responsible for his problems or for getting him out of them."

"Listen, you're the best lawyer our family has, and you owe it to us to get Uncle Louie out of this fix."

Phil leaned against the kitchen's granite counter. "Drew, don't flatter me with empty accolades. I don't owe anybody anything. Did he murder those guys?" He had to be careful not to divulge any of the information Kathryn had told him.

"You can talk to Uncle Louie yourself at the Perkins County jail to find that out."

Phil yanked the phone away from his ear, considered chucking it out the window, then he returned it to its original place. "I'm not going."

"You will if you know what's good for you."

"You threatening me? I have a life here in Cedar Key. I can't just leave it and go back to defending guilty people. I'm not going to do it!"

"Yes, you are, and I'm coming down there to make sure you do!" The line went dead.

Phil stared at his phone, trapped in a crazy nightmare. He'd left behind his family's manipulation when he left New York. Why did he have to go through this again? He needed to go for a run. He had to clear his mind.

CHAPTER 6

Kathryn and Sadie walked along G Street, the palm trees swaying in the breeze and seabirds soaring in the air. The sun warmed her skin, still chilled from her swim. Details of the case filled her brain to overflowing, but her heart remained tucked away in its own little corner. Where had her passion for solving this case gone? What had happened to her today?

Like the piles of palm fronds and sand on the sides of the road, Kathryn shoved her eagerness to get that promotion aside. She could win this case, but it no longer had the power to define her. This morning in church, a freedom had flowed throughout the building and the people. Kathryn wanted that freedom.

She held tight to Sadie's leash as a car passed on her left. A man in a straw hat with a cigar in his mouth waved at her. She waved back and smiled. This man obviously knew Cedar Key's secret for happiness.

Secrets.

Some secrets are better left buried.

Kathryn shook her head as she rounded the bend in G Street. No, the secrets to the Ezzo case were not better left buried. The missing gun and the truth of Ezzo's innocence or guilt, she'd find them. She had to.

Kathryn stopped and let Sadie walk on to the tiny patch of sand in the bend in the road, boulders holding back the rising tide. Out in the water stood the dilapidated shack she'd seen yesterday. Why didn't someone tear it down? It was quite an eyesore.

"Kathryn! Hey, wait up."

Kathryn turned around as Phil jogged toward her in cargo shorts and a black tank top. A gust of wind tousled her hair, and the sight of him, glistening with sweat, almost knocked her over.

"You admiring the old shack?"

She returned her gaze to the remnant of something that had possibly been beautiful once. "I guess. It must have some sentimental meaning around here or else someone would've torn it down by now. Looks like the ocean is taking care of business."

"Yeah, I'll have to tell you the story behind that some time. What've you been up to since lunch?"

"I went for a swim and decided to bring Sadie for a walk to process things."

"Making any headway?"

"Well, I—" She twisted her toe into the sand.

He held up both hands. "I know. You can't tell me anything until you do my background check."

Kathryn nodded. What more could she say?

"Did you get my email?"

"When?"

"About an hour ago."

"No, sorry. What's up?"

"I've got to tell you something about the case. I hope it'll prove to you how trustworthy I am."

She pushed her hair away from her face, but the wind whipped it back again. "Okay...don't be so mysterious."

"Can we sit?" Phil motioned to a large rock on his left.

"Sure." Kathryn sat and pulled Sadie to her side. Sadie tugged away from Kathryn and plopped down beside Phil. The gulf ebbed and flowed at their feet, sea grass swayed in the current.

Phil sighed and rubbed Sadie's ears. "I have to tell you something, but I need you to remain calm."

"Calm?" Kathryn gulped and wiped a bead of sweat from her brow. She stiffened her back and rubbed the back of her neck. This didn't sound good.

Phil squeezed his hands together and then laced his fingers. "Earlier, you let the name of your suspect slip."

"Yes, I know. I should've been more careful. I'm not usually that vulnerable."

"I'm glad you let it slip. I—"

Kathryn turned to face Phil. She searched his eyes. Where were his glasses? Without them, flecks of gold sparkled uninhibited. Something else showed in his eyes though. Concern? Fear?

A sandpiper landed a few feet away. Sadie darted toward it, pulling Kathryn into Phil. "Excuse me." Kathryn righted herself with his help and then motioned for him to continue.

He studied the shack, obviously avoiding looking at her. "I don't really know how to say this, so I'm just going to say it." He looked up at the sky. "I don't know how something like this could have happened. I've been trying for the last hour to figure out the probability of it all." He waved his hands as he talked, and his lips quivered. "It doesn't make sense. It's like some weird slap in the face by fate, and I don't even believe in things like that."

Kathryn touched his arm and stopped his rambling. "Phil, what is it?"

He groaned and raked his hands through his hair. "Louie Ezzo is my uncle."

Kathryn froze. "What?!" All the blood drained from her head, and she steadied herself on the rock with her hand. "Your uncle?" How could this be? Had Phil followed her here? Was he behind the threats? She wasn't safe with him. She jumped up off the rock and yanked Sadie's leash, causing Sadie to yelp.

Phil bolted off the rock after her. "Wait! It's not what you think."

She turned around and screamed into the wind. "What do I think? That you followed me here? That you're the one who's been threatening me? Why would I ever think something like that?" she scoffed.

"Kathryn, think! How could I have followed you here? I live here." He cradled her elbow in his hand.

She jerked her elbow away and tugged Sadie up next to her leg. "How do I know that? What are the chances that the one person I connect with in Cedar Key is the nephew of my suspect? It's bad enough that you're the ex-fiancé of one of my friends."

"I've been trying to figure it all out. I even thought maybe you were the one coming after me to get information."

Her mouth flew open. "What? That's ridiculous."

"You approached me on the peer while I was fishing. I didn't run my car into yours on the road or pretend to be your pool man."

"I would never do such a thing."

"I believe you, but do you see how it looks from my point of view? It looks bad either way. I promise you, I didn't know that's who you were prosecuting. I didn't know until you said his name."

"I promise you that I didn't seek you out to find out what you knew. I was shocked when I realized you were Maria's ex. You saw my shock. If I had known who you were when I came here, I would have already known those two key pieces of information about you." Kathryn turned away from him, but Phil stepped back into her path.

"So we've established that neither of us knew about the other before we met on the pier. I was so distraught when you said Louie's name, I called my Pops as soon as you dropped me off after lunch. He confirmed that Louie was in trouble. He asked me, if you want to call it that, to defend him, but I refused."

"This is too much to fathom. Absolutely too much." She threw her hands in the air. "The one time I let my guard down and trust someone…"

"I'm not the bad guy here. You can trust me."

Kathryn glared at him through squinted eyes.

"Look, I could get in a lot of trouble with my family for helping you. I mean, a lot of trouble. So trust me."

She shook her head. "Helping me? I can't let you help me now. Why would you even want to?" She covered her face with her hands to shut out this nightmare then she tore her hands away from her face. "You can't help your uncle's prosecutor. Talk about a conflict of interest."

"Look, I want to help. I'll find a way around this conflict." He locked his jaw and beat his right foot on the ground. "My cousin, Drew, said I have to defend Louie, and he's coming down here to make sure I do. I don't want to think about the trouble I could be in if I don't defend him. I might have to go into the Witness Protection Program." He laughed, but ran his fingers through his hair and groaned. His hands shook, and his lips quivered again.

Kathryn grabbed his shoulders. "Phil, you have to get as far away from me as possible. Now! You need to go back to Savannah. I can handle this case myself. We're in danger if we work together."

"You can't handle an Ezzo. Not without me. I'm not leaving Cedar Key until this case is solved, and I'm not leaving you." He paced a few steps away, Sadie trying to follow him, and then returned. "Let me see your file. Maybe I can tip you off to where the weapon is. If I can't figure it out, I'll leave you alone and not see you again until we're in court."

Kathryn's heart plummeted to the bottom of the sea. How could she not see Phil again? How could the next time be a face off in court as two virtual strangers on opposite sides of a case, never being allowed to see where this could go? "Phil..." Her phone rang. She yanked it from her pocket and looked at the screen. "It's the D.A. I have to take this."

Phil nodded and stepped out of earshot.

Kathryn cupped her hand over her right ear to block out the roar of the wind and surf. "Hello, Mr. Schwartz." She released the tension on the leash and let Sadie stand by Phil, who kneeled and stroked her fur.

Schwartz cleared his throat. "Kathryn, you've been removed from the Ezzo case."

She lurched forward. "What? Why?" Phil's head shot up, and he crinkled his brow. She shook her head.

"You were seen fraternizing with the defense attorney."

She spun around to face the Gulf. She couldn't let Phil overhear this conversation. "Fraternizing? When?"

"In a restaurant this afternoon."

She laughed. "I was having lunch with a man I met down here. Who said that? Can't I have a moment of privacy?"

"You're down there on business not pleasure. You shouldn't be trying to meet men while you're working a case. Besides, this man just so happens to be Phillip Tagliaferro, the defense attorney, Kathryn."

"He's not the defense attorney. At least, he's trying not to take the case. Louie Ezzo is his uncle, and they're trying to force him to defend him."

"So you do know him?"

"We met Friday night."

"Sounds a little too convenient to me."

"It's not like that."

"You knew he was Ezzo's nephew, and you're befriending him—or worse?"

Was he accusing her of inappropriate behavior with someone she just met? Was he accusing her of getting too involved with someone just to find out information? "Sir, I'm not sure I approve of your line of questioning. I met him Friday night, learned that he was a former attorney, and asked him questions about Cedar Key to try to locate the weapon. I didn't know he was Ezzo's nephew until a few minutes ago. He doesn't want to defend him, but they're threatening him into it."

"I'm sorry. We can't risk losing this case. It's best if someone who's neutral handles it from here."

She stomped her foot. "Neutral? I *am* neutral! I'm so neutral that I'm not convinced Ezzo is guilty. I want to see justice served on the person who deserves to be convicted of murder—if Ezzo isn't."

"Tagliaferro has already clouded your judgment, Bellamy. You're thinking like a defense attorney."

"No, that's not true. I already felt this way before I met him. It doesn't make sense that Ezzo would dirty his hands over a few nobodys."

"Kathryn, the decision is made."

Kathryn hated to beg for anything, but this case meant everything to her career. And her reputation was all she had. She couldn't let her good name be soiled and be the cause of a potentially guilty man going free. "Please listen to me. We can't pin the murder on him if he's innocent. Let me try to find the gun. Without it, you have nothing. He'll go free. If he's guilty, you can't let that happen."

"That won't happen. The truth will come out with or without the gun. I've assigned the case to someone else who won't get mixed up in the personal lives of the parties involved. Enjoy the rest of your time there. Take a vacation. Stay away from Tagliaferro. We'll have a new case for you when you return."

Her hair whipped across her face, and she shoved it away with fury. "Wait, please. What do you mean by neutral?"

"We know you've had a former personal connection with Tagliaferro, and now you're dining with him when you should be working on the case against his uncle."

This was unbelievable. They'd been snooping into her private life? Digging up her past? "He was engaged to one of my college friends. That's all. I met him on Friday and didn't realize until Saturday that I'd met him before. I wasn't friends with him. I only met him once."

"Kathryn, sit this one out," The D.A. barked.

"Do I have a choice?"

"No. Besides, you're probably safer where you're at anyway."

"Safer? Are you saying the threats I've experienced do have something to do with the Ezzo case?"

"The least amount you know the better. We'll see you in a week." The phone went dead, and a tidal wave of tears gushed from Kathryn.

Phil rushed to her side, and Sadie pawed at her legs. "What's wrong?"

Through skips and blubbers, she told Phil the news. "Now my career is ruined and my reputation—all because of you." She clinched her jaw and narrowed her eyes.

Phil pointed to his chest. "Because of me?"

She stomped her foot. "Yes. If I hadn't met you, I'd still be working. This case would've sent me straight to Senior Assistant D.A. They don't give peons like me a second chance at these things."

"I'm sorry, but I hardly think that's my fault."

She glared at him.

He stepped closer to her. "Kathryn, I'm just as much a victim in this as you."

"I have more at risk though."

Phil huffed. "You clearly don't understand the complexity of this situation and how powerful my family is."

She slumped. "Sorry. You're not responsible. Neither of us is. I just needed someone to take my anger out on." She squeezed her eyes shut and let out a scream. "How is this happening? It's like we've been set up."

"Maybe it's not such a bad thing though." Phil tipped her chin upward with his thumb. "I can vouch for the fact that a life without all that crime is a peaceful life."

Kathryn felt herself melting into Phil. His concern poured over her and sifted away her sadness, like the ocean carried away the sand on the shore. "But I don't have anything else but law. And Sadie. You have a great life here." She motioned to the water and the town a mile away.

Phil let go of her chin. "Kathryn, I promise you God has something better in store for you. I know it hurts to be removed from the case, but ride the tide."

"What?" She scrunched up her face.

"Ride the tide. Go with it. Let it take you to new places."

"Is that what you're going to do?"

"I'm going to stay right here with you. And I'm going to call my cousin later and tell him I won't represent Uncle Louie." He smoothed the hair away from her face. "How about we get our minds off this ridiculous distraction and I take you for a picnic on my boat?"

"A picnic? On your boat? I—I don't know." She popped her right hip out and twisted the toe of her left foot in the sand again.

"You're on vacation now. Remember?"

Kathryn laughed. "I guess you're right."

"Do you want me to pick you up in my boat or do you want to come back over to my house?"

"I'll meet you at your house."

"Still not ready to trust me, huh?"

"I'm getting there."

CHAPTER 7

Kathryn had started the day with a hunt for local gossip at church, ended up at lunch with Phil, was dismissed from her case, and now she was going boating and picnicking with a man with whom she had too many forbidden connections. No one could accuse her of living a boring life now. She'd always expected the unexpected, but this day produced a roller coaster high even in her.

Kathryn fed Sadie and checked her water bowl. She grabbed a sandwich baggie out of the drawer and zipped her cell phone into it. In case the boat turned over, she'd spare her phone from destruction.

She changed into her white-and-navy floral halter-top sundress. She'd wear her swimsuit underneath it, but she wasn't getting into that water with sharks and marshy sea grasses and who-knows-what-else.

"Sadie, I'll be back in a bit." Sadie tucked her ears and whimpered. "I'm going out with Phil." She reached for the remote and turned on cartoons to keep Sadie company until she returned. She slipped on her white rhinestone-clad, braided sandals and headed out the door with her keys and phone in hand.

It took a brief two minutes to arrive at Phil's house, where she rolled her Honda in place behind his SUV. Her gaze trailed along the white railing up the stairs to the porch and found Phil leaning against a post waiting on her. Dressed in white drawstring cotton pants and a black button-down short-sleeved top, he slid his sunglasses away from his face and grinned. Her attention froze on his face, and her heart jumped to her throat. Phil wasn't wearing his glasses again, and he'd shaven off his beard. From his spot above her, a strong jaw and full smile greeted her.

"What have I gotten myself into?" She climbed out of her car and made her way to the stairs. "Hey."

"Hi there. You want to come up and see the place or are you ready to hit the water?"

"Well, if you're ready, I'm ready. I think." She giggled. "Actually, I'm pretty terrified to get out there in a boat."

"Have you never been in a boat before?"

She tucked her phone and keys into her skirt pocket. "Living out in the country, I've gone tubing on a lake and ridden in a boat many times. But I've never been on a boat in the ocean."

"Well, I promise to be the best captain you've ever had then." He lifted a red cooler off the deck. "If we get out there now, we'll have plenty of time to tour around before the tide goes out."

Kathryn grimaced. "We can get stuck?"

"Not likely. My boat can float in ten inches of water."

"That's a relief. I'd hate to leave Sadie for too long."
Of course, Kathryn could think of worse things than being stranded on a boat with Phil. Who cares if he was Maria's ex and Louie Ezzo's nephew? This was the closest thing she'd had to a date in years, and since she was on a forced vacation

from her duties, she might as well enjoy it.

"Do you want to go water skiing?" Phil stepped off the last step and sidled up next to her, motioning with his head to a pair of water skis leaning against the storage area.

"Ha ha, funny! I don't think so."

"Okay, if you're not feeling adventurous. Maybe we can do a little fishing though."

"Sure. As long as you don't bring in another giant shark."

"Giant? That was a baby."

"Well, keep the sharks out of the boat."

"Yes, ma'am. If you insist."

She nudged him with her elbow. "I do."

Phil led the way through his backyard to a dock on a canal and stepped on to a white Carolina Skiff. He placed the cooler on the floor of the boat and then reached for Kathryn's hand. "Watch your step, miss." He winked before he slid his sunglasses onto his face.

Kathryn sat on the bench behind the steering wheel and adjusted the strap on her dress. Her insides felt like spaghetti.

Phil adjusted several knobs on the console then untied the rope that secured the boat to the dock. "You look very nice, by the way."

"Thanks. You do too. I like your face." Kathryn gulped and erased her words with her hands. "I mean, the lack of beard and glasses. I mean, I liked the beard and the glasses, but your bare face is nice too." *Shut up, Kathryn!*

"Grazie. I like your face too."

Oh, he was speaking Italian to her now? The stakes just got higher.

"It was getting too hot for a beard. And the

74

glasses...well, they're just for looks. I can see fine without them."

"Just for looks, huh? So you're a trend follower?"

"Sometimes. Only when it makes me look better though."

She giggled. Nothing could make Phil look bad. Beard. No beard. Glasses. No glasses. Mud on his face. Food on his clothes. He'd look great no matter what. She'd already seen him covered in fish bait and shark blood and even they didn't detract from his charm. Kathryn fanned her face. The heat was getting to her.

Phil put the boat in reverse and then directed it toward the open water. He waved at some of his neighbors, who sat on their docks. "I thought we'd go over to Atsena Otie Key for our picnic, if that's okay with you. It's got a gorgeous beach."

"I saw some pictures of it in a scrapbook at my condo. It's beautiful, but I read that there are a lot of snakes on the key." Kathryn shuddered.

"Yes, there are a lot of rattlers and copperheads, but I know how to watch out for them. Stick close to me, and you'll be fine." Phil straightened his back and puffed out his chest, playing the role of the guardian.

He wanted to protect her? She'd gladly let him. "Don't worry. I will." Kathryn shook her head and grimaced at her boldness then she pointed. "There's my dock right there." She had to turn the course of this conversation away from too much closeness with Phil. Without the umbrella of business over their heads and without the security of the accountability she had back home, this time together could catch her off-guard and take a turn in a taboo direction before she knew what had happened.

"You're right there? I know the owner. You're not far from me. I could've picked you up in the boat." Phil maneuvered the skiff around a bend, watching on both sides to steer around the shallow spots. "You can stand up here with me, if you'd like. You'll have a better view, and we won't have to yell over the wind once I open her up."

Kathryn eased herself up from the bench, finding her sea legs, and inched her way to Phil, who laughed. "Don't make fun of me."

"Sorry. I've done enough of that already, right?"

"Right." Kathryn let her shoulders relax, although she held on to the bar around the console. The shade of the awning reduced the heat she'd felt earlier, but her insides still tingled from her closeness with Phil. Her head told her to protect her heart, but her heart wanted to experience some fun and some attention from a man. This man.

Phil whipped the boat around to the right, causing her to lean into him. She grabbed the bar tighter and smiled until her lips stuck to her teeth from the wind. Phil dashed around small sandy spots and gave her the local's tour of the area. Then he slowed the boat and turned to face her. "Here we are. Isn't it beautiful?"

The key, surrounded by cerulean water, an azure sky, and trees and grasses in various shades of green and brown, couldn't have been a better place for a picnic. "It's gorgeous. Kind of feels like you're a million miles away from the world."

"That's why I like to come out here."

Phil helped Kathryn out of the boat and went back for the cooler and a quilt. He held up the beach umbrella, but Kathryn shook her head. She could use a little sun on her shoulders. Phil returned to her side, kicked off his sandals, and ripped off his T-shirt, sending Kathryn's internal temperature to new heights. Maybe she needed the freezer pack from the cooler to cool her down.

"So how does it feel to be on vacation?"

"I haven't been on a vacation in years so I don't have much to measure it against, but I'd say this one is off to a pretty good start." What girl wouldn't love an afternoon on a beach with a hunk of a man like Phil? She'd better behave herself. It had been too long since she'd had so much as a kiss. She wouldn't fight him off if he tried to kiss her, but she'd have to refrain from making the first move. She bit her lip and tucked her chin. Heat darted through her body like a pinball in a pinball machine.

Phil tipped her chin upward. "I'm thrilled to be a part of your vacation."

The best part of it so far. Was she losing her senses? In a few days when she returned home, they'd be on opposite sides of this case.

No, they wouldn't. She had her freedom. The first bit of freedom she'd felt in a long time. She was free to fraternize with this man all she wanted to.

"I'm glad you came with me out here. I'm sorry that you got taken off the case, but I'm not sorry you're still here in Cedar Key."

"I'm glad I'm still here too." Kathryn accepted the bottled water Phil offered her and forced herself to focus on something other than his attractiveness. She'd never been this shallow before. "You know, this morning I came to church hoping to hear some gossip that might lead me to the gun. Your pastor's words hit me like a runaway elephant right in my heart."

"How so?" He pulled containers of fruit and

sandwiches out of the cooler and placed them on the quilt.

"I don't know much about church, but I've always known—felt that God was out there somewhere watching me." She waved her hand in the air. "This morning, I realized that He's not just watching me. He's watching over me, and He's not as far away as I thought. I don't deserve to be cared for like that, but I'm glad He's there."

Phil laughed. "No one deserves God's love and protection. That's what makes it so great. He created us and so I guess you could say He has a vested interest in us. I believe we're never somewhere without God ordaining it first. I think He ordained you to be there this morning to hear that message."

"What do you mean?"

"I knew when I saw you the second time, when I ran into you at the sandwich shop, that you needed some kind of reassurance. I didn't want to pry, but I knew you were feeling hurt. You cried this morning in church, and I prayed that God would speak to your heart."

"Thanks. I—I don't know if that's what you call it, since I don't know religious terminology, but I felt the ice thawing a bit. I think you call it faith. Facts have always been easier for me to believe in than things I can't see."

"Then I'm glad my uncle inadvertently brought you here to Cedar Key."

Kathryn's shoulders had a pink hue, and her skin had started to sting. Phil was tanned from being out in the sun, so he didn't seem to mind the direct sunlight. She poured some of her bottled water into the palm of her hand and patted her shoulders to cool them off.

"You're getting a lot of sun on your shoulders, and

your nose and cheeks are pink. Are you ready to head back?"

"I'm fine to stay a bit longer, if you'd like. You know the tides better than me."

"We've got a little more time. Would you like me to get the umbrella from the boat?"

"That would be great!"

Phil hopped up off the quilt and sauntered over to the boat. Confidence dripped off him like the sweat that dripped off her forehead. He had probably been a beast in the courtroom. Too bad he wasn't still practicing law. What a thrill it would be to see him in action. If he ended up defending Ezzo, she'd attend the trial just to see him work.

Phil returned and staked the pole in the sand. Then he attached the umbrella and opened it. The angle of the umbrella created the perfect shady spot for both of them. "Do you mind if I squeeze under here with you? I'm a bit toasty." His lips parted, and he half-grinned.

"I'd be happy to share my shade with you. Thank you for thinking to bring the umbrella. I wouldn't have survived much longer out here without it." She placed her hand over her heart.

"You're used to being inside in a courtroom and not outside in all this grandeur." Phil nudged her with his arm and let it rest against hers. The heat wasn't going to get any better if he stayed this close to her.

Time to turn the conversation in a different direction once again before she got herself into trouble with this alluring man. If only she could drown out the sound of her pulse thumping in her throat. "I've been thinking about the probability of us meeting. It's not as far-fetched as I first thought."

"I'm listening." Phil pulled a container of fruit from

the cooler and offered some to Kathryn.

She reached in and slipped out a slice of pineapple. "There are churches where I live that are three times the size of Cedar Key. People run into each other at the store all the time, and they recognize each other easily even though twelve thousand people live in my town. It isn't unthinkable that our paths would have crossed at some point here."

Kathryn took a bite of pineapple and wiped the juice from her chin. She held up her index finger. "Plus your family has connections here, so Cedar Key isn't all that random of a place for me to end up or for you to be here. If your uncle or his goons had any sentimental attachment to the gun at all, it makes sense that they'd hide it here in Cedar Key. They certainly wouldn't want to hide it somewhere in New York where investigators would find it, and they wouldn't have hidden it in Georgia near where those two murders took place."

Phil paused with a strawberry in front of his lips. "Valid." He popped the strawberry into his mouth and nodded.

"You live here. I came to find the weapon. No biggie."

"Still, we might not have met had you not come to the pier with your dripping ice cream Friday night."

"Had you not been reeling in monsters from the sea and bringing all sorts of attention upon yourself." She laughed.

"Yeah, that's me. The total narcissist. Seriously, I'm glad we met. You've spiced up my life. It'd gotten a little too safe—too much like a vacation." He laced his fingers behind his head and rested it on the blanket.

"I can't imagine. I think I could use a little bit of that

kind of life for a while. I've gone straight from high school to college to law school and to working in the system. It's exhausting."

"Now's your chance then. Just rest."

Kathryn wrapped her arms around her bent legs. "Sadly I can't. I can't get the case out of my head. Where could the gun be? How does the D.A. expect to win without it? He's taken me off the case, but is he going to send the new prosecutor down here to finish what I started?" She huffed.

Phil tapped her on the shoulder. "You're supposed to be on vacation."

"I know. But how can I relax fully when that gun is out there somewhere?" She pointed to the Gulf.

Phil sat up and folded his legs to his chest. "All right. What makes you think it's out in the water?"

Kathryn pushed her hair out of her face. "The file mentions that the evidence was washed away. Washed away means in water. But where? Cedar Key is surrounded by water. Of course, the guy at the store said some secrets are better left buried, so maybe the gun is buried somewhere?" She sucked in a deep breath. "That's really getting to me, and I'm still puzzled by the fact that there was only one shooter."

"Are you sure there was only one?"

"Yes, ballistics proved the bullets came from the same gun."

"Then what puzzles you?"

"Two men who were shot in the hands and feet before being shot in the head are going to stand there while a man shoots them? No. One would fight the shooter to protect the other man or he'd run off and hide. It's not like the gun was a machine gun or some other rapid firing gun. What kept the second victim there?"

SHERRI WILSON JOHNSON

"What if the men were tied up first? Then they couldn't fight the shooter."

"Good point! I hadn't thought of that. You deserve a cookie." She laughed and pointed to the cooler.

Phil reached in and grabbed a cookie for both of them, handing one to Kathryn. She took a bite of the lemon-iced delight and wiped the crumbs away from her lips.

"Have you been able to find any connection to Cedar Key and the crime?"

She widened her eyes. "Uh, yeah. You."

He sketched circles in the sand with a piece of driftwood. "Besides me. Forgetting that it's my uncle with a familial connection to Cedar Key that has been arrested for the crimes, why would someone choose this place specifically to hide or bury a weapon? There are closer beaches and tons of lakes."

"That brings us right back to the Ezzo connection here in Cedar Key. That's why it has to be your uncle or one of his associates. Could it be hidden underneath a dock or in a crab trap? They're everywhere around here. What do you think of that theory?"

Phil raised his eyebrows. "It's a good one. But do you know how many there are? How many places they could be out in the water?"

"Exactly. It's like trying to find Waldo in a crowd of red-and-white striped shirts."

Phil rolled back on the quilt with laughter, grabbing his stomach. "Kathryn, you're so awesome!"

"Thank you. But we've still got a missing weapon out there."

"You're not going to rest until you find it, are you?"

"Nope."

"What can I do to help you relax?"

"Point me to that gun."

"I think the only way I can do that is to ask my uncle where it's at."

Kathryn shrugged and raised her eyebrows.

"Kathryn, if I do that, I wouldn't be able to tell you because of attorney-client confidentiality."

"Assuming you were to defend him."

"If I ask, then the assumption would be correct. So I'm in as much a predicament as you."

She puffed. "I'm going to keep studying the file and find the missing piece to this puzzle. I'm curious why he cares enough about the gun to hide it and not just throw it away somewhere."

CHAPTER 8

Phil waved as Kathryn pulled away from his house, grabbed the cooler off the ground then bounded up the stairs like a teenager. Giddy, was he? He'd never felt like this before. Not even with Maria. Others might think the taboo nature of their association had him dancing in his mind, but his heart told him something different. Kathryn was a unique woman with a genuine heart, and he had to get to know her more.

Phil unloaded the cooler's contents into his refrigerator and pantry and stretched out on the couch. He grabbed the remote off the coffee table, but after finding nothing to watch, he gave up. He couldn't stop thinking about Kathryn. Her countenance, her beauty, everything about her had taken him prisoner. How, in two short days, had she stolen his desire to remain carefree and unattached and replaced it with a longing to spend every moment with her?

A strong, independent woman on the outside with an internal yearning for love—that was Kathryn. She'd had the encounter at church which proved her heart wasn't too calloused yet. No matter what damage had been done to her in the past, her heart was fertile soil, ready to receive God's goodness. Kathryn wanted to belong. She craved acceptance. Phil could help her find it. He'd point her right to the One who would love her unconditionally. Could he be more to her than that though? Would she allow him to visit her in Mitchell's Crossing and take her on a real date?

His phone vibrated, and he rolled over onto his side and dug it out of his pocket. Judging by the area code, it was Kathryn. Panic coursed through Phil's body like an incurable virus, and he jumped up off the couch, ready to go into attack mode. "Hello?"

"Hey, it's Kathryn."

"Are you okay?"

"Yes, I'm fine." She laughed.

Phil relaxed his shoulders and let out a heavy sigh.

"I was wondering…I know we've already eaten but…I found an ice cream maker here at the condo and thought maybe you'd want to come over in a bit and eat some ice cream and dig into this file with me."

"I'd love to. What about the background check?"

"I can't exactly do that now, can I? I'm not even supposed to be acquainting myself with the case anymore."

"I guess not. Then I must say thank you for trusting me enough to have me over for ice cream. Do you have your ingredients?"

"No, but I'm going to run back to the store. I want to revisit that manager or owner or whatever he is."

"Kathryn, you're off the case. Remember?"

"Oh, I remember, but he doesn't know that. Even if I don't get to talk to him, I need groceries if I'm going to stay the week."

"How about I go with you?"

"No, I'll be fine. Thanks though."

Independent women—why was he attracted to them? They never knew how to let a man be a gentleman. He chuckled. "Okay, if you're sure. What time can I come over?"

"Give me an hour. I'm going to hurry so I don't miss—"

"The sunset?"

"You guessed it!"

"You had better hurry because the store closes at 8:00 p.m."

Kathryn said goodbye, and Phil did a disco spin in the middle of his living room. He scratched his stubbly chin. He shouldn't get too excited. Kathryn was three-fourths business and one-fourth personal. This was about solving the case. But as he trotted off to his room to shower and change clothes, something blossomed inside his heart that had been dead a long time. Hope.

* * *

Kathryn fluffed her hair and straightened her T-shirt when Phil rang the doorbell. Sadie jumped up from her spot beside the sliding glass door and beat Kathryn to the door. Kathryn sucked in a deep breath, determined not to let Phil sweep her away by his presence. "Come on in. You walked?" She motioned outside to the path where his vehicle should have been.

"Sure. It's nice out. And you're so close." Phil handed Kathryn a bottle of chocolate syrup and a bag of mini chocolate drops. "For the ice cream." He leaned in and placed a soft kiss on her cheek, sending a jolt of heat to her toes, the scent of exotic spices and wood tickling her nose.

She smiled and stumbled away from the door, dizzy

with glee. "Thanks! And thanks for coming over." Trying not to let this man affect her was a useless battle.

"Thanks for inviting me. This is a beautiful place, isn't it? They've updated it since I was here last."

"I like it. It's got everything a vacationer could need." Kathryn mixed the ingredients for the ice cream, poured them into the canister, stuck the dasher into it, then snapped on the lid. She added the rock salt and ice and turned on the machine. "The ice cream should be ready in about twenty-five minutes."

"I can't wait to try it." Sadie sidled up next to Phil and put her paw on his leg. He rubbed her ears, so Kathryn didn't scold her for being a pest. "Do you make ice cream often?"

"I know my way around an ice cream maker." She curtsied. "It's my mother's famous chocolate fudge recipe. You'll love it. We can sit out here on the patio, if you'd like." Kathryn led the way through the living area, and Phil and his shadow, Sadie, followed.

"I'm glad you're staying in Cedar Key this week."

Kathryn sat in one of the lounge chairs and motioned to the one beside her. "Did I have a choice?"

Phil lowered himself into the chair and kicked off his flip-flops. "You could've gone home. Or somewhere else."

"True, but I needed a place like Cedar Key. Lazy and low key. And…I wanted to get to know you a little better."

"You just want to know what I know about my family."

"Not true." Kathryn giggled then got up to check on the groaning ice cream freezer. Disappointment would pour down on top of her if this freezer quit working. She'd been craving ice cream since she'd gotten here Friday and thus far, it had played hide-and-seek with her. She could hardly count the melting concoction she'd had on the pier. When she returned to the patio, she handed Phil a bottled water and returned to her chaise.

He nodded and took the bottle from her, their fingers touching in passing. "So you don't dislike me?"

Kathryn paused with her water bottle halfway to her lips and peered at him out of the corner of her eyes. "I don't dislike you."

His foot shook like a nervous squirrel. "Would— would you consider going on a date with me?"

"I thought the boat ride and picnic was kind of a date."

"You did?" He grinned. Then he sat up and turned to her, finding her eyes with his. "Well, I'd like to take you on a real date once this case is over."

There went her heart again. Fluttering like a butterfly. Sweat trickled down between her shoulder blades and across her forehead, and it wasn't from the heat. A real date? She'd almost forgotten what a real date was like. Since her break-up with Zeke over a year ago, she'd turned down every request for a date, not that there'd been that many. She'd be crazy to turn down a date with Phil. "You wouldn't have a problem with the fact that I'm Maria's friend?"

He shook his head and shaded his eyes with his hand. "You aren't really her friend anymore, are you?"

"Good point." Sadie left Phil's side and returned to the cool of the condo. "Let me go check on the freezer again. It's making a weird noise." Kathryn followed Sadie indoors and added a bit more ice and rock salt to the machine. The churning was slowing so the ice cream would be ready soon. When she rejoined Phil, he sat on the edge of the pool with his feet swirling in the water. Kathryn sat beside him and slipped her feet into the coolness.

Phil nudged her with his elbow. "Besides, you should feel more hesitant about going out with me because I'm the ex-fiancé. You were just an innocent friend."

She touched him on the forearm. "You're an innocent ex-fiancé."

"Ha, I've never been accused of being innocent. But I was innocent—or naïve—about her whereabouts most of the time. Of course, I spent a lot of time focusing on my career and didn't put enough time into pursuing her. So you can't really blame her for finding someone else."

"I don't believe that one bit. You're a kind man. Maria is a fool for messing that up."

"Thanks." He took a swig from his water bottle and wiped his mouth with his hand. "So would you go on a real date with me?"

She splashed the water with her feet. "Of course."

"Awesome." He pumped his fists in the air. "How did things go at the store?"

"As I expected. That guy wasn't there, so I didn't get any new information. I'm still not sure your uncle did it, but there's no doubt he was present, and he probably gave the command."

"It's definitely looking that way. I'm surprised that he went all the way to Georgia for something like this instead of just sending someone to take care of things for him. There is obviously something extremely personal about this situation to him for him to make his presence known and risk his freedom."

Kathryn rubbed her forehead. "I think there's going to be a mistrial if the weapon isn't found."

"You'll get charges to stick because he was there."

"Yeah, but I want the charges to be enough to put him away so he won't do this again."

"Putting Louie away doesn't mean he won't do it again. He has a long reach and lots of goons."

Kathryn groaned. "That's why I can't give up even though they took me off the case. I still think the gun is somewhere out there in the water, but I don't know where. The only other lead I have is a mention in the file of a honeymooning couple. Something about the couple having a secret. But who would that couple have been?"

"Wait! A honeymooning couple?"

"Yes."

Phil pulled his legs out of the water and slapped his knees. "Okay, you know the rundown shack out in the water?"

"Yes." She swirled the water with her toes.

Phil did a pretend slam dunk motion with his right hand and let out of puff of air. "That's called the honeymoon shack."

"What?"

"Yes!"

"Do you think somebody hid the gun out there?"

"I don't know, but it's worth a shot. We could get my boat out there tomorrow when the tide is high and look for it."

"But it's about to fall into the water. How would someone have gotten a weapon out there?"

"Very easy. Just go out there on a boat."

She grabbed his shoulder. "Do you think that's where it's hidden?"

"I don't know, but that's the first thing we're going to do tomorrow. I'll pick you up at your dock, and we'll go and see for ourselves."

The sun dipped behind the trees, waving goodnight to
Kathryn and Phil as they sat on the dock finishing their ice
cream. Sadie sat at their feet and woofed every time a pelican
attempted to land on the rail.

Phil's phone buzzed. He pulled it out of his pocket
and looked at the screen. He hit the decline button and
placed it on the table between them.

Kathryn pulled her hair back into a ponytail. The
wind beat her senseless. "Did you need to take that call?"

Phil turned up his lip. "No. It's nothing that can't
wait." He squeezed the back of his neck and sighed.

Something bothered him. A darkness had come over
his face as soon as he'd looked at the phone's screen. Kathryn
had seen that look before. She'd made that face too many
times to count. When the phone vibrated on the table again,
Phil silenced it and tapped his forehead with his fist.

Kathryn cut her eyes sideways at him. They'd been
sharing the serenity of the sunset and swaying to the current
before his caller had interrupted. They'd theorized about the
weapon, reviewed the details of the murder, and savored
every bite of the ice cream. Now Phil's foot shook, and his
hands tapped on his knees. Whoever had called had ruined
the mood.

His phone buzzed again, and he groaned.

"You can get that if you need to. It must be
important."

He puffed. "I'm sorry." He picked up the phone and
hit the answer button. "What's up?" he barked. Phil massaged
the back of his neck again and looked out into the darkening
sky as he listened to the caller. "Um, I'm not at home."

After a moment, he stood and paced around the dock. The wind was violent, but Kathryn was able to catch most of his words. "Why do you want to know where I am?" He paced like a caged lion. Then he leaned on the rail and buried his head in his left hand.

Whoever was on the other end of that call was obviously someone he didn't want to talk to. If Phil was a dog, his hackles would be raised by now. Kathryn scraped the last bite of her ice cream out of her Styrofoam cup and tried to focus on the final glimmer of sun going down, the pink and orange sky displaying God's glory. He must care about the world to create such splendor.

Phil shoved his phone into his pocket and plopped down next to Kathryn.

"Is everything okay?"

"Not really. That was my cousin, Drew. He's here in Cedar Key and looking for me."

That couldn't be good for either one of them. "What did you tell him?"

"That I wasn't home. I've got to stall him until we can get out there to the shack."

CHAPTER 9

Kathryn paced in front of the sliding glass door, wearing a groove in the peacock-colored shag area rug and waited for Phil to pull up at her dock. What was taking him so long? He'd walked home to get his boat an hour ago, and he should've been back fifteen minutes ago.

Phil had spent the rest of the night in the spare bedroom to avoid running into Drew after Kathryn had taken him home and they'd discovered his Mercedes parked in his drive. Something must have happened to Phil. Had Drew taken him to Georgia to see Ezzo? Surely, he would've called to warn her. "Where are you, Phil?"

Her phone chimed on the counter. She ran to retrieve it, tripped over Sadie, and stumbled into the edge of the glass coffee table. "Ouch!" She grabbed her shin and hopped the rest of the way to the kitchen. "That's going to make a terrible bruise, Sadie." She picked up the phone. A text from Phil waited for her in her messaging box.

Kathryn, Drew is here. I'm trying to stall him and get to you as soon as I can. We have to get to the gun before he does. Be waiting. Phil

Kathryn collapsed on the bar stool and dropped her phone to the counter. She buried her head in her trembling hands. This was like a mafia movie. How were they going to find the weapon before Drew got to it? He obviously knew where it was. Could her life be in danger for associating with Phil?

She uncovered her face and slapped the top of her legs. How had she gotten herself into this mess? She needed protection. But who would protect her if Phil was unable to? What if Phil was a threat to her, after all?

I will.

Kathryn lifted her bowed head and turned it to both sides. Who said that? Great! Now she was hearing voices in her head.

She needed a plan of action in case Phil didn't return to her—in case she couldn't trust him. Things like that always happened in John Grisham novels. She popped up off the stool and darted over to the phone directory on the foyer table. She flipped to the boat rental section. If she had to, she'd rent a boat herself and find the gun. Then she'd call D.A. Schwartz and tell him not to let Louie Ezzo out of jail. She'd contact the local police and have them arrest Drew, and maybe Phil, on suspicion of being connected with the murders.

A beeping sound repeated several times out back. Kathryn ran to the back door. Phil was at the dock in his skiff, waving at her with both hands, like a hitchhiker trying to get a ride on the side of the road. She grabbed her cell phone and keys, locked the back door, and left without saying a word to Sadie.

Kathryn ran across the tree-lined patio, branches whacking her in the face, and down the walkway to the dock, careful not to trip on the uneven boards. "Where've you been?" She took Phil's offered hand and jumped into the boat. "I was worried sick!"

"I told you. Drew was at my house. He insisted on taking me to see Uncle Louie." Phil shoved the boat into gear, and Kathryn grabbed on to the rail. "I told him I had some business to attend to before I could consider going anywhere."

"Phil, I'm scared. Are our lives in danger?" Kathryn yelled over the rushing wind.

"I don't think so. At least I hope not."

Kathryn's fear and anxiety churned her stomach into a mass of molten lava. She gripped the railing and braced herself for what they'd find at the old honeymoon shack. Her fear must've been painted across her face because Phil reached his arm around her and drew her to his side. She stepped closer to him and let his presence blanket her in security.

The skiff bounced on the waves, and the waves reciprocated by pounding into it, splashing the sea onto Kathryn and Phil. The engine roared as Phil pressed the skiff to its maximum speed, begging the boat to take them to their destination with haste. Kathryn's heart pounded against her chest. The moment she'd waited for since she'd arrived Friday evening was finally here.

"Phil," she yelled. "If we find the gun, we have to remember not to smudge the fingerprints."

"I've got a plastic bag we can use to pick it up." He lowered the gear, and the skiff bumped along the waves, rocking them from side to side.

Thunder rumbled and lightning clapped in the distance. Kathryn grabbed on to Phil's forearm with both of her hands. If it rained, they'd never be able to climb the rickety pylons to the remnants of the shack and find the gun.

Phil pulled the skiff up to a pylon and tied a rope around it. "You stay here. I'm going to climb up and see if I can find the gun." He steadied himself as the boat rocked in the waves.

"Let me go. I'm lighter than you, and I can probably climb easier." She stepped toward the edge of the skiff. Thunder rumbled again, and Kathryn lost her balance. She teetered on the edge of the boat and fell back onto the driver's seat. "Never mind. You go."

Phil laughed. "Oh, so now it's okay for me to put my life at risk?"

Kathryn covered her mouth with her hand and winced. If her choices were to stay in the safety of the boat or climb up what was left of the shack and possibly fall into the dark Gulf, she'd pick the safety of the boat. "Sorry. I'm more of a coward than I thought."

Phil winked at her and hoisted his way up onto the post.

"Be careful!"

"I will." He found his footing and then pushed himself up to a strip of what must have previously been the floor of the shack.

The skiff banged into the side of the pylon, and Kathryn squealed. What would she do if it turned over? What if Phil fell into the water? She turned to the back of the boat. Two lifejackets were pinned to the underneath of the bench seat. She rushed back there, put one of the lifejackets on, and then brought the other one to the front with her.

A pelican balanced on one of the pylons and stalked Phil. Sea gulls and egrets soared in the increasing wind, and waves crashed against the boat and the shack. A dark cloud rolled in overhead, casting its gloom upon them.

Kathryn cupped her hands around her mouth and screamed, "Do you see anything?"

"No, nothing. There's nothing here."

"Then come back down. I'm afraid we're going to get struck by lightning or that the boat is going to turn over." After another clap of lightning, the sky opened up, and rain poured down on them. Kathryn wrapped her arms around her waist and squeezed her eyes shut. This had to be the craziest stunt she'd ever allowed herself to be involved in. Finding the weapon was not worth risking her life—or Phil's. "Phil, please come back to the boat!"

"I'm coming." Phil eased his foot off the top of the pylon, sending the pelican into the burgeoning storm.

The boat slammed into the pylon, and Kathryn tumbled to the back. When she righted herself, Phil was nowhere. "Phil! Phil!" She slipped to the front of the boat and leaned over the edge.

Phil reached his hand up out of the water. "Help me up!"

Kathryn reached for the lifejacket, but it was floating away beyond the shack. The wind must have blown it out of the boat. "Hold on! I'll get you." She reached over the side of the boat as far as she could but couldn't get to his outstretched hand. "Reach, Phil!"

Phil went under the water and crashed into the pylon. Then he popped up at the edge of the skiff. Kathryn reached again and grabbed him by the back of his T-shirt. She held on to the railing and pulled on Phil until it felt like she would go overboard too. She groaned and tugged with all her might using every bit of strength she had in her.

Phil coughed and gagged then grasped on to Kathryn's arms. She yanked, and he pulled, and finally they got him back into the boat. They fell to the back, saturated from the rain, gasping for air.

"Thank. You. Kathryn." Phil coughed and sucked in as much air as would fit into his lungs.

"You're welcome, but don't ever do that again." She beat at his chest. "I thought you were a goner."

"I almost was." Phil pushed himself to his feet and offered Kathryn his hand. He helped her to the bench. "Sit here. I'm going to get us out of this storm."

* * *

Kathryn handed Phil a towel and went into the kitchen to brew some coffee. Sadie sat at Phil's feet. "What about your cell phone? Did you have it on you?"

"No, it was in the boat's glove compartment. I've learned my lesson about having my phone on me when I'm around water."

"Smart move." She slipped the single-serve cup into the slot, shut the lid, and pressed the brew button. "If you falling in and the boat crashing against the pier hadn't been such a scary experience, it'd kind of be comical."

Phil towel-dried his hair and tossed the towel on the coffee table. "I say we go ahead and laugh about it because if we get distraught, it's just going to make things worse."

"I'm glad you were the one who climbed up there because if I had fallen into that water, I'd probably have had a heart attack before you could've rescued me."

"Not true because I would've jumped in as soon as your body hit the water."

She pinched his beardless cheek. "Aww, thanks."

"Let's not waste anymore of our time thinking about

my near drowning or the case today."

Kathryn propped her hand on her hip. "How do you propose we do that with your cousin lurking around Cedar Key?"

"I'm going to go home and take a shower then take you for breakfast."

"It's almost lunch time." Kathryn laughed, letting the aroma of the Columbian roast ease her stress.

"Okay, we'll go for lunch." Phil punctuated his sentence with the waving of his hands.

If he insisted on persuading her, Kathryn would share a table with him again. She giggled under her breath. Who was she trying to fool? It wouldn't take any persuading at all. "Lunch sounds good. I still don't see how you can just push the case aside completely. We've hit one big dead end after another. I can't believe the gun wasn't at the shack."

"It may have been at some point. Someone may have gotten to it before we did since you were asking questions about it. Or it could've gotten knocked off by a bird or a storm."

"You know that means your uncle is not going to go down for murder if he's guilty."

"I refuse to believe that. All we need to do is find somebody who knows what happened."

"You make it sound so easy. Since I no longer have access to the information, and you don't want to defend him, I don't see how we can get our hands on any more evidence."

"You're right." He accepted the red-and-white lighthouse adorned mug from Kathryn.

She sat next to him on the sofa with her mug in her hand.

Phil stared into her eyes and drank from his cup.

"This is good!"

She smiled at his compliment. Oh, to forget all about the case right now and focus on what was happening between them—but her mind couldn't let it go. Too much hinged on this case. She blew on her coffee and sipped its richness.

"Kathryn, why do you care so much?"

The way he said her name, it sounded smooth like honeysuckle dripping off the vine. She could sit and listen to him say it a million times and never tire of it.

"Kathryn?"

She cleared her throat. "I told you. I'll never get another chance at a case like this."

"So?"

"So…my career will be over."

"And?"

Kathryn huffed, "And I'll be unemployed, for one reason, but I'll also let a lot of people down if I fail at this."

"Like who?"

"You're nosey, aren't you?"

"When I have to be. I know there's something you're not telling me."

Kathryn took a long sip of her coffee and placed the mug on the coffee table. She wasn't used to revealing so much of her heart to people she barely knew, but it felt like she'd known Phil for a lifetime already. "My father wants me to be a Supreme Court Justice. So much so that he almost convinced my mom to name me Justice when I was born."

"Seriously? Then you would've been Supreme Court Justice Justice. I'm sure you'd have gotten a lot of snickers with that."

"Exactly!" She rolled her eyes. "Nothing wrong with being named Justice as long as your occupation isn't being a justice in the Supreme Court system. In order to get there though, regardless of my name, I have to be a judge first. In order to be a judge, I have to become District Attorney. My county is small and is run judicially mostly by men. They're all good old boys. It takes a lot of work to get their approval. This case could get me closer to my goal."

"You mean your dad's goal." He touched her knee with the lightness of a butterfly's wings, leaving behind a sensation that left Kathryn breathless.

She shrugged. "True."

"Is that what you want?"

"I don't know anymore. But if not this, I'm not sure what I'd do."

They lingered over their coffee and watched the pelicans and seagulls soar outside in the post-storm afternoon heat. Sadie tapped her tail on the floor and pinned her ears back every time a bird swooped in front of the door. Phil stretched out his legs, letting his thigh rest against Kathryn's thigh. Could she believe this meant something? That he was interested in her. Could it be possible?

"Do you know the whole story about why Maria found someone to replace me? My best friend, at that?"

Kathryn grimaced. "Great subject change."

"Sorry. Do you?"

"No, but do I want to know? That's part of your past, and it's private."

"I want to tell you." He turned toward her, placing his mug on the coffee table.

"Okay." Kathryn changed her position and faced him.

"Unless you don't want to hear."

"No, I'd love to know what happened."

"Promise not to laugh."

Kathryn raised her right eyebrow. "I can promise, but since you've already broken that promise to me twice…" She twirled a tendril of hair and stared out the window.

He bent his neck until he captured her gaze with his. "All right, all right. Guilty as charged."

Kathryn patted his knee. "I promise not to laugh."

"Maria wanted to be more physical than I wanted to be. I know that sounds like I'm some kind of freak or something, but I was trying to do things differently than the men in my family. I didn't want any unplanned children, and I didn't want there to be deep scars if we didn't make it, the kind you get when you're physically attached to someone. Apparently she wasn't willing to wait."

"Yeah, well, that doesn't make you a freak. It makes you admirable. It shows you respected her even if she didn't respect herself. For the record, I didn't know any of that. I just always assumed y'all were…involved."

"I think a lot of people thought that. Maria liked it that way."

"That's kind of how things happened with me and Zeke. He did a lot of unwarranted talking. I probably wasn't as chaste as you were, but I'd been raised pretty conservatively and wanted to keep my reputation clean, so I wouldn't move in with him when he asked me to and wouldn't spend the night. As a side note, my dad was cheating on my mom the whole time he was telling me to remember that people were watching me and that I'd better live an upright life."

"Crazy."

"I know. Such a hypocrite. I thought I'd marry Zeke, but he wanted to test drive the car first, so we were at an impasse. He was too busy being a playboy to realize how much I cared for him. When we broke up, he moved in with a friend of mine a few weeks later, and I pretty much swore off men."

"So we've both had the same situation happen to us. Has it made you reluctant to get involved again?"

"You have no idea. I figure all men must be cheaters, so I'm better off focusing on my career." Kathryn raised her eyebrows and shook her head. She'd succeeded at everything but love. Phil waited for her to continue, seeming to take everything she said in seriousness. "I'm not good at relationships. I fell in love in high school, or thought I did, and that ended poorly like most high school relationships do. I fell in love again in college, and that was a disaster because he wanted me to put him through med school and promised to put me through law school after he graduated but had no plans of marriage in his future. I knew that would end one-sided, leaving me without a ring on my finger and no law school while he had trysts with nurses in the hospital."

"Yeah, it wouldn't be the first time something like that happened."

"See, you see my side of things. Thank you for that. When I got to law school, I met Zeke. I didn't know how to have a successful relationship because I'd never seen it modeled before. I saw too many of my friends fall in love with the wrong person—or be the wrong person, like Maria. With the way my parents' hypocritical relationship was, and the way things turned out with Zeke, I figure I'm not going to be any good at it for a long time."

"I'm not a gambling man, but I'll bet that's not true."

CHAPTER 10

Phil pulled away from the dock at Kathryn's rental condo, as she waved at him from the porch. Lunch had possessed a different flavor than their lunch on either Saturday or Sunday. How in just two days had they formed a bond that felt like they'd known each other their entire lives? They couldn't be more different. She, the Southern belle of the courtroom. He, the runaway attorney whose voice reverberated like a cymbal.

Something in Kathryn's eyes told him she was open to exploring the possibility of getting to know him more. The distrust he'd seen in them earlier had melted away. Could he show her the flipside of what men could be like? Could he prove to her that not all men were cheaters?

Was knowing him dangerous for her? His life could be in danger if he didn't defend Uncle Louie and his goons, so hers could be by association, as well. There had to be a way to keep her safe yet allow him to spend time with her.

"Lord, you know what I need. You know how lonely I am. I'd love an opportunity to make Kathryn a part of my life. But despite the danger, there's also her trust issues. She doesn't trust men, and I'm not sure if she trusts you. Please work in her life."

In the stillness of the afternoon heat, a gust of wind blasted across Phil. God had always spoken to him through the wind. He'd take comfort in the breeze that now blew and trust God to resolve the barriers that threatened to keep them apart.

Phil eased up to the dock, his shoulders slumping. Drew's black Mercedes sat underneath the fifty-year-old Live oak and the scraggly palms. "What is he doing here again?" He tied the skiff to the dock post and sprung out of it onto the dock. He tossed his sunglasses onto the front seat of his SUV through the open window when he walked past it on the way to the stairs.

If it were possible for his blood to boil, it would be boiling right now. It was bad enough that Drew had to come to Cedar Key uninvited, but to show up uninvited at his house again was ridiculous. Phil climbed the steps to the porch, taking two at a time. He opened the screened door and slid his key into the lock.

Drew cleared his throat from where he sat in the swing at the end of the porch, facing the water. Without turning around, he called out in a gruff voice, "I've been waiting for you to get back. Are you done with business? I'd like to get on the road."

Phil wrenched his key out of the lock and let the screen door slam behind him as he stepped to the side porch. "No, Drew, I'm not. You can't just come down here and expect me to drop everything to help our uncle."

Drew stood from the swing, sending it into a frenzy, hiked his shorts up higher on his waist, and closed the distance between them. He towered several inches over Phil and outweighed him by thirty or forty pounds. He stared into Phil's eyes with clear blue eyes hooded by thick-lashed eyelids, the scar over his right eye contributing to his menacing guise. "Why not? It's what families do."

Phil stepped back and scowled. "Family? Family is when you're there for each other all the time. Mutually. Unselfishly. Not just when you're in trouble and need someone to bail you out."

Drew lifted his ball cap off his head and wiped away his sweat with the back of his hand. "Yeah, yeah, whatevah." He returned the cap to his head.

"Whatevah is right." Phil turned away and headed toward the front door.

"You're coming with me." Drew grabbed Phil by the arm, yanking him around to face him.

"Get your hands off of me!" Phil yanked his arm free and locked his knees. If Drew wanted to go a round or two, Phil welcomed it. "This is ridiculous." Phil turned away from Drew and unlocked the door. He stepped in and then turned back to his cousin. "I'm not coming to Georgia with you."

Drew followed him into the house. "Are you coming on your own then?" He lit a cigarette and plopped down on Phil's sofa.

"Maybe. I'm going to call Uncle Louie this afternoon." He grabbed the cigarette out of Drew's mouth. "Don't smoke in here." He carried the cigarette over to the sink and shoved it into the disposal. He turned on the water and clicked the switch to turn the disposal on. His hands were as unsteady as a new surgeon in his first surgery.

"When did you become such a jerk? And a traitor?"

Phil swung around to face Drew. "I'm not either of those things. I've just learned to take care of myself and to live without being manipulated by others. You should try it sometime."

Drew rubbed his face and chuckled. "No thanks. I like the security family brings."

"Some security. Doing the dirty work for someone else will come back and bite you in the..." Phil shook his head. It was useless trying to explain things to Drew.

"In the what? Mr. Goodie-goodie can't curse anymore? Is that it?" Drew slid another cigarette out of the pack and twirled it through his fingers almost daring Phil to try to take this one from him.

Phil poured a glass of water from the pitcher on the counter, and he gulped it down in a few swallows. Sweat trickled down both sides of his face, half from anger, half from fear. "I'm not a goodie-goodie, Drew. I'm living my life better now."

Drew stuck the cigarette behind his right ear and folded his hands in mock prayer. "For *God*, is it?"

"Yes. For God. Now, if you will, leave so I can get the rest of my work done." He motioned toward the door.

"Can't we stay here?"

Phil tipped his head. "We?"

"Yeah. Me and Barney."

"Barney is here with you? Why did you bring him? He'll cause more damage than good." Phil sighed. His cousins held less sense in their heads combined than a mindless sheep.

"He's the best one for convincing people to do what we need them to do. Capisce?"

"No, no capisce. I don't want to hear anything about your plans, and I don't want any part in them. Now leave." Phil shoved his hands into his pockets.

"We seriously can't stay?"

Phil shook his head.

"Well, that's okay. I've got to pay a visit to the D.A. who's here in Cedar Key trying to dig up dirt on Louie."

The freight train of Drew's words collided with Phil's heart and pinned him against the wall. He couldn't let his cousins endanger Kathryn, but he couldn't let on that he knew her either. "Wait! What are you talking about?"

Drew's gaze roamed over Phil's face, obviously picking up on Phil's nervousness. "If you must know, some D.A. named Kathryn from Perkins County is here. Sam at the grocery told me she's been snooping around the last few days."

"So what? She's not worth the effort, I'm sure. If there's something here that ties Louie to the murder, it's probably been taken care of. Right?"

"How should I know, Phil?" Drew roared with laughter.

That confirmed it. Drew knew where the gun was. So why didn't he just go get it and get out of Cedar Key? Why did he feel the need to stay and harass both Phil and Kathryn? Phil's throat locked up on him. Drew must know they'd met. He had to convince Drew to stay under the radar. "Why bother with a woman? She's no threat."

"I wouldn't be so sure about that, man. They say she's like a rabid fox on a hunt when she's after evidence. I can't risk letting her slip through the cracks. I already tried to warn her, but she doesn't take hints too well."

Phil ran his fingers through his hair and then held on to the back of his neck. If he could take Drew down right here in his kitchen, he would. But his confidence dissipated like the coolness of the morning breeze. "Drew, just go back to New York. Haven't you gotten into enough trouble already?"

"Not nearly enough."

"You're going to end up turning the attention on you and Barney, and you'll be brought in for questioning."

"Already was, and we're out on bond. We're untouchable, Phil. When are you going to learn that?" He laughed and walked out through Phil's screen door, letting it slam behind him.

From the doorway, Phil stood, hand on cell phone, waiting for Drew to pull away. Drew and Barney were the two associates Kathryn had told him about. Well, they weren't missing anymore.

* * *

Kathryn leaned against her car, waiting for Phil to answer his phone, her orange sherbet sundress blowing in the hot breeze. She tried to return to the calm state she'd been in earlier, but it wasn't working. She'd convinced herself that the rest of the week would be as smooth as an adventure around Cedar Key in a sailboat. Slipping through the water. Wind in her hair. Phil by her side. What a mistake that had been. Here she stood on the side of the road surrounded by nothing but trees, both of her back tires flat, almost shredded.

"Hello?" Phil's voice created a balm on Kathryn's spirit, like ointment on skin after a sunburn.

"Hey, Phil."

"Kathryn? Are you okay? I was just about to call you."

"I'm okay, but I can't say the same for my car. I've just had two flat tires."

"*Two* flat tires? Did you hit something?"

"No."

"Where are you?"

With no road signs in sight, how could she point Phil to her exact location? "I'm stuck on Florida 24. I was headed to follow up on a lead I found in the file."

"How far out are you?"

"About thirty minutes. I'm out in the middle of nowhere. I haven't seen a car since I stopped."

"I'm on my way now. Stay in your car with the doors locked, in case someone followed you."

She looked in all directions. "I doubt anyone did. I'm out here alone except for a dead armadillo. Why would someone have followed me anyway?" She walked around the back of her car and shut the trunk hatch. She would have changed the tire herself if there had only been one flat.

"You've been getting threats, right?"

"Not since they took me off the case."

"Listen to me. I have reason to believe you're in danger."

"What?" She might as well have stepped on a rattlesnake for all the adrenaline that shot through her body.

"Drew was at my house when I got back from lunch with you. My cousin Barney is here with him. He's the one who does the convincing, if you know what I mean. They know you're here."

She squeezed her scalp. "They know I'm here? Are they the ones who threatened me?"

"Drew didn't admit to it, but I'm positive it's them. I'm 99% sure they're the associates you said were with Louie."

"What are their legal names?"

"Matthew Bernard Ezzo and Andrew Thomas Ezzo."

"That's them!"

"I pretended not to know you and tried to discourage

Drew from pursuing you. If they're following you, they're hoping to catch you defenseless."

Kathryn jumped into her car and locked the doors.

"Phil, I'm freaking out! What if one of them—or both—is following me now?"

"How long have you been sitting there?"

She stared into the rearview mirror. "I—I don't know. About fifteen minutes."

"Okay, that's good. If they were following you, they'd already have come up to you. Probably pretending to assist you. Unless—" Phil groaned.

"What?" She ducked her head.

"Unless they're waiting to see if I'm coming to help you."

"But you said they didn't know you knew me."

"Yeah, well, they're not always as dumb as I'd like to think they are. Drew did look at me kind of funny when I tried to convince him to leave you alone."

"What should I do?"

"Exactly what I said. Just sit there in the car with the doors locked and windows rolled up. Don't take help from anyone but me. I'll be there in twenty minutes."

"Okay." Kathryn cranked the car and rolled up her windows. Somehow, she'd tricked herself into believing there'd be no more threats. Not smart. Whoever leaked it to the D.A. that she'd been seen with Phil could just as easily have leaked it to Ezzo's goons--his nephews. Or they were the ones who leaked the info in the first place. She wouldn't be safe until Louie and everyone involved with him lived behind bars.

Kathryn pressed the seek button on her radio to find something soothing to listen to until Phil got to her. Old rock-n-roll wouldn't do the trick today. Neither would hip-hop. Old love songs were too depressing. On the fourth try, an ambient sound with a guitar solo caught her attention. That would do. She sat back in her seat and closed her eyes. Phil should be here in fifteen minutes.

> *Are you lonely and in need of a friend?*
> *Are you scared and need a rescue?*
> *Call out to the Father and let Him come in.*
> *He wants to take care of you.*

Kathryn's eyes popped open, and she sat straight up in her seat. The song continued, but she heard no other words after the ones that had spoken directly to her heart. It's as if the song was her song. Written just for her. On the radio screen, there was nothing. No artist and no song title.

Kathryn shivered. Was this song even playing on the radio? Was it a message to her from God? She laughed and shook her head. She'd obviously lost her mind from all the stress of this case. God didn't work that way.

Did He?

She rested her head on the headrest and closed her eyes again. The chorus repeated twice more, and the song ended without fanfare. It left behind a feeling of peace though. She wasn't alone. No matter how lonely she felt at times and how scared these threats made her, someone was watching out for her.

A knock on her window made her jump out of her seat. She turned to stare straight into the tiny blue eyes of a scraggly bearded man in greasy overalls. Was this one of Phil's cousins?

He tapped on the window again. "Miss? Do you need help?"

She shook her head as she pressed the lock button

making sure she'd locked the car. "Someone is on the way. Thanks."

"You sure?"

"Yes, thanks."

"Alrighty then. Have a good day." The man walked behind Kathryn's car and climbed into an old beat up wrecker. He honked his horn as he passed her and waved.

Kathryn let out her breath and ran her fingers through her hair. That was close. She had to stay alert. If that had been one of Phil's cousins, she could have been overpowered. She turned up the radio and let the next song fill her mind with something besides her fear.

CHAPTER 11

When Phil arrived, he honked his horn before approaching Kathryn's car. Now that was a gentleman.

Kathryn hopped out of the car and ran to him. He wore khaki pleated dress shorts, a white golf shirt, tucked in, and brown leather sandals. This was the most businesslike he'd looked since she'd met him, and the look suited him well. Casting aside all inhibitions, she embraced him. Phil encircled her waist with his arms.

"Thanks so much for coming to my rescue. No one has ever rescued me before."

"You're welcome." He pulled back and looked down into her tear-filled eyes. "No one?"

"No. I suppose it's because I'm usually acting as if I don't need help. But I'm starting to believe that that's the wrong approach to this life. It's not such a bad thing to need others."

"Life lessons learned in Cedar Key, huh?" Phil squeezed her waist and then released her. "Let's have a look at what we've got here." He bent to look at the back left tire, then walked around to the other side. When he stood, he sighed. "This doesn't look good."

"What do you mean?"

"Your tires were slashed."

"Slashed! How can you tell?"

"Come over here and look."

Kathryn walked around to the back right side of the car. Phil pointed out the cut marks in the tire. "I can't believe this. Who would have—"

"Who do you think?"

"Your cousins are serious about their work, aren't they?"

"You have no idea. See why I said you can't handle an Ezzo alone?"

"Yes, I see now. So what do we do now?"

Phil pointed at her trunk. "I'm assuming you don't have two spares in there."

She shook her head.

"Okay. Let me call my mechanic, Elmer. I'll get him to bring two new tires over from his place, and he'll put them on here."

"How far away is he?"

"Oh, his shop is just a few miles up the road. If he was further, I'd recommend towing your car. But he's pretty quick and always handy." Phil dialed a number and waited. He winked at Kathryn.

Despite the seriousness of the situation, Kathryn almost planted a whopper of a kiss on Phil's face. Of course, that wouldn't have been a ladylike thing to do. Unless she played the part of the damsel in distress. She giggled. She was losing her tough woman image, and it didn't bother her at all.

Phil raised his eyebrows, obviously wondering what she was laughing at. "Hey, Elmer? This is Phil. Yeah, I've got a friend's car over here on 24. She's got two sliced tires. Can you bring some replacements out here and put them on for us?" Phil waited, then knelt down beside the back left tire. "Yeah, they're P215/60R16. Thanks, man." Phil hit the end button and leaned back onto the back quarter panel. "Elmer will be here in a bit."

Kathryn leaned against the car beside Phil and circled her elbows with her fingers. "Did he say how much they'd cost?"

"No, but probably a hundred per tire."

"Ugh! This little trip is starting to eat away at my savings."

"You need me to cover you?"

"No, thanks. I've got it. I just hate spending money I don't have to spend."

Phil bent over and looked between his legs at the busted tire. "Looks like this is one of those times you have to spend money."

"You're funny. Truly funny." She smacked his arm. "You can turn it in on your insurance depending on what your deductible is."

"I suppose. I guess we could sit in the car in the air conditioning."

"If you want. Or we could just stand out here in the breeze with the armadillo and chat."

Kathryn laughed. "This isn't a breeze. This is a burst of hot air."

"Then into the car we go."

"Would you mind terribly if we sat in your car? I want a working mode of transportation in case we need to escape without much notice." She chewed on her forefinger.

"Absolutely. This way, ma'am." Phil escorted her to his SUV, opened the passenger side door for her, and shut it behind her.

Kathryn inspected the inside of the vehicle. Clean. Detailed. Not a gum wrapper in sight. No surprise. Although, he'd said his vehicle was worse than hers. He'd probably made it sound as if he was messy in order to make her feel better about herself. How sweet. After Phil slid into the car, he cranked it and turned down the radio then pointed the air vents toward her.

"Okay, so tell me about your cousins and how they plan to convince me not to prosecute your uncle—even though I'm actually not prosecuting him anymore."

"What do you want to know?"

She pulled her hair back into a ponytail, securing it with a brown hairband she'd had on her wrist. "What do they look like? How dangerous are they really? How do I get away from them permanently and not have to worry about joining you in the Witness Protection Program?"

Phil chuckled. "They can both be dangerous, but not in a deadly kind of way. They're the ones who know how to break a leg or cut off a thumb. They do the ground-level dirty work."

"Oh, that's comforting." Kathryn widened her eyes and shook her head at Phil. "You may be wrong about them though because remember they were arrested in Perkins County after the shootings along with your uncle? At least one of them has to be the shooter. That doesn't sound too harmless to me."

"True. I'm sure if Louie asked them to do it, they would have. They'll do anything to remain on the payroll. Now you see why I had to get out?"

She nodded.

"As far as the Witness Protection Program goes, I

wouldn't mind going into it if you could be by my side."

Kathryn nudged him with her elbow. "How sweet."

"Seriously. I could think of worse things than having to start over with a new name and occupation with someone like you beside me. If nothing else, it's better than going it alone."

Kathryn peered at him out of the corner of her eye, heat crawling up her spine. The tight cockpit of the SUV made it impossible for her to resist Phil's charm. What was happening to her tough shell? "You're slick."

"Slick? I'm being serious, Kathryn. I like you."

She faced him. Boy, he was close. "I—I like you too."

"I mean I really like you. As in I think it would be incredible to get to know you better."

"Well, I kinda think it would be amazing to get to know you better too, although it seems weird to say that to someone I didn't know three days ago. You think it has anything to do with the fact that it's virtually impossible for us to be anything more than acquaintances?"

"It's not impossible for us to be more than acquaintances, and if it were, that wouldn't be why I like you. I have nothing to prove to anyone. I don't need to be rebellious and throw my efforts into something or someone that's taboo. I like you because you're intriguing, sweet, funny, and…and quite lovely." Phil drummed his knees with his fingers.

"Okay, well, I don't have anything to prove to anyone either when it comes to my dating life. If I did, I would have already either made a move on you to prove that I could have any kind of guy I wanted, or I would have run away from you in an effort to impress whoever it is I was trying to impress."

"Because I'm that bad?"

"No, you goof. Because if I was trying to impress someone, you'd be at the bottom of the list of eligible candidates given our current situation."

"True. So why do you hang around with me?"

"Let's see." Her face and neck burned, and it wasn't from sitting in the car with the sun beating down on the windshield. She counted off the reasons on her fingers. "Although it seems like the two of us together breeds trouble, I'm apparently safer with you than without you."

"And?"

"You wrangle sharks."

He rolled his eyes. "And?"

"You've got a boat."

He laughed. "And?"

She smiled. "You're kind and interesting and…I think you're easy on the eyes. But you are a little irritating because you didn't tell me what your cousins look like. I think one of them came up to the car right before you got here."

Phil jumped in his seat and grabbed the steering wheel. "What? What did he look like?"

Kathryn shivered at the memory. "A scraggly-looking man with a beard. Piercing blue eyes. Drove a wrecker. Wore overalls."

Phil slung his head back onto the headrest and erupted with laughter. "You obviously know nothing about Italians. Especially ones born and bred in New York."

She punched him in the arm. "You're laughing at me. Again!"

"Sorry." He laughed into his hands.

"So what you're saying is they don't look like country folks from Georgia? They look more like the mafia guys in movies?"

"Something like that. Maybe not quite so stereotypical. But close." Phil scratched the back of his neck. "You would've known if one of them had approached you."

"How?"

"Because we probably wouldn't be sitting here right now." He pointed beyond the windshield. "There's Elmer now."

"That—that's Elmer?" Kathryn giggled and covered her face with her hands. "That's who I thought was your cousin."

"Nope. He's my buddy. He usually goes fishing with me. I figured that's who you were talking about when you described the man who approached you." Phil opened the car door and joined Elmer as he stepped down out of the wrecker, reaching his hand out to Phil.

Now that she had a better look at the man, it was clear that Elmer was the same man from the pier who congratulated Phil on his big catch. Kathryn was a poor judge of character by nature and too often critical and judging of innocent people. Sometimes she even had them convicted in her mind before the evidence had been fully disclosed. To be fair to herself, this critical attitude came with the job. She needed to learn how to be more discerning in the future. At least Elmer was one more advocate in Cedar Key. Kathryn needed all of them she could get.

She stepped down out of the SUV and introduced herself to Elmer. The sooner he could get her tires changed, the sooner she could see where the rest of this day would go.

"If you don't mind, I'd like to take pictures of this evidence before you start working." Kathryn whipped her phone out of her pocket and pulled up the camera app.

"Sure thing, ma'am." Elmer pulled his jack from the

back of his wrecker.

"And would you be able to keep the tires in your possession in case we need them for evidence later?"

"Anything for a friend of Tag's."

Tag? That was Phil's nickname? Not too shabby.

* * *

After Elmer changed Kathryn's tires and took her debit card information, he shook their hands, tipped his cap, and drove away.

Kathryn swiveled toward Phil, her hands cupped in front of her. "Thanks again for coming to my rescue."

He nodded. "My pleasure. Do you want to file a police report?"

"Against a mystery man? No thanks. I don't need to draw more attention to myself than I already have."

He shrugged. "If you're sure."

"I'm sure. Would you want to go with me to follow up on this lead?" She raised her shoulders up to her ears and grinned like a child asking for one more hour of reading time before bed. Phil looked at his watch, and Kathryn's heart plummeted. He'd already helped her more than she could ever repay him. She shouldn't have asked him to go with her. He obviously had other things to do.

"Where is it?"

"Somewhere in Chiefland. Off Highway 19. I'm not staying long because of Sadie. But I called and asked if I could come interview this man."

"You were going to go alone?"

Kathryn twisted up her mouth and nodded. "I know, not the smartest thing I've done today."

"You said it. Not me." Phil tossed his keys in the air. "I'll follow you."

A light drizzle landed on Kathryn's windshield and thunder rumbled in the distance as she pulled back onto Highway 24. She looked around her visor at the darkening sky then switched on the wipers. "If ever I need it not to rain, it's now." Mr. Ballew was waiting on her, and she needed a clear path in front of her to find his place in Chiefland. "GPS don't fail me now."

Kathryn turned on to County Road 345, and the GPS fired off directions to go six and a half miles and turn left onto Rocky Creek Road. Her destination would be on the left. She glanced back into her rearview mirror. Phil was right behind her. The lightning charge that had been running through her before Phil had come to her rescue was as dormant now as winter's trees.

She'd never been a part of a team, except a few times in law school. Even her staff seemed to exclude her most of the time. But Phil was there to help her, and he didn't care if he benefited or was harmed. That made Kathryn want to laugh or dance or go bungee jumping. Somehow, some way she'd express her joy when this was all over.

The rain disappeared as quickly as it had come. Within fifteen minutes, Kathryn pulled up to the old white farmhouse, rows of corn in the field to the left, pecan trees in the field to the right. Two brown-and-black mutts ran out from under the rusty old tractor beside the red barn, and chickens scattered across the lawn. Phil pulled in behind Kathryn.

A sun-baked man in overalls and a soiled white T-shirt climbed out from underneath the tractor and called to the dogs. He removed a green can from his back pocket and loaded his jaw up with what looked like tobacco, then returned the can to the pocket with a shove. He hollered at the dogs, and they ran into the crawlspace underneath the house. Hopefully, this man would lead her right to the weapon.

Kathryn straightened her sundress and slipped her sunglasses onto the top of her head. She reached her hand out to the grubby farmer, his brawny hand swallowing hers. "Mr. Ballew? I'm Kathryn Bellamy, Assistant District Attorney for Perkins County, Georgia. We spoke earlier on the phone."

He eyed Phil and wiped his neck with a blue bandana. "Howdy. You didn't say nothin' on the phone about bringin' nobody out here with ya."

"Oh, I'm sorry, Mr. Ballew. I had some car trouble back there on 24, and my friend came to help. He followed me here to make sure I didn't have any more trouble."

Mr. Ballew scratched his stubbly chin. "Mmhm, well, I don't 'xactly like the thought of talkin' in front of him."

Kathryn held up her right hand. "I understand. He's okay though. You can trust him. This is—"

Phil stepped forward, but Mr. Ballew retreated. "I know 'xactly who he is. And that's why I ain't comfortable talkin' with him around."

Kathryn held her hand up to push Phil toward his SUV, but Phil stepped closer to Mr. Ballew. "Excuse me, sir. You know who I am?"

The man nodded. "Yep, I do. You's one of those guys from New York."

Phil locked his knees and shoved his hands into his pockets. A less forceful posture might work with this simple farmer. "Yes, I am from New York originally, but I live in

Cedar Key now."

"Yeah, I know you do. You belong to that family. I—I ain't gonna talk with him around, miss."

Kathryn stepped closer to him and folded her hands in front of her. What did he know about Phil? If this man didn't trust him, should she? "Please, Mr. Ballew. I need to know what you know. I'll have him wait in the car." She glanced in Phil's direction and begged with her eyes.

"No, if you're associated with him, I'm not gonna talk to you neither."

Kathryn's heartbeat pounded in her head and threatened to explode out her ears. How had her budding trust in Phil turned into uncertainty in a matter of minutes? Trusting others had always proven to be a mistake. Was it going to happen this time too?

Phil rocked on the balls of his feet. "Sir, what family are you talking about?"

"The ones who keep murderin' people and breakin' arms and legs. No way I'm gettin' myself in the middle of things."

So he did know the Ezzo family. "Mr. Ballew, I can subpoena you for court if I have to. I really don't think you want me to do that. Do you?"

He swatted a fly and shook his head. "No, no, I don't. Listen, his family is bad news." He pointed at Phil.

"But I'm not, sir. I'm a former attorney and a private investigator. I am here to help her put the bad guys in jail permanently."

"Even if they's your family?"

"Even if they are my family, yes."

Mr. Ballew tightened his overall straps and scratched his chin again. "Two guys came down here with a gun that supposedly was used to kill a couple of people in Georgia. They hid it on the property of someone they know."

"You don't know any names?" This case was like a mosquito bite that wouldn't stop itching. Kathryn wouldn't be satisfied until she solved it.

"No, ma'am. That's all I know."

"Okay, I see." She tapped her chin. "Would it change your story if I told you your name was in the file?"

"Uh…"

"You apparently talked with investigators when they came down here trying to locate the weapon. It's reported that you claimed the evidence was washed away. Now you're saying it was hidden on someone's property. Which is it, Mr. Ballew?"

"Uh, well, I don't rightly know."

"Where did you get your information? Did someone threaten you not to talk to the police?"

He rubbed his chin again. "I heard it from a friend who heard it from a friend. Ya know? Like that old song from the 80s. It's just a rumor, I guess. Shoot, this town and Cedar Key are too friendly for something like that to go on." He kicked at the dirt with his right boot.

He was going to try to change his story to get out of testifying against the Ezzo family. Understandable, but not acceptable. "Mr. Ballew, I beg you to tell me what you know. Please, just a hint. Today, someone slashed the tires on my car." She pointed behind her at her car. "I almost wrecked on the way here. I could've been killed. I've received threats ever since I've been here. This place isn't as nice as you'd like to think it is."

"Well, I—"

"You wouldn't want a little old thing like me to fall

into any trouble, would you? I'm just as innocent as you are. And my friend here, he's innocent too." At least she hoped he was. "We want to put these guys away."

Phil held his hands out to Mr. Ballew. "Sir, please tell her what you know."

Mr. Ballew narrowed his eyes into slits and moved his gaze back and forth from Kathryn's face to Phil's face. He spit brown juice from his mouth onto the ground and wiped his chin with his bandana then scratched his balding head and whistled. "Lordy, Lordy, why does trouble always find its way to me? I try to work hard. I go to church almost every Sunday. And still, trouble always finds me."

Kathryn wiped the sweat from beneath her eyes. "How do you think I feel, Mr. Ballew?" She was no different from this man. Innocent, yet wrapped up in something ugly. Except she didn't go to church. But neither one of them deserved this trouble.

Phil reached his arm around Kathryn's shoulder and drew her close to him. "Please, sir."

He threw his hands up in the air and turned a few circles before facing them again. "Okay, the man you need to talk to runs the grocery in Cedar Key."

Kathryn laughed. "Already tried that. He won't talk to me."

"Of course he won't. He knows what's good for him. But he knows the man that hid the gun. Now I ain't tellin' you no more."

"Thank you, Mr. Ballew. You've been very helpful." Kathryn waved to him, and she and Phil returned to their cars.

Phil widened his eyes. "Wow, that was intense."

As Mr. Ballew slid back underneath his tractor and

the dogs ran out from under the house to join him, Kathryn opened her car door. "I'm shaking."

"I'll follow you back to the condo and help you get your things. I'm going to put you in one of my rental properties. You'll be safer there."

Kathryn knotted her brow. "There's no need to do that, Phil. I'm sure I'll be safe."

"Kathryn, I won't hear of it. Someone, probably my cousins, slashed your tires. In your driveway. I can't believe they didn't go flat sooner or even shred while you were driving."

"I think they only partially punctured them so I would have time to get further away and would be caught out alone and vulnerable."

"Exactly." Phil emphasized his meaning with bulging eyes. "All the more reason you need to be somewhere else for the next few days. Or you need to return home."

"We'll talk about it when we get there." Kathryn climbed into her car and followed Phil back to the condo. On the way, her heart squeezed with worry for Sadie. Was she safe? When she left earlier, she had no way of knowing her tires had been slashed and no need to fear for Sadie's safety. The thirty-minute ride back to the condo felt like the road trip from home to Cedar Key. She couldn't get there fast enough.

Kathryn closed her eyes for a brief moment. "Please keep Sadie safe."

Who was she talking to? God? She'd never cried out to him before, that she remembered. Would He watch over Sadie until she returned? He'd watched over her so far. Kathryn turned up the radio and let the soothing inspirational tunes ease her concern.

CHAPTER 12

Phil pulled in behind Kathryn and hopped out of his SUV before she could get out of her car. He pushed his shoulders back and scanned the property with eyes that normally portrayed joy. Kathryn smiled at the protectiveness that oozed from him. He'd proven his trustworthiness to her. Enough so that she could give up her quest for justice and let the Ezzo case solve itself. That's how much she wanted to spend the next few days getting to know Phil better.

Phil returned from around the back of the condo, pushing his way through the palm trees that lined the side of the building, and gave her the okay sign. Kathryn shut her car door and together they went inside, where Sadie greeted them by jumping in the air and licking their hands.

"You're safe!" Kathryn bent to receive love from her baby.

Phil walked down the hall to the bedrooms and returned with a nod. "I'm glad Sadie is safe. Looks like everything's in order here. I feared my cousins would've ransacked the place while you were gone."

"Me too. That's why I brought everything that was important with me—everything but Sadie." She held up her laptop bag. "See, everything's safe, and I'm safe here."

Phil shook his head and turned up the left corner of his mouth. "Let's examine the evidence, counselor. Exhibit one: a threatening note. Exhibit two: a threatening phone call. Exhibit three: your tires were slashed while your car sat out in the drive. You're not safe here. I'm going to have to take you into protective custody."

The tone in his voice sent shivers of delight down her spine. She could get used to having Phil as her security guard. "Oh, you are, are you?"

"Yep." Phil took Kathryn's laptop bag from her hands and put it on the sofa. Then he wrapped his arms around her waist. She draped her arms around his neck. Her legs trembled, and she had to pull all her strength together to remain standing. Phil captured her into a hug, tucked his chin, and placed his cheek against hers. "I want to keep you safe, and I haven't felt this way about anyone in...well, ever."

She pressed her cheek against his. He smelled like coconuts and pineapple. The sweet scent flooded her mind, bringing her back to their picnic on the beach. "Thank you."

Phil released Kathryn and leaned against the bar with his hands in his pockets. "Let me put you in one of my rentals."

Kathryn pointed out the sliding glass door and pouted. "But the sunsets."

"You're as stubborn as they come, A.D.A. Bellamy. With that attitude and determination, you'll make it as far as you want to go. But I'm not taking no for an answer on this one. I'll put you in a unit that's private and has the best view of the sunset in all of Cedar Key."

"I'm not sure I can afford that."

"I wasn't going to charge you. However, I could use

your help on a project."

"What's that?"

"I'm in the process of repainting the bedrooms and bathrooms in the unit. You interested in assisting me?"

Kathryn smiled and nodded at the idea of working as a team with him on something other than the case. "I'd love to help! We can try to figure out where the weapon is while we work."

"You're hopeless." Phil shoved his hands onto his hips.

"Yeah, I know, but I feel like we're so close now. After meeting with Mr. Ballew, I know that gun is here."

"One thing's for sure: you must be on to something or my cousins wouldn't bother with you."

"Exactly!"

"Then let's pack your bags and get you over to the other place." He looked at his watch. "I'm getting hungry for dinner. I'd like to take you to get some seafood."

"I'd like that." Kathryn hooked Sadie up to her leash and walked her to the sliding glass door.

Phil asked, "Are you ready to go to dinner now, or do you want me to give you time to pack?"

Kathryn stood at the back door and extended Sadie's leash so she could go outside alone. "If you don't mind coming back in about thirty minutes?"

Phil pulled his keys out of his front pocket. He rotated the keys on the ring until he found the one he was looking for then he removed the key and placed it on the bar. "Here's the key to the house. I'll text you the address. It's probably best if we don't head over there together anyway."

"Why?" Kathryn ducked her head out through the door and clicked to Sadie.

"I don't want Drew to find out I moved you. He obviously knows where you're staying now. I don't want him to know I know you."

"Good point." Sadie ran into the condo. When Kathryn unleashed her, she ran to Phil and begged. Kathryn laughed. "She wants her treat."

"Where are they?"

"In the puppy paw jar by the sink."

Phil opened the jar and gave a biscuit to Sadie. "I'll call Drew and find out where he and Barney are. I'll text you and let you know it's okay to go on over. Then I'll come get you for dinner." Phil winked at Kathryn and stepped out onto the porch.

Kathryn danced on her tiptoes to the bedroom to pack her bags, Sadie on her heels. Phil had held her so close, close enough to kiss her. Yet he'd held back. He was a true gentleman. Maybe too much of a gentleman. She giggled.

* * *

Phil flipped through his mail from the swing facing the canal. The greenish-brown brackish water lapped against the tree-lined shore, boats trolled to their docks after a day out at sea. Instead of the estuary's usual smell of sea grass and algae, dread filled the air as he waited for Drew to answer his phone. Thankfully, he hadn't been waiting for him when he returned from Kathryn's.

The ringing stopped and Phil straightened, tossing the mail on the swing beside him.

"What?"

"Well, hello to you too, Drew."

"Did you call Uncle Louie?"

Phil grabbed his forehead. He'd forgotten to call. When Kathryn called for help, he'd dropped everything and gone to her rescue. "No, I didn't get the chance. I'll call tomorrow. I doubt they'll bring him to the phone though."

"You're trying to get out of it. Aren't you?"

"Drew, I told you I'd call. I'm a man of my word."

"You've yet to prove that."

"I'll call tomorrow. When are you headed home?"

"I've got one more visit to pay to the D.A. and then I'll go. Barney is staying until she goes back to Perkins County."

"So you met her?"

"Not exactly."

"What do you mean?" Phil paced the porch.

"I sent her a message to mind her business."

Phil knew enough about what Drew had done, and he didn't want the details. "Don't tell me. I don't want to know. The more unapprised I am of your actions, the better." He squeezed the back of his neck and leaned against the railing. Drew had no conscience. He didn't care who he hurt as long as he achieved his goal.

What if the slashed tires had caused Kathryn to wreck? What if she'd died out on Highway 24? Phil would have nothing but his speculation and no proof that his cousins had been responsible. *Thank You, Lord, for keeping Kathryn safe.*

"Phil!"

"Sorry. Look, I've got to go. Where are you now?"

"I'm at the yacht club. Barney went clamming with a group of locals."

"Clamming?"

"Yeah, something he's always wanted to do

apparently."

"Let me know when you leave. And take Barney with you."

"He won't go until she goes."

"I'm going to call him. He needs to leave her alone. She's just a woman and probably won't find what she's looking for."

"You seem awful certain of that. Maybe I should get you to take care of her and not Barney."

Phil stepped into the house and dropped on to the sofa. Should he tell Drew he'd take responsibility for getting Kathryn out of Cedar Key so they'd leave her alone?

"Yeah that's a great idea, Phil. Why don't you convince her to leave the case alone?" he snorted.

"I know what you mean by convince, and I'm not the guy for that. But I'll tell you what I will do."

"What's that?"

"I'll call Perkins County tomorrow and see what I can find out. Then I'll call Louie." After Phil hung up with Drew, he sent Kathryn a text that he'd pick her up in fifteen minutes.

* * *

Kathryn gripped Sadie's leash as she unlocked the door to Phil's rental. The last thing she needed was for Sadie to rush in and break something. She walked through the foyer and before she made it ten steps into the home, she gasped.

The blue two-story stucco possessed vaulted ceilings with windows from floor to ceiling along the back wall, granite countertops and stainless steel appliances in the kitchen, and ceramic tile floors throughout the downstairs.

Oil paintings of ocean scenes hung on the walls in the living area, and oversized tan leather furniture waited for her to make herself comfortable. The place screamed opulence.

"Sadie, I'm not sure we're fit to stay here. We might mess this place up." Sadie woofed as if she knew what she'd said, and Kathryn laughed.

She took Sadie off her leash then explored the rest of the five-bedroom dream home. She meandered through the downstairs and upstairs rooms until she found her way back to the two-story living area and to the back porch, which overlooked Daughtry Bayou. She opened the paneled glass door and sucked in the Gulf breeze—hot and healing. A small plane took off from the runway behind the house and joined the pelicans and seagulls in the pale-blue sky, blotted with the occasional cloud.

Kathryn's phone chimed and interrupted her bliss. She unlocked the screen and pressed the messaging button.

I'm in the drive.

She didn't mind the interruption from Phil, and she appreciated his advanced warning instead of knocking on the door and scaring her. She bounced on her toes and turned away from the view. "Sadie, Phil's here!" Sadie turned in circles and whined. Kathryn returned to the front door. "I'll be right back. I'm going to get my things." She shut the door behind her and waved at Phil from the porch.

He stood beside his SUV with his keys in his hands, sunglasses covering his eyes. Were they smiling as usual behind the shades? "Is the place okay?"

Kathryn's heart begged to leap out of her chest and right into Phil's hands. "Okay? It's perfect. I'm almost afraid to stay here. I might mess something up."

"Nonsense."

"Do you think Sadie will be okay? She doesn't normally mess things up, but I'm a little nervous with her being left in a new place without me."

"She'll be fine. If she messes anything up, it can be replaced. I mean, she'd not a furniture eater, right?"

"No, she's not." Kathryn's chest warmed. Phil's generosity had no end.

"You ready for some seafood?"

Kathryn tried to control the tingling that dashed throughout her body as she bounded down the stairs toward him. "Yep! Let me get my things into the house first." She popped the trunk and grabbed her grocery bags and laptop bag.

Phil reached into the trunk for her luggage.

"Thanks for helping me unload and for letting me stay here. The house truly is amazing and the view is gorgeous. No trees to block the sunsets."

"I know. It's one of my favorites. My grandparents used to stay here before they bought the other properties. Then they bought this one. When Grandpa died, Grandma stayed in a bungalow until my folks made her move back to New York."

Kathryn opened the door, and Phil followed her into the house. "What happened to the bungalow?"

"My parents own it. They stay there whenever they come for a visit. Pops doesn't come much because he says there's nothing to do here in Cedar Key and he thinks I abandoned the family, but Ma comes a few times a year now that Grandma is gone."

"She comes alone?"

"Sure. She loves the shops and the locals, loves to spend time at the library and read. There's a quilt shop she goes to too. I don't know if she's making a quilt or if she just likes to hang out with those ladies."

"That's neat that she doesn't mind traveling alone. My mom rarely goes anywhere now that she doesn't have Dad as a travel partner. I'm sorry for your loss, by the way."

"Thanks." On the way down the stairs and to Phil's SUV, Phil stopped.

Kathryn halted too. "What is it?" She focused her gaze on the street. Hopefully, Phil hadn't spotted one of his cousins.

"I just thought of somewhere the gun might be."

Kathryn grabbed Phil's forearm. "Where?"

"It's a longshot, but there's an old cemetery about five minutes from here over on Gulf Blvd. You said the guy in the store said something about buried secrets. I didn't even think about an actual cemetery."

"Can we go?" Kathryn clapped her hands. Who cares if she looked like a child?

"Sure. I'm willing to search anywhere."

"Now?" She batted her eyelashes. What was happening to her professional demeanor? She'd transformed into more of a woman since she'd been here than she'd ever been.

"Aren't you hungry?"

"Yes, but I want to find that gun. If we wait until after we eat, it will be getting late. I'm not going to get stuck in an old cemetery at dark."

Phil laughed. "Okay, we'll go there now. We can poke around and see if anything looks disturbed."

Kathryn would dance the rest of the way to the SUV, but why celebrate prematurely?

The entrance of the cemetery wasn't at all what Kathryn had expected. Two nice concrete columns marked the entrance, one with a plaque with the name of the cemetery etched in it. She'd assumed it would be a neglected and overgrown parcel of land. "What's that walkway there?" Kathryn pointed to a wooden walkway that led out into the water.

"That's the boardwalk. A lot of people fish out there. I've gotten a whopper or two out of that backwater myself on occasion. We can walk it once we've checked out the cemetery, if you want to."

"Okay, sure." If they found the gun, she'd skip down the boardwalk.

Phil pulled his SUV over to the side of the path. "Let's get out and walk. It will be easier to spot if something has been tampered with. Do you want some mosquito repellant?"

"Yes, thanks."

They exited the vehicle, sprayed themselves with repellant, and started on the first loop around the graves. Shaded by two-hundred-year-old oaks and cedars, the graves were covered in moss and dark stains. Some had iron fences around them, some had elaborate headstones on them. Others had small plain headstones, and others had nothing but a jagged rock placed at the head of the body to represent the loved one who'd passed so long ago.

"I'm surprised these graves have survived the harsh ocean winds and the flooding that comes with hurricanes."

"I know. When I first found this place, I remember being surprised that they would have sited a cemetery so close to the water. But I suppose in the 1800s, they didn't think about things like that."

"Maybe not. Do you see anything yet?"

"Not yet. Let's keep walking. Back here in the back there are some unmarked graves. Maybe the gun is buried in or around one of them."

Kathryn shivered. "I hate cemeteries. They are so creepy. Especially with the Spanish moss dripping from the oak trees and the cedars shadowing the graves."

"Yeah, it's eerie back in here. Oh, I forgot to tell you to watch out for copperheads."

Kathryn squealed and jumped like she'd stepped on a snake. "Phil! Don't scare me like that."

He laughed. "Sorry. But you do have to watch out for snakes around here. They definitely can be up in these leaves."

"Gross. I'll just stay here on the pavement. You go fish around for the gun."

"So you'd let me risk my life for your murder weapon?" He stabbed himself in the heart with his fists and pretended to fall back.

"Yep!" Kathryn shooed him to commence his hunt for the gun.

Kathryn and Phil walked around every loop in the cemetery and turned up nothing. Not one single hint of a disturbed or freshly dug grave.

"I'm sorry we didn't find anything. I told you it was a longshot, but I didn't want it to go unchecked." Phil squeezed Kathryn's shoulder.

"It's not your fault they didn't bury it here."

"You ready to walk the boardwalk?"

Kathryn pouted. "No, can we just go to the restaurant? I'm so bummed. I just want to stuff my face with shrimp."

Phil threw his arm over Kathryn's shoulder and led

the way to the SUV. "Anything you want, ma'am. I'll take you anywhere you want to go."

CHAPTER 13

Phil escorted Kathryn up the steps to the Tropical Winds restaurant near the city park where they'd run into each other on Saturday. He acted like a skittish deer, looking past people, jumping whenever a baritone voice rang out. They were at a table together, but Phil's mind was somewhere else.

Who was Kathryn to interfere with his thoughts though? She'd been lost in plenty of her own over the last few days. She'd obsessed over solving this case, one that she no longer had any obligation to solve. She'd rehearsed over and over in her mind what she'd say to Daddy when she got home, how she'd tell him she no longer wanted to pursue his dream.

She'd also practiced her speech to Maria if Phil pursued her once she left Cedar Key, how she'd explain their meeting and their instant attraction to each other although they were on opposite sides of this case.

Kathryn shook her head. Her imagination was like a wayward runaway child. She couldn't assume Phil would want to see her once she left this island refuge. She'd do herself a favor if she forgot about these wild ideas. "Phil? You okay?"

He cleared his throat and scratched his whiskered

chin. "Yeah, I'm sorry."

"What's up? You were so quiet in the car on the way over here."

"Me quiet? You were quiet too."

Kathryn acknowledged with a nod. "Guilty as charged."

"I'm upset that I haven't been able to help you find the gun."

"That's not your fault. It's either already been found, or it's been removed by forces beyond our control."

"Or it's out there waiting for us."

"You know that's what I'm hoping for. What else is bothering you? You're antsy."

"I'm on the lookout for Drew and Barney. Barney went clamming today with the locals. Since he's a big eater and this is the best restaurant in town, he could appear at any moment."

"Then why did we come in here?"

"I'm beginning to wonder that myself."

Kathryn chewed on her thumbnail. "So he's not just here for business then?"

"I wouldn't say that. He's either trying to make money somehow, or he didn't really go clamming. He may have taken a boat out to where the weapon is hidden."

"Did Drew say where Barney went specifically?"

Phil's gaze darted around the restaurant. Sweat beaded on his upper lip. "No, but he did say Barney was staying here until you leave. They're going to keep watching you, which means they'll figure out we know each other."

Kathryn shook her head. "Not good."

"No, not good."

"Which means, Phil, it was a mistake to come out in

public together."

"We probably shouldn't do this again. They know you're tenacious and won't give up."

"My reputation follows me everywhere, doesn't it?"

"Indeed. Drew even called you a rabid fox."

Kathryn threw her head back and laughed. "Oh, he has done his homework, hasn't he?"

"I'm afraid he knows too much about you. Too much for my liking, anyway. So we'd better stay out of public for the rest of the time you're here."

"I agree. But we've got to find that gun."

Phil nodded and gulped down his water.

The waitress took their order then Kathryn continued, "I've been thinking about what Mr. Ballew said." With her finger, she traced the border of the paper placemat on the table, a map of Cedar Key, and outlined invisible circles around the islands which surrounded this quaint place.

"What's that?"

She tapped her index finger on the table. "If the gun was hidden here because the killer, your uncle, had connections to Cedar Key, it stands to reason that you're the connection."

"You're saying I know where the weapon is?" Phil stiffened his neck and cracked his knuckles.

"No, sorry." She erased her words with her hands. "I mean that you're connected to the family, so maybe they hid the weapon on one of the family properties you now own."

Phil puckered his lips and raised his eyebrows. "You may have a point."

"How many properties do you have?"

"Five. Including my own home."

"Do any of them have a hideaway? A cellar? A fort?

Are any of them on the canal where there could be crab traps or some other connection to the water?"

"They're all on the canal or the bayou including the one you're in over by the airstrip."

Kathryn nodded and straightened in her seat. "We need to check each place off the list until we eliminate them or find that gun. Time is running out. I've got to go back home, and the trial is coming up."

"Okay, we'll start first thing in the morning. I told Drew I'd call Uncle Louie, although I doubt they'll let him talk on the phone. He suggested that I convince you to forget about the case. I'm going to tell him I found out you're off the case. Maybe they'll drop their quest and go home."

"They won't go anywhere until they secure the weapon."

"Which means we're bound to have a run in with them at some point."

"I was afraid you were going to say that."

* * *

They returned to the house, and Kathryn accepted Sadie's greeting by kneeling down to ruffle her ears then poured a glass of water. She drank a little and cleared her throat. Her meal must have been saltier than she'd realized while eating it.

Phil unlocked the storage closet beside the laundry room and pulled a gallon of paint, two poles, two rollers, a drop cloth, and a paint tray out into the hall. "You sure you don't mind helping me paint?"

Kathryn cleared her throat again. She must have gotten a flake of pepper lodged in the back of her throat. "Not at all. As long as we can take a break and watch the sunset."

"Definitely!"

"Let me go change into something that I don't care if it gets paint on it. Because it will if I'm doing the painting." Kathryn smiled.

Phil raised his right eyebrow, obviously puzzled by her throat tickle. "I didn't consider the fact that you might not have any casual clothes with you."

"No, I do. I've got some ratty old T-shirts I like to lounge around in."

"Okay, good."

Kathryn coughed. "Excuse me. I don't know why I'm having a problem here."

"Was the food too spicy?"

"Maybe. I'm not sure." Kathryn grabbed her suitcase handle and wheeled it to the master bedroom at the end of the hall. It had a private balcony overlooking the bayou. She imagined the captivating view of the sunsets from it. She cleared her throat again. Why did it feel as if she'd swallowed a feather?

Phil hollered from the kitchen, "You're trying to get out of painting, aren't you?"

Kathryn laughed, but a cough interrupted. She changed clothes in the master bathroom, the giant Jacuzzi calling her name, and hung up the clothes that would wrinkle.

By the time she returned to the living room, Phil had opened a can of light terra cotta paint and stirred it with a paint stirrer. "What do you think of—" He looked up into Kathryn's face. "Whoa! You'd better sit down." He abandoned the stirrer and dashed over to her side. "Are you allergic to seafood?"

Kathryn cleared the tickle again and plopped on to

the tan leather sofa. "I don't think so. Why?"

"Your face is swollen. Did you not notice when you were in the bathroom?"

"No. I didn't even look in the mirror." This must be a strange reaction to the shrimp because not looking in the mirror to check her appearance when in the presence of a man was out of character for her.

Phil squatted beside her. "Do you feel okay?"

Kathryn blew out a puff of air. "Not really. I kind of feel spacey."

"I'm calling 9-1-1."

"No. I don't want to go to—" Her tongue felt like it was the size of a t-bone steak wedged in her mouth.

"You're probably right anyway. The closest place is thirty minutes away. We don't have time for that. I'll call Mrs. Barnes down the road. She's a retired nurse. Just sit tight."

Kathryn swallowed hard and massaged the front of her neck. "Who's Mrs. Barnes?"

"She's a neighbor a few doors down. Real sweet. She goes to the church." Phil searched his phone for her number, hit dial, and waited. He joined Kathryn on the sofa, and Sadie rested her chin on Kathryn's knee.

Was she having an allergic reaction? She'd had shellfish before and had never experienced anything like this.

"Mrs. Barnes, it's Phil. Hi, yes, I'm doing well, except I have a friend over here at the rental on Airport Road, and I think she's having a reaction to the seafood she ate earlier." Phil listened and took Kathryn's hand in his.

Phil explained that Kathryn didn't want to call the paramedics or go to the hospital. She tried to cough, but her throat felt like someone had a hold of it. She swallowed again, and her tongue stuck to the roof of her mouth. "Phil?" She squeezed his hand, and pleaded with her eyes for him to get help fast.

"Can you hurry over here?" Phil studied Kathryn's face. "Thank you." He ended the call. "She'll be here in two minutes. She's going to give you liquid antihistamine. If that doesn't work, we're calling an ambulance."

"I'm sorry." Kathryn whispered.

"About what? You didn't know this would happen. I don't care about anything but making you better."

"Do you think someone poisoned me?" Kathryn squeezed his hand.

"No. No one would've done that. Your eyes are swelling, Kathryn. I'm worried."

Kathryn nodded. She leaned her head back on the sofa and shut her eyes.

"Don't go to sleep on me now. I need you to focus on breathing."

"Okay." Sadie jumped on to the couch and put her paws in Kathryn's lap. Kathryn stroked her head.

A knock sounded at the door, and Phil jumped up and bolted to answer it. He opened the door and pointed to Kathryn, and with an elevated tone in his voice, he explained to Mrs. Barnes the latest on Kathryn's condition.

She kneeled at Kathryn's feet. "Well, honey, you're a sight. Can you breathe?"

Kathryn nodded.

Phil took Sadie by the collar and pulled her off Kathryn's lap. Sadie whined. "Not now, Sadie. Kathryn needs help."

Mrs. Barnes measured out a dose of antihistamine in the plastic cup that came with the bottle and offered it to Kathryn. "Here drink this."

Kathryn sat up and took the cup. She sipped the cherry flavored thick and grainy liquid, forcing it down her throat.

"Can you swallow?"

"Yes, ma'am. I think so." Kathryn's eyes burned and her tongue itched. How could her tongue itch? What if— what if she died?

"Drink it down now. We'll wait a few minutes and see if you need more. Let me check your pulse."

While Mrs. Barnes checked her pulse, Phil paced from the front door to the back. He opened the door to the deck and went outside. He paced in front of the door and then returned. Had he come to care for her in these few days of knowing each other? If she died today, at least she'd have someone with her who showed concern for her well-being.

"Your pulse is normal. Let me look in your mouth." Kathryn rolled her head back onto the sofa and opened her mouth. Mrs. Barnes held up a mini-flashlight and pointed the beam of light down Kathryn's throat. "Everything looks okay. There's some swelling, but your throat is open. Do you have an epi pen?"

"No. I've never—" Kathryn swallowed and shook her head. "I've never had a reaction like this before."

"Okay. Let's take one more tablespoon. It's probably going to knock you out, but it'll most likely take care of the reaction." She poured the liquid into the plastic cup and handed it to Kathryn.

Kathryn groaned, and Phil came back to her side. "Drink it or you're going to have to go to the hospital by ambulance."

She sighed. "Okay."

"Phil, will you be able to stay here with her? She

shouldn't be left alone."

"Absolutely."

Kathryn shook her head. "I'll. Be. Okay." Her words came out like a slow drip from the faucet. The medicine was kicking in; her tongue wasn't stuck to the roof of her mouth anymore, and her throat felt looser.

"You're a funny girl. I wouldn't leave you alone if a hurricane was pounding Cedar Key right now. I'll be here all night."

Mrs. Barnes put the cap back on the antihistamine bottle and placed it on the coffee table. "I'll leave this here with you. She might need some more later. The swelling around her eyes should go down here in about thirty minutes or so. If not, give her one more tablespoon. She may need to see a doctor tomorrow though."

"Thank you, Mrs. Barnes." Phil walked her to the door.

"You call me if you need me."

Kathryn closed her eyes while Phil whispered with Mrs. Barnes at the door. His voice lulled her into a tranquil state. Sadie jumped into her lap, and Kathryn draped her hand over her back. She didn't have the energy to stroke her. She'd rest here for a few minutes and then help Phil paint.

* * *

After an hour of watching for signs of emergency in Kathryn, Phil returned to his house to get his laptop, a change of clothes, and other items he'd need while standing guard for the night. He returned to the rental, making sure neither Drew nor Barney had followed him, and parked behind the shed around the back of the house, where he'd also moved Kathryn's car earlier.

Drew called, but he ignored it. If he had to defend Uncle Louie, he would. And if Louie turned out to be guilty, so be it. His family couldn't hide the truth forever.

But right now, Kathryn was his top priority, not worrying about his uncle or his two brute cousins and their insistence that he defend Louie. His focus was on getting their minds off Kathryn, to help her find the murder weapon, and to get her reinstated to the case.

He walked Sadie one last time for the night, and she returned to Kathryn's side on the bed in the master bedroom, where he'd carried her after she'd fallen asleep on the sofa. Phil brushed Kathryn's hair out of her face. Her breathing was as steady as the sway of a dock on the water, and her face glowed from the light of the moon coming in through the window. The allergic reaction was unfortunate and had caused the poor thing to miss the sunset, but Phil didn't mind the opportunity to watch over her for a little while longer. She'd leave Cedar Key in a day or so, and he might not get another chance to spend this kind of time with her again.

If Pops knew he'd befriended the prosecutor—former prosecutor—for his ex-brother-in-law, he'd charter a private flight to Cedar Key and give Phil a lashing or two with his tongue, if not with his fists. To Pops, there was nothing more important than protecting the family name, especially not a woman. If he found out that Kathryn had been friends with Maria, he'd pass judgment on her before hearing anything else about how kind and innocent she was. A friend of Maria's would be a traitor to the Tagliaferro family, in Pops' eyes.

Phil sighed and opened the can of paint. He'd work a little in one of the bedrooms for a while and hopefully come up with a plan for finding the gun.

CHAPTER 14

Kathryn pulled the covers up to her chest and yawned. The ocean-blue luxurious sheets felt like Egyptian cotton; they had to be 1,000-thread count. Blanketed by a blue, gray and silver feather-light spread boasting of interlocking geometric shapes, she protested leaving this haven with its vaulted ceilings and skylights. But the smell of bacon filtered into the room, and her stomach growled in response.

Delight flooded her soul when her gaze landed on the painting above the dresser on the wall opposite the bed. The turquoise ocean waves crashing against the shore. The sea foam lingering behind as the waves rushed back to the depths of the ocean. The sea oats glimmering in the sunset. The lone gull soaring in the breeze. Clearly, this was not a painting of Cedar Key, but of somewhere in the Gulf. There was no mistaking its beaches and surf.

The beach had always conjured up such relaxation in Kathryn. She'd solved problems while sitting on a sandy shore which might as well have been a therapist's couch. From her spot near the crashing waves, she'd dreamt of days where rejection and pain had no place. Yes, the beach held all of her secrets and her heart close to its own. She could bottle up the sugar white sand and collect seashells galore, but she couldn't adequately capture the essence of this marvel of nature or the emotions that stirred within her every time she sat before it. The artist of this painting, however, had somehow done it, and Kathryn would forever be grateful to her for it.

She yawned again and stretched then bolted upright in the bed. Where was she and what day was it? How had she gotten here into the bed? The TV resounded in the living area, so she wasn't alone. Alarm raced down her spine, and the hairs on the back of her neck stood to attention. Who was with her? Where was Sadie?

She slipped out from underneath the covers and tiptoed down the hallway. She peeked around the corner into the kitchen. Phil stood in front of the stove, and Sadie sat at his feet. Kathryn smiled and scurried back to the bedroom.

In the bathroom, she brushed her teeth then her hair and pulled it back into a messy bun. She washed last night's make-up off her face and studied her puffy eyes. Why did she look like a blowfish? Ah, that's right. She'd had an allergic reaction. Phil must have stayed all night with her. Warmth smoothed the apprehension away from her body.

Kathryn turned too quickly leaving the bathroom and caught the door facing with her shoulder to keep from falling. The antihistamine had done a number on her, but it had obviously worked. She inched her way into the kitchen down the hallway, sliding her hand along the wall for support.

And there he was. Standing in her kitchen—his kitchen—in slim-fitting charcoal gray shorts, a gray heather round-neck T-shirt, and black Chuck sneakers. Was it the leftover antihistamine in her system that made her feel light-headed or was it the sight of him? Oh, it was the sight of him, no doubt. She straightened her T-shirt, tucked a strand of hair behind her left ear, and shuffled into the kitchen.

Phil's eyes smiled. "Well, good morning, little Miss Sunshine. I thought I heard you fumbling around back there." He sidled up next to her with two giant steps and placed a kiss on her cheek. His citrusy cologne combined with the savory scent of the bacon swirled around her. "You look much better this morning than you did last night."

She dismissed his compliment with a wave of her hand then brought it to her cheek on the spot he'd kissed. Both of her cheeks must have been as red as a rose judging by the heat searing through her flesh. "Oh, please. I look terrible, especially with no make-up."

"There isn't an ounce of truth in that statement, counselor. You're a natural beauty."

"Thanks." She cut her eyes at him. He had a knack for flattery.

"Did I wake you with my clanking around in the kitchen?"

"No, it was the smell of bacon that woke me. You sure do make big breakfasts."

Phil returned to the stove and tapped the spatula on the frying pan. "It's not really breakfast anymore. It's already noon."

Her eyes bulged, and she rubbed her temple. "Noon? I've been asleep since 9:00 p.m. last night?"

He pointed at her with the spatula. "You guessed it. I checked on you all throughout the night, and you seemed to be okay, so I didn't wake you."

"Thank you. Did you put me in the bed?"

He squinted. "Yes. I hope you don't mind."

"No, thanks." He'd carried her to the bed like some

kind of hero from a romance novel. Wow!

"How did you sleep?"

"I don't know." She laughed, still fuzzyheaded. "I guess pretty well. I was confused like never before when I woke up a few minutes ago. I couldn't remember where I was. What did you do while I slept?"

"I ran home to get some things I needed then I spent some quality time with Sadie. She's a great dog."

"That she is." Kathryn patted her leg, and Sadie ran to her side.

Phil removed the bacon from the pan, and placed it on a paper towel to drain. "Then I painted one of the bedrooms."

"I thought I smelled fresh paint."

He picked up a piece of paper off the counter. "And I made a list of my properties and all the possible places someone could hide a weapon."

Kathryn slipped the paper from Phil's grasp and examined it. "So you didn't waste any time?"

"No way. We don't have any to waste."

Kathryn slid on to the bar stool as Phil pulled the biscuits from the oven. Surely, they weren't homemade. They were two inches high with nooks and crannies just waiting for butter to puddle in them. Kathryn's stomach growled again.

"Do you want your eggs scrambled or fried?"

"Scrambled is fine. Just two."

"How do you feel?"

"Refreshed. I haven't slept that deeply in years." She studied the list of properties.

"I guess that's one benefit of having an allergic reaction."

"I suppose so."

"And you've never had a reaction to seafood before last night?"

"Nope, but I think my dad might be allergic. I'll have to ask him when we talk next. That was really scary."

"Tell me about it."

She turned her attention to him. "I'm thankful you were here with me. If you'd dropped me off and left, I don't know what would've happened."

"We don't want to think about that. I was here for a reason."

She folded her arms and leaned on the bar. Phil sprinkled salt and pepper on his edible masterpieces with care, in the same way he did everything else. In the four days she'd known him, she'd come to realize that he was an intentional kind of guy. He wouldn't be there with her now if he didn't care about her. What a crazy situation. How had she managed to attract the attention of a man who couldn't have been more taboo for her?

"You know, you may be right. Since I've been here in Cedar Key, I've had an awful lot of protection." This had to be the work of something higher than her. Or someone. Maybe God? She shrugged. Thinking about God's providence was too big a subject for her right now. "I don't think that's a coincidence. Do you?"

"No, ma'am. I do not." Phil served the eggs, bacon, and biscuits onto the bar. "Let me say a quick prayer for us."

Kathryn bowed her head and closed her eyes. A lump the size of Georgia grew in her throat at Phil's sweet words. When he finished praying, Kathryn wiped a tear from the corner of her left eye and sliced her biscuit in half then spread butter on each piece. It melted as soon as it touched the steaming bread, like her heart had melted at Phil's prayer, and her mouth watered. "Do you want to tackle this paint job after we eat?" She took a bite of the biscuit and rolled her eyes up toward the ceiling. She'd never tasted anything like it.

"I didn't think you'd feel like doing it after what you went through last night." Phil bit into his biscuit and grinned. He must have agreed with Kathryn about their perfection.

"Sure, why not?" Kathryn licked the butter off her lips and dropped a piece of bacon into Sadie's begging mouth.

Phil agreed with a nod, licking bacon grease from his fingers. "Why don't we first go explore my properties and see if we can figure out if the gun is hidden in any of them? We can always paint later today."

"Okay." Kathryn scooped up the last bit of her eggs, and her mouth formed into a frown. She should have eaten more slowly and savored each morsel. "You know what I'm sad about?"

"What?" Phil gulped down the last of his coffee.

"Two things: that my breakfast is gone..."

"You want some more? I can whip up a few more eggs." He started to hop up off the barstool.

Kathryn reached for his forearm and stopped him. "No, I'm good."

"Okay. What else?"

"I missed a sunset."

"Yeah, you did, didn't you?" He laughed and patted her hand, sending electric shocks throughout her body. "Maybe you can stay one extra night to make up for it?"

"I just might have to do that." Kathryn slid her hand from underneath his and headed to the bedroom to change clothes. Was she ready for another full day with this man? Her wall of defense was beginning to crumble, and that scared her more than swimming with the sharks out in the bayou. But she had to start somewhere. It was like learning to swim or ride a bike. If she didn't allow someone to teach her how to accept kindness and friendship, how would she ever learn to navigate life's waters?

She scanned the items in the master bedroom closet she'd flung in there last night after dinner. She needed something comfortable for their day of exploring but something cute, also, to make a lasting impression on Phil. Her black drawstring shorts and gray V-neck with her pink sneakers would fit perfectly with his look. That's what she'd wear. She dressed in a flurry and walked down the hallway with a bit of a foxtrot in her step.

* * *

Kathryn juggled her keys, phone, and laptop bag in her hands, as she locked the beach house door and followed Phil around the back. A plane buzzed overhead, the birds and katydids serenaded them, and the ocean's breeze guided them toward their day of adventure despite the escalating heat.

"I like your outfit." Phil looked over his shoulder and winked. "Sporty."

"Thanks." Kathryn's stomach tightened at the compliment. Then her purse strap fell off her shoulders and landed in the crook of her elbow, causing her to tilt to the left and step off one of the steppingstones that led to the shed. The antihistamine still affected her balance. Or maybe Phil's compliment was the culprit. Thankfully, he hadn't seen her stumble. She pulled the strap back up onto her shoulder and followed him to his SUV. "You moved my car around back?"

"Yep. I didn't want my cousins scouting every street until they found it. In Cedar Key, it's easy to do that. I parked mine back here, too, so they wouldn't find me either."

"Good call." Kathryn waited as Phil opened the passenger's side door of his SUV for her, and she climbed in. "So where should we go first?" Phil shut her door and went around to the driver's side.

Phil hopped in, shut the door, and pulled his sunglasses from the visor. "I think we'll head over to the tree house first." He slid the sunglasses onto his face and tipped his head toward her as he cranked the car.

There was that confident, almost cocky, attorney she knew was buried somewhere behind that cool and genteel façade. And there was that tingle again. She gulped and blew out her breath. "Tree house?"

He eased the car out from behind the shed and around to the front of the house. "Yep, it's a one-bedroom built up in a giant oak tree. It's the smallest one, so I figured it'd be easiest to check out first. Cross it off the list. Plus, no one is staying there right now."

"What are your other places like?"

"Besides the tree house and the one you're in, which is the most luxurious, I've got one in the old mill complex over by the city park, and two cottages over on 4th Street. I doubt the gun is in the one in the complex though. Not private enough for burying evidence."

"It seems like it would have to be somewhere secluded, if it hasn't been tossed out to sea. We already know it's not at the honeymoon shack or buried in the cemetery." Kathryn's phone rang, and she swiped her finger across the screen to unlock it. Beverly. What could she possibly want? "I need to get this."

"Sure." Phil turned down the volume on the radio.

"Hello," she answered the Clerk of Court's call.

"Hey, Kathryn. Sorry to bother you on your vacation."

Some vacation. "That's okay. What's up?"

"The D.A. shuffled your cases around for you since your time off came up suddenly, but he postponed a few of them because there were too many details that you were wrapped up in."

"Okay. That's what he said he'd do when we talked on Sunday."

"Oh, you talked to him? Okay. So they'll be waiting on you when you return."

"Okay, thanks." She had to be fishing for something. Otherwise, she wouldn't have called. The office gossip ring must be too silent right now.

"So when are you returning?"

Seriously? Was it that impossible to get a break from the office? "I'll be in Monday, if not sooner."

"Monday?"

"Yes. D.A. Schwartz gave me the week off, so I'm going to take it."

"Are you coming back in town before then though?"

Kathryn sighed. What was this all about? "I don't know. Why?"

"Well, a man has called three times wanting to know when you'll be back. He won't leave his name. Kinda sounds mysterious. I wondered if he might want to ask you on a date."

"What did he say?"

"He asked if you are available for appointments, and I just figured it might be for a date."

"Why would you figure that?"

"Oh, I don't know. I'm just a romantic. Now that you

make me second-guess myself, he did get kind of angry when none of us would tell him more information."

"Okay. Do me a favor. Tell D.A. Schwartz about him. And if he calls back, don't give out any information about me. At all. I'm afraid it could be related to the Ezzo case."

Phil jerked his head toward her and questioned with a raised eyebrow.

Kathryn shrugged. "I don't want him or anyone else who calls to know I'm off this case, and I don't want him especially to know anything about me."

"You got it. What have you been doing?"

She wasn't going to give up until she found out something gossip-worthy. "Relaxing. Having reactions to seafood. You know, the usual."

"You had an allergic reaction?"

"Sure did. Still under the influence of the antihistamine a bit."

"Oh wow! Did you know you were allergic?"

"Nope. I wouldn't have eaten it if I'd known." Kathryn sighed.

"Oh, yeah, obviously. Did someone help you or did you have to call 9-1-1?"

"Yes, I had help. Didn't have to go to the hospital." Kathryn sighed again.

"Is Cedar Key on the Atlantic side or the Gulf?"

"It's on the Gulf down past the Suwannee River. It's a nature preserve, so there's no white beaches. Just salt marshes and estuaries, lots of fishing and great sunsets." She was through with sharing information about her time in Cedar Key.

"Sounds great! Well, take care. Catch some sun for me."

"Okay." Kathryn ended the call.

"She sure was nosey."

Kathryn shrugged. "Unusually so."

"What's happening back at the office? Did I hear correctly my uncle's name?"

"Yep. Someone's been calling trying to find out information about me. He won't leave his name. It's probably one of your cousins."

"Your coworker didn't say anything to him?"

"No. She thought it was somebody wanting to ask me on a date. Like when does that ever happen?"

Phil laughed. "You sounded like you were using discretion when talking to her."

Kathryn nodded. "I'm not close to her. Not sure how much I can trust her yet. She's the new clerk for my judge, and she favors the men attorneys in the office over the women. I think she doesn't like women being in positions of authority. She doesn't take direction from me too well."

"She sounds intimidated."

"Maybe."

"You think she'd tell someone where you are?"

"I don't think so, but she might paint a bad picture of me to her coworkers. So I don't talk about my private life." Kathryn crossed her arms and rubbed her elbows.

"I don't miss that about practicing law. Your whole life is an open book."

"Yeah, I hate that part of it. I hate a lot about it."

"Well, you don't have to think about it anymore today. Let's try to find the gun so you can prosecute my uncle."

"Phil, you're terrible!"

"Why?"

"You know I'm off the case. Plus, why would you want your own uncle prosecuted?" She laughed and shook her head.

"I want the truth to come out...even if it means my good old uncle is guilty."

"I want that too."

"And I want you to be reinstated to the case, if that's what you want."

"Yeah, I'm still thinking about that. But for now let's get on with our investigation."

"Hang on!" Phil slammed the brakes on and jammed the SUV into reverse. Gravel and crushed shells spewed out from underneath the car.

Kathryn grabbed on to the dashboard and braced herself with her feet pressed almost through the floorboard. "What are you doing?"

Phil put the car into drive, pressed the pedal to the floor, and nodded toward a house that fit the description of the tree house. "That's Drew's car."

CHAPTER 15

The black Mercedes with dark tinted windows looked like a monster waiting to devour them. "What's he doing there?"

Phil turned left onto a desolate gravel road and stopped the vehicle. "I can only assume he's looking for the gun." He yanked off his sunglasses, rubbed his forehead, and pressed his fingers into his temples.

"What does this mean? What does this mean? What does this mean?" Kathryn couldn't stop waving her hands in the air. She'd felt anxiety and panic before, but this was the worst. Sweat broke out on her upper lip, and her pulse tapped out a beat in the notch between her collarbones.

"I don't know." Phil drummed the steering wheel.

"Did he hide it? Or did he just figure out that that's where it most likely was?"

Phil groaned. "Who knows? But I'm not taking the chance of him seeing us here together."

Kathryn buried her face in her hands. "No way!" Now they both needed protection. Who was going to protect her protector?

"We'll go into town and check out the rental at the old mill complex and wait it out at the park. We can come back by in a bit."

Kathryn slapped her legs and turned toward Phil. "What's the point? If he knows where the gun's at, it won't be here when we get back."

"What are you suggesting?"

"Drop me back off at my place and then come back and confront Drew yourself."

"Or..."

She slapped the console. "Phil, come on! If he's collecting the gun, it'll be gone! We'll never know."

Phil grabbed her hand and turned sideways in his seat. "Look, Kathryn, I don't want to get killed over this. If Drew's responsible for the murders, who's to say I won't be next? Especially if he realizes I know you."

She slumped. "We can't chance that." Kathryn tapped her foot on the floorboard. "Call him."

Phil puffed and ran his hands through his hair. "What?"

"Call him and get him to meet you somewhere else. I'll come here by myself and try to find the gun."

Phil turned off the ignition. "No way! You're forgetting one big problem. Barney. He doesn't care who he hurts."

"Make sure Barney is with Drew. Get them to help you do something at your grandmother's cottage. Distract them both, and I'll try to find it."

Phil groaned again and pulled his phone out of the console. "This is an impossible situation. I feel like I'm a married man trying to hide his mistress."

Kathryn giggled. "Well, you sure know how to turn an impossible situation into something comical."

Phil didn't laugh; he stared at Drew's number on the

phone's display but didn't hit the call button.

"Look, Phil, if you don't want to call him, don't. If you've got a better solution, tell me."

"No, I'll call him. I don't want you to think I'm a coward."

"Coward? How could I? You've done nothing but protect me ever since I arrived. You're not a coward. I understand if you don't want to get involved any further in this case. Really, I do."

Phil nodded and hit the call button. Kathryn couldn't read the look in his eyes, flecks of something painful clouding them. Was he frightened for her? Or did it go deeper than that? Was he really in fear for his life?

"Hey, Drew. What are you and Barney doing right now?" He squeezed the steering wheel with his left hand. "You're still in Cedar Key?" He nodded to Kathryn.

Drew's voice boomed through the earpiece, and her heart pounded.

"Yeah, can you guys come over to Grandma's place and help me move a few things around? I'm going to be painting in there next week, and I need to move the furniture to the center of the room." He squeezed the back of his neck and planted his gaze on the headliner. "Yeah, I called. She's not on the case anymore. Someone else is prosecuting." He listened. "Why are you still interested in meeting her? She's not a key element of the case anymore."

So Drew was still determined to come after Kathryn. Phil should have told him that she'd had gone back to Georgia. Why couldn't things be as peaceful as they looked outside the car window? Light breeze. Birds fluttering in the bushes. Sunlight streaming through the trees.

D.A. Schwartz had thought he was ensuring her

safety by removing her from the case and making her stay in Cedar Key, but he'd been wrong. Not even in Cedar Key was she safe.

Phil sighed. "I suppose the case will be dismissed without the murder weapon."

Could he convince Drew that there was no need for them to stay in Cedar Key? Maybe if they left, Kathryn could enjoy the rest of the week with Phil unthreatened. And maybe they'd find the gun.

"No, I didn't talk to Louie. I'll call the public defender later today and see what the evidence is, if he'll tell me." Phil cranked the car. "Okay, I'll see you over there in a few minutes."

Kathryn buckled her seatbelt. Somehow, she'd unbuckled it in her moment of panic, ready to flee the vehicle for the wooded area if the need had arisen. "He didn't suspect anything?"

"I don't think so." Phil pulled into the drive and around the back of the house. He slipped a key off his key ring and handed it to Kathryn. "Here. This is the key to the tree house rental. You follow me over there. If they're gone, you go in. If they're not, stay back. Don't let them see your car. They know what it looks like, remember?"

"Right. Got it." Kathryn's nerves erupted like an earthquake, and her entire body shook.

Phil grabbed her trembling hand. "Are you sure you're up for this after your allergic reaction?"

"Yes, I want to get this over with. The sooner we find the gun, the sooner we can get this case behind us."

He squeezed her hand. "And move forward?"

She nodded. "If you'd like to."

"Oh, I'd like to." Phil leaned over and placed a gentle

kiss on her lips.

When he pulled away, Kathryn leaned forward for a lingering moment. Why did it have to end? His lips were soft and comforting, yet there was passion in them. She could feel it.

"Kathryn?"

Her eyelids fluttered open. "Yes?"

"We had better get going. Unfortunately."

"Yeah. Unfortunately."

He cocked his head. "Maybe we can pick up with this later?"

"Rain check." Kathryn laughed and hopped out of his SUV. She skipped to her car with the same foxtrot she'd had earlier, almost forgetting about the threat to her life and his. Almost.

* * *

Drew and Barney were waiting on Phil when he arrived at Grandma's old cottage. Drew leaned against the car, and Barney stood on the front porch, looking as out-of-place here as Phil would look at a poker game with Uncle Louie's employees in the backroom of his shipping company.

Phil yanked his sunglasses off, grabbed his phone, and jumped out of his SUV. He straightened his shoulders and sucked in a deep breath preparing himself for his interaction with his cousins.

"Hey, Cuz. Thanks for making us work while we're down here." Drew dropped his cigarette on the ground and smashed it with the toe of his leather loafer.

"I needed the muscle power, and I figured you needed something to occupy your time other than looking for the gun."

"How do you know we're looking for the gun?" Barney tossed a toothpick on the ground.

Phil sent a disapproving look toward the litterbugs. "Aren't you?"

"Drew wants the gun. I'm looking for that D.A. The gun is probably long gone by now. Fun with the D.A. is a job perk."

Phil was just about to reach his boiling point. He'd just as soon cut Barney's arms off than let him put one single finger on Kathryn. *Stay calm!* "I told Drew she's not on the case anymore. What makes you think she's even here?"

"I told *you* that we heard she was down here, and we're going to convince her to drop her search."

He threw his hands in the air. These buffoons were relentless. "Who cares if she's here, guys? She's off the case."

"So what. It'll be fun to mess with her." Barney rubbed his hands back and forth against each other and grinned.

"You mean more than you already have?" Phil couldn't ask them about Kathryn's tires because if they found out he knew her, they'd force him to tell them where she was. Or they'd follow him to her. "You're ridiculous. Don't you have better things to do with your time?"

Barney unwrapped a stick of gum, folded it into his mouth, and threw the wrapper on the ground. "Not really."

Phil stepped up onto the front porch and glared at Barney. "Pick that wrapper up. I'm not your mama."

"Whatever. Let's get this done. I'm getting hungry."

Phil unlocked the door, and the two lumbering men followed him inside the dark and stuffy cottage. He kept the blinds drawn to keep the heat out and to keep vandals from knowing the place was unoccupied.

Drew ripped off his silk button down shirt revealing a white V-neck T-shirt underneath. "It's hot in here."

"Yeah, that's summertime in Florida. I don't run the air if nobody's here. You know Ma and Pops. They don't like to waste electricity."

"Yeah, they're cheapskates." Drew laughed.

"No, they're smart with their money. They're a lot smarter with theirs than you are with yours, I'm sure." Phil clicked the thermostat to come on. His two cousins provided more than enough hot air for this tiny place.

Drew scoffed, "Maybe but I always seem to find my way to more when I need it."

"Okay, okay, you guys, let's quit with the insults and get busy moving this furniture. I hate manual labor." Barney was dressed in a yellow-checkered silk dress shirt and black dress pants, as if he was going to a business dinner. What a way not to fit in here in Cedar Key.

They began in the living room shifting the flower-patterned plush furniture and wooden end tables and coffee table to the center of the room.

Barney grunted. "Why are you painting in here?"

"It hasn't been freshened up since Grandma lived here. Ma and Pops wanted to change things around and update. They're thinking of retiring here to be close to me. Well, that's Ma's idea. Not sure Pops could give up his golf course."

Barney nodded as if it made sense to him. "Yeah, remember coming down here during the summer when we were younger?"

Drew whacked Phil on the back, knocking him off balance. "Yeah, those were the days."

Phil grunted and put some distance between him and

his cousins. "*Some* days. All I remember is defending myself against you two thugs. And trying not to drown in the swimming pool. About as bad as when we used to go to Cayuga Lake."

Drew let out a whoop. "Yeah, now those were great days."

Barney closed the distance between them and pinched Phil's right cheek. "We just tried to toughen you up, Phil. You were always such a mama's boy."

"That's not true. I've just never been one to fight."

Drew glared at him with squinted eyes. "Yeah, what about in high school when you beat the snot out of Jimmy Mulligan?"

"Again, I was defending myself."

"Yeah, right."

"He's right, Drew. Phil was more the type for loving the ladies."

Phil shook his head. "Nope, I wasn't after what you guys were after."

"Your loss."

"Yeah, whatever, Drew. Let's get this finished up."

They moved the furniture to the center of each room, standing the mattresses up on their sides in the bedrooms, and then Phil had had enough of his cousins. He needed to get back to Kathryn. Maybe she'd found the gun.

"So we're done here?" Drew asked, moved to Phil's side, and held out his hand.

Phil accepted Drew's gesture. "Yeah, guess so. Thanks. I couldn't have done it without you guys." As much as he hated to admit it, he couldn't have moved everything without their brute force.

"Anything for family. Right, Drew?" Barney moved to

Phil's other side and slapped him on the back.

"How about I buy you guys something cold to drink in town?" Phil took a step back and walked toward the door.

"Maybe next time. You can return the favor by calling Louie."

Phil nodded. He'd promise them anything to get rid of them.

* * *

Kathryn ran up the stairs to the front porch of the tree house cottage and fumbled with the key to unlock the door. She scooted inside and locked the door behind her, then leaned against it to catch her breath. Sweat poured down her face and between her shoulder blades, and her heart raced.

The cottage, streaming with sunlight, was no bigger than a singlewide mobile home, decorated with salmon-colored cushioned rattan furnishings and straw mats on the tile floors. There couldn't be too many places to hide a gun in this quaint getaway, but she'd never know if she didn't get started. She began by lifting the cushions on the sofa and chairs, then bent to her knees and looked underneath all of the furniture. She lifted the mats in case there was a hidden compartment underneath any of them. Nothing. Only someone desperate to escape quickly would hide a weapon in the living area of a cottage.

She moved on to the kitchen, which looked like a tiki bar; a thatched awning balanced on cane poles and a grass skirt covered the bottom of the bar. Imitation pineapples and coconuts hung on the kitchen walls, and tiki lights lined the ceiling around the cabinets. Any other time, this scene would have brought forth a thrill from her body. Right now, there was no time for glee.

She opened each kitchen cabinet, the refrigerator, and the freezer. Empty except for essentials. In the storage closet, she dug through the mops and brooms but found nothing. The laundry room was the same except for a washer and dryer, and she found no gun underneath, behind, or inside them. In the bedroom, nothing hid underneath the mattress or the bed, behind any of the picture frames, or in the drawers or closets. She searched everywhere that could possibly have a hidden compartment. There was nothing.

Out back on the porch in the deep freezer, nothing was inside, underneath, or behind it either. She let out a scream that scared the egrets nesting in the nearby oak trees, and she covered her mouth. The gun had to be here somewhere. This was the most likely place. But she needed to be quiet or she'd disclose her location to those rotten men.

She ran down the stairs and into the yard, and searched around the giant oak tree, but there was no evidence of anything buried there. No turned up soil. No clumps of leaves. She stomped around the entire foundation and found nothing. She sighed and brushed her hair out of her eyes, the taste of sweat on her lips. This wasn't as easy as she'd thought it'd be.

At the canal, the crab traps sitting on top of the dock were empty, and there weren't any traps sunken in the water. It was hopeless. If the weapon had been anywhere near the tree house cottage, Drew and Barney would have gotten it already. Her phone chimed, and she dug it out of her pocket.

A text from Phil: *I'm on my way.*

She pushed her hair out of her face, sweat dripping

down the side and off the end of her nose. She slapped a
mosquito that buzzed around her arm then sent a text back:
Okay. I didn't find anything here at the tree house.

He returned a text: *I'll be right there.*

CHAPTER 16

Phil pulled up outside, and Kathryn waited for him at the top of the stairs. He opened his door and tossed his sunglasses onto the seat. "So you didn't find anything?"

She shook her head.

"All right, that's okay. We'll just keep looking." Phil joined her on the porch.

"I'm so frustrated. What if they already found it?"

"I—"

"Well, well, dear cousin. What have we here?" Drew rolled up to the driveway and jumped out of his car, Barney following him.

Phil jumped and turned around to face his cousins, goose bumps on the back of his neck. "What's your middle name?" he whispered, grabbing Kathryn's hand where it hung by her side.

"My—my middle name?" she whispered in his ear.

"Yes. Give it to me," he whispered with urgency chasing his words.

"It's Elizabeth," she whispered back.

Phil squeezed her hand and nodded to Drew and Barney as they reached the bottom step. "What do you mean?"

Drew's gaze roamed Kathryn's body from head to foot and back up again. "Who's the chick? No wonder you haven't had time to call Uncle."

Drew's eyes were clear blue, and his eyelids looked like he wore eyeliner. He had a scar over his right eye that crossed his eyebrow. Encircled in a cloud of cigarette smoke, his round face resembled Phil's, but the obvious years of smoking had aged him. And his voice, raspy and thick, was a casualty of the cigarette smoke. He looked to be taller than Phil by about an inch or two and had the build of a football player. He'd probably played in high school and smashed every player he came in contact with, even his own teammates.

Barney, with his buzzed head and acne-scarred face, towered over Phil and Drew. His eyes were blue, like Drew's, but were deeper in color. And shifty. His lips were full, and his crooked smile spoke deeply about his character. He wore a gold nugget ring on his right pinky finger and an earring in his left ear. He smelled of cheap cologne, the kind the old men in the public defender's office wore. Surprising, considering he dressed as if he came out of a high-fashion catalog.

"Not that it's any of your business, but this is Beth. I'm showing her my rental properties."

"I bet you're showing her more than that." Barney laughed.

Despite the intense fear that coursed through her body at the possibility of either of them touching her, Kathryn raised her right eyebrow and rolled her eyes at Drew's chauvinistic comment. She'd dealt with plenty of scumbags like them in the courtroom and refused to be intimidated.

"Barney!" Phil let go of her hand and shoved his hands onto his hips.

Barney tossed his hands in the air, as if to throw Phil's chastisement away. "What?"

"That's rude and inappropriate." Phil turned to Kathryn. He blew out a puff of air, and his nostrils flared. He was like the bull in the pasture beside her house. "Please excuse him." He turned back to face Barney. "You're letting her see your bad side, man."

"Yeah, well, I'd like to let her see my good side." He pushed his way past Drew, but Phil blocked him from getting to Kathryn, and her entire abdomen quaked with fear.

"Easy man." Drew grabbed his arm. "She's a client of his."

Barney shrunk back with a groan.

"Is there something I can do for you two? If not, I'd like to continue with my tour."

"We'll wait."

"For?" Phil folded his arms and spread his feet apart, like an Indian chief from an old Western.

Kathryn stepped away from Phil with trembling legs while the men strutted their peacock feathers. She didn't have to stand around and listen to this.

"We wanted to check out the place too."

"You're planning on renting it from me?"

"No man. Besides, we're family. We shouldn't have to pay to rent one of your places."

"These rentals are my livelihood. I give discounts to family members but no freebies. Listen, you guys go on into town, and I'll meet you there in a bit."

Kathryn turned away from the roosters, followed the porch around the side of the house, and pressed her body against the wall. The fact that they were Phil's relatives turned her stomach. He could be like them if he didn't let God lead his life. Just like Zeke, who only thought of himself, and Daddy, who cared too much what his colleagues and clients thought of him, Phil could be wild and untamed if it weren't for his belief in God. Was God really that important to one's life? Was she missing out on something valuable?

Drew's engine turned over, and two car doors slammed shut. Kathryn's knees buckled, and she squatted on the side porch. The porch shook at the weight of Phil bounding the rest of the way up the stairs.

"Kathryn?"

"I'm around here." Hot tears sprung from her eyes, and as Phil turned the corner, she swiped them away from her face. Why did he have to see her so vulnerable again?

Phil knelt at her side. "It's okay to cry, Kathryn."

"No, it's not. That's all I do around you. I'm not a weak person, I promise."

He took her hands in his. "I know that, Kathryn. Tears aren't a sign of weakness."

She wiped away a straggler tear that had landed on her upper arm. "They're not?"

"No, they're not. Are you okay?"

"I thought I was, but that scared me so much. I thought they were going to force themselves on me."

"I wouldn't have let that happen. I was more afraid they were going to figure out your identity. They obviously haven't spent any time on the internet or looking at photos taken by their spies, or they would've recognized you as the A.D.A."

"Oh, man! I didn't think about them recognizing me." She pulled herself up to her feet, and Phil stood up beside her. She dusted off the back of her shorts.

"I don't know how they didn't recognize your car either."

"Now that's weird. There's no reason why they wouldn't have noticed that that's the car they messed with."

"Unless they had someone do their dirty work for them."

"That's a possibility. We're too dangerous for each other, Phil."

"Nonsense." He leaned in close enough to kiss her, and her heart stalled. "I happen to think we're kind of good for each other."

She ran her tongue along the back of her teeth and smiled. "The truth of that remains to be seen. The evidence states otherwise. What are we going to do?"

"That depends on what you found."

"I told you. Nothing. It's not here. They already found it, or it never was hidden here."

"Or it's still hidden."

"I don't know where it could be. I've looked everywhere."

"Let's go check out my other two condos and then go for a swim."

Kathryn's mouth fell open. This guy was crazy! "How can you think about swimming at a time like this?"

He shrugged. "I'm hot, and I'm wound tighter than the cables on Brooklyn Bridge. I need to clear my head and look at this from the killer's point of view."

"You mean your uncle's point of view?"

"Or the point of view of one of my cousins."

She slapped her thighs. "I wish someone would confess. It'd make things a whole lot easier."

"I agree. But that's not likely to happen. At least not until the weapon shows up." He reached into his shorts pocket and pulled out his keys, jingling them in the air. "I'm going to go by my house and get my swim trunks and some steaks. I'll meet you back on Airport Road."

Kathryn trailed behind Phil down the stairs to their vehicles. "I think I'll follow you. I don't want to be alone. Not even for a moment."

"Sounds good to me."

* * *

Kathryn followed Phil to his house and waited in her car for him to gather his things. Then they went to the rental and parked around back behind the shed again. Sadie barked at the sound of their car doors shutting. "She misses you when you're gone, doesn't she?"

"She's used to my long hours away."

"But she's had more time with you this week."

"True." Kathryn unlocked the door, and they slipped inside. Sadie ran to greet them and pawed Phil's legs.

Phil plopped his bags down on the kitchen counter and rubbed Sadie's ears. "Hey, girl. We're going for a swim." He turned to Kathryn. "Let me tenderize the steaks before we swim." He washed his hands and opened the package of steaks.

Kathryn went into the bedroom to change into her swimsuit. Good thing she'd brought her one-piece. She wasn't ready to swim in a two-piece alone with a man she'd only known for a few days.

Kathryn handed Phil a frosted glass of lemonade and took a sip from her own glass. Lounging next to him on the white teakwood chaise, with his shirtless tanned body glistening with sweat, Kathryn needed all the cooling down she could get. Maybe they should've gone into town for some sightseeing. Or maybe she should've gone alone and taken a break from this addictive man.

She slipped her sunglasses off the top of her head and covered her eyes with them. Maybe that would help distract her from Phil's masculinity. "So, um, you don't have a pool at your place?"

He licked his lips of the lemonade residue that lingered on them and smacked. "Nope, I figure with all the pools to choose from at the rentals, there's no need."

"Good point. Tell me about your place in Savannah." Did she really care about it or did she just need a huge distraction? She studied a bird on a branch in the oak tree beside the window and then shifted her gaze to him.

"It's a great place on Tybee Island. A little bungalow. I bought it when I started my practice in Savannah. I intended to stay there and rent out these units remotely, but then my plans changed. It's for sale now. That's why I was going home. I had a prospective buyer."

"I'm sorry I messed up your plans."

"No worries. I got a realtor friend to show them the place."

"Why did you decide to move here?"

"I closed my practice because of all the garbage with my family, and I didn't see the need in staying somewhere so crowded if I wasn't going to be working. Ma had asked me to manage the places since Grandma couldn't, and it just seemed like the right fit. When Grandma passed, I stayed and bought the properties from her estate."

"When did you become a P.I.? And why?"

"While I was there in Savannah, I became curious about detective work. Watching too many episodes of *Law and Order*, I'm sure." He laughed. "So I got my license. I haven't done much P.I. work though." He stood, adjusted his swim trunks, dropped his sunglasses on the chaise, and did a cannonball into the pool.

The splash soaked Kathryn and Sadie. "Oh, I'm going to get him!" She bolted upright, ripped her sunglasses from her face, and did a cannonball as he surfaced. When she surfaced, he splashed her in the face, and she splashed back. Sadie barked and ran the length of the pool before settling on the edge beside the pool filter. "You're a beast! Finish your story." Kathryn wiped her face and smoothed back her hair. She probably looked horrible.

Phil spit water from his mouth and laughed as he swam to the edge of the pool where Sadie sat. "When I moved here, I realized very quickly that I could make more money renting out these units than I could make as a detective or as a lawyer and avoid most of the headaches I'd had for years."

Kathryn cocked her head and swam to the edge. She leaned against the wall and paddled in the water. "More money?"

He held up his left hand. "Well, let me clarify. More money with less hassle equals more money to me, even if it's not more money in the bank."

"Got it!" So he wasn't money-hungry like Daddy or Zeke. That was good. "You're fortunate to have found something to fall back on." Kathryn was no closer today than she'd been when she arrived on Friday to knowing what she wanted her future to look like. If she gave up law, what would she do?

"I suppose." Phil let go of the wall and floated beside her. Good thing the water was cooling her off. "Did you not have any hobbies or thoughts of what you wanted to do before you followed your dad's path for your life?" Phil pushed himself part way out of the water and grabbed two green-and-white striped vinyl mesh floats. He pulled them into the water, climbed on to one, and held the other for Kathryn.

She dragged herself onto the float, trying to look graceful. Sadie woofed and whined. Kathryn clicked to her. She wouldn't jump in, Kathryn was sure. "Hobbies? I love to read crime novels and pretend I'm the detective. I used to play detective when I was younger with my neighborhood friends, mostly boys. I brought a stack of novels with me to read while I was here, but I haven't gotten around to reading one single page. Are you surprised?"

He chuckled. "No, I'm not surprised at all, what with the hunt for the weapon, the flat tires, and the allergic reaction to seafood."

She splashed him. "Yeah, it's a wonder I haven't gotten to any of them." She laughed and kicked his foot.

"Was there something else you wanted to be before you studied law?"

She stared up at the sky. She needed her sunglasses to hide behind. Should she reveal her innermost desires to him? Was he safe? "Don't laugh."

"I won't."

"When I graduated from high school, I didn't want to go to college right away. So I went to dental hygienist school and became a hygienist."

"No way!"

"Yep! I graduated with honors and paid for my

college degree with my income."

"Wow! That's impressive. I never would've guessed. Why did you want to be a hygienist?"

"I thought it'd be cool to join an organization that went to impoverished areas of the country and even out of the country to do dental work for free."

Phil sat up and balanced himself on the float. "That's awesome, Kathryn. Did you ever get to do a trip?"

She shook her head and raised the left corner of her mouth. "No, I went straight to law school after college and the rest is—well, you know how it is."

"I'm sorry, but maybe you'll get to do something like that one day."

"Maybe. I don't know. When I become frustrated with law, I think about returning to the dental field."

"Why don't you?"

"Daddy would have a conniption." Kathryn rolled her eyes then Sadie jumped into the pool and paddled over to them. "Sadie! What are you doing, girl?" Kathryn grabbed her collar and pulled her onto the float with her.

"A conniption?" Phil lost his balance and tumbled off the float. When he surfaced, he laughed and questioned her meaning with a raised eyebrow.

"Yeah, a fit. You know?"

He tipped his chin. "I sure hope you're able to find the right path for your future when all of this is over. I'll pray you do."

Kathryn slipped off the float and swam with Sadie over to the steps. Sadie plodded up the steps to the stamped-concrete patio, and Kathryn returned to her float. "You're a big prayer person, aren't you?"

"What do you mean?"

"You pray before every meal, and your faith seems to be ingrained in you."

"I can't imagine living a day without the security of my faith."

Security? She hadn't felt secure in a long time. And when she had, it hadn't been true security. It'd been founded on fear of failure and rejection. Would she ever know the kind of security Phil knew? "I've never thought of religion as security. It always seemed to be confining. Lots of rules. But I'm beginning to see the benefit of having faith."

"You are? How so?"

"It offers protection from harm, from people like your cousins."

"Not always. Bad things still happen. But when they do, God is always there. That's where the true element of faith comes in, knowing He'll provide for you and protect you. Mainly, it's about being certain of your future after your death. That's the best aspect of faith."

Kathryn crinkled her eyebrows. It seemed contrary to what she'd known as a lawyer. Facts were something one could trust in. She swam to the steps and dried off then stretched out on the chaise. "So what's your theory about the gun? You know I need to head home tomorrow or Thursday. With or without further evidence."

Phil joined her on the patio, shook the water from his ears, and stretched out on his chaise. "I wish you didn't have to go."

She slipped on her sunglasses. "Phil, let's not make this complicated."

"Complicated? It's already complicated. Nothing we can do to change that."

She shook her head. "I have to go back."

Phil slid Kathryn's sunglasses down onto the edge of her nose uncovering her eyes. "Oh I know. Believe me, I know. But I don't have to like it."

She smiled even though now was the time to end things before they started. That was the best way to avoid getting hurt. She tucked her sunglasses on top of her head. "Your theory?"

"Needle in a haystack."

She scrunched her face. "What?"

"It's a needle in a haystack. I don't know if anyone will ever know where that gun went."

"What about the honeymoon couple?"

Phil bent his neck forward. "You think there was one?"

"Maybe not a real one. But maybe two people posing as a couple on their honeymoon?"

"Maybe."

"Can you check your records to see if a couple rented one of your units?"

Phil gulped down the rest of his lemonade. "I can, but couples rent from me all the time. It's nothing unusual."

"Any right after the murders?"

"I'll check my records when I go home."

"Why don't you go home now and get your records while I grill the steaks and make a salad?"

"You're not going to let this go, are you?"

"Nope." Kathryn smiled and fluttered her eyelashes. Why did she feel the need to flirt?

Phil clawed the air with both hands like a grizzly, his lack of desire to leave her obvious. "I can't imagine how tenacious you are when you're actually assigned to a case."

"You have no idea." She giggled and pointed toward the house for him to leave on his assignment.

CHAPTER 17

While Phil was gone, Kathryn grilled the steaks, made the salad, and replayed in her mind everything about the inside and outside of the tree house cottage. The fierce looks on Phil's cousin's faces told her the gun was there. But where? There had to be a hidden clue somewhere. Where had she not looked?

Kathryn's phone vibrated on the counter. She washed her hands and answered without looking to see who the caller was.

"Kathryn."

"Hey, Mom. How's it going?"

"Well, things have been better."

"What's wrong?"

"I suppose since you're out of town you haven't seen the news?"

"No, I've been trying to vacation even though it was forced upon me. What's been on the news?"

"Your face."

"My face?" Kathryn stumbled back and caught herself on the counter. Why was she on the news?

"Yes, and your dad is extremely upset with you."

Mom's stern schoolteacher voice shot verbal daggers at Kathryn.

"Why? What did I do to him? Wait, you talked to Dad?" Something must be severely wrong for Dad to call Mom. The two rarely spoke since the divorce.

"Yes, I did. I had no choice. He called me infuriated."

"About what? Wait, why is my face on the news?"

Mom sighed. "They're saying that you've compromised the investigation by consorting with one of Louie Ezzo's relatives. The news station showed a picture of you at a restaurant with some young man."

Kathryn's mouth fell open. The ramifications for her connection with Phil were just beginning. "Oh."

"Oh? Is that all you have to say for yourself? How could you do this to your dad, and how could you screw up this case?"

"Mom, why do you care how Dad feels after everything he's put you through?"

"Kathryn, that's not the point. Our family has a reputation to uphold."

"Mom, I've been trying to outlive that reputation ever since Dad left you."

"Kathryn…"

"Mom, please listen. I'm not sure how any of this affects Dad directly, but..."

"Because you've made a fool of yourself. Of him. And of me."

"A fool? If I did, I'm just following in his lead. You're obviously making that call based off what the media is saying. Don't you want to hear my side of the story?"

"Only if it will change things."

Kathryn paced the house until she ended up on the

balcony off the master bedroom. "I hope it'll change the terrible opinion of me that you obviously have. I came down here to find the murder weapon because none of the investigators had been able to find it. The first evening I was here, Friday, I met a guy on the pier who was fishing. He looked familiar to me, but I couldn't place him, so I didn't think much of it. The next day while eating lunch, he came in the restaurant and asked to sit with me. His name is Phil, and it turns out, he's Maria's ex-fiancé."

"Oh."

"Exactly. But it gets worse. Phil is also Louie Ezzo's nephew, and the family is trying to force him to defend him."

"Yes, he's the one they showed on the news."

"He's no longer practicing law. He lives here and runs a condo rental company. I told him what I was here for long before I knew who he was. I let Louie Ezzo's name slip, and he confessed that Louie was his uncle. He's been trying to help me find the gun because I've been receiving threats since I've been down here. He's been with me so much to try to protect me because his two goon cousins are down here trying to find the weapon too. And they want to make sure I don't prosecute their uncle. Phil told them I'm not on the case anymore, but they don't believe him."

Maybe now Mom and Dad would stop thinking of themselves for one tiny moment and realize that she'd done nothing shameful or selfish. She may have ruined her chances of becoming Senior A.D.A., but that was okay with her.

"How do you know he's not with them? It doesn't seem like a coincidence that you'd meet him when you're down there to find the evidence."

"That's what I thought at first too. But he's really a good guy. He doesn't want anything to do with them. He's a member of a local church here and seems to be well-respected in the community. I've come to trust him with my life." Had she really just said that? She trusts him?

For at least ten seconds, Mom was silent. Then with softness in her voice Kathryn had never heard before, Mom said, "You never trust anyone."

Kathryn nodded, although Mom couldn't see her. "I know, but I trust him. Now do you see what kind of predicament I'm in? I'm not consorting with the defense. Phil isn't defending his uncle, even though his cousins are threatening to hurt him if he doesn't."

"I'm speechless. I'm so sorry for assuming the worst."

Kathryn rubbed her face with the pad of her hand and blinked away the tears that threatened to consume her. "It's okay, Mom. Please tell Dad what's happening if you talk to him again. I wanted to call him, but I knew he'd think the worst and that we'd only get into an argument. I know this makes him look like a failure, in his eyes. But it's really not about him. Not everything is."

"I know, honey. I know. I'll tell him. Just be careful. If your face is on the news with this Phil person, then his cousins are likely to see that you know each other."

"Thanks for the warning."

Kathryn ended the call, exhausted, and noticed a text from Phil in her inbox.

I'll be a little while longer. Got held up.

She texted him back saying she had a bit of news from home she couldn't wait to fill him in on when he returned. He didn't return a text.

Kathryn fed Sadie her dinner and walked her along the side of the house, careful to watch for a surprise attack from Drew and Barney. If they figured out who she was, then she didn't have much time. She had to find the gun and get it to the D.A. before they got to her. She should call Phil and tell him what Mom had said, but there wasn't enough time, and she shouldn't disturb him.

She walked Sadie back into the house, wrapped the steaks in foil, stuck the salad in the fridge, and grabbed her phone and keys. "I'll be back, Sadie. I've got to check something out."

She drove back to the tree house cottage, barely putting her car into park and turning off the engine, and ran up the steps, checking behind her to make sure the cousins weren't after her. She still had the key, so she went in and locked the door behind her. Her gaze raked over every surface in the living area as if it were the first time she'd seen them and finally landed on a spiral-bound notebook on the end table by the hallway. A guest book! Why hadn't she noticed it before?

Panting, she ran to the table, grabbed the book and plopped on to the sofa. She opened the book to reveal page after lined page of guests and their notes of pleasure about their visits. She flipped to the back of the book to the last entry, which happened to be on the day after the murder.

Thanks for letting us stay here on such "short notice". We love this little "hideaway". Everything about it, including the old fashioned well in the backyard, was perfect for our "honeymoon".

Kathryn reread the note, and the hairs stood up on the back of her neck. What was with all the quotation marks? *Honeymooners* here on *short notice*? That was unlikely. They loved the *hideaway*? Of course they did if they were hiding a weapon. These people, if there were two of them, had to be who had hidden the gun. But where would they have hidden it? It wasn't in the old honeymoon shack out in the bayou. It wasn't in a crab trap here on the property. It wasn't in the cemetery. So where then?

Kathryn placed the book back on the table then picked it up again. She'd need it for evidence. She sprinted to the kitchen window and peered out to the backyard. The well! She hadn't noticed it out there when she'd been here before, but there it was. A stacked-stone well, about five feet in diameter, with a shingled roof, hidden amongst a cluster of cedar trees. Could it be? Would they have hidden it in there?

She yanked open the pine cabinet underneath the sink and grabbed a plastic grocery bag; she'd seen them in there on her hunt earlier. In the storage closet, she snatched a flashlight then bolted out the backdoor and down the stairs to the well. She stopped in her tracks, checked for signs of Drew or Barney, and clicked on the flashlight. She directed its beam down into the well and searched for the gun.

In the late afternoon sunlight and with the aid of the flashlight, the gun showed itself. On a ledge just below the surface, it rested. Adrenaline shot through her body. She slipped her hand into the bag, leaned over the edge, and reached with all her might.

* * *

Where was Kathryn? Sadie barked inside the house, but Kathryn didn't answer the door when Phil knocked. He shifted his weight to his right leg, knocked a second time, and still she didn't answer. He squeezed the back of his neck and sighed. What could he do but wait? He couldn't use his key. To go in and find her in the shower or otherwise indisposed would startle and anger the independent and guarded woman.

With the aroma of the grill lingering in the air, he

went around to the back of the house to see if she was at the pool or possibly still grilling the steaks. True to his suspicions, Kathryn's car was gone. He paced the backyard and tapped his knuckles on his temples. Where was she? Why did she leave when she knew he was coming back? There was only one place she could be. She'd gone back to the tree house.

Phil groaned and ran toward the front yard, but his buzzing phone halted him. He dug it out of his pocket and unlocked the screen. Pops. Why did he have to call now? He'd call him back later. He ran to his SUV while shoving the phone into his pocket and jumped in. As he cranked it, he began his prayer.

"God, please protect her. I should've never let her out of my sight. I should've known a strong-willed woman like her would never leave this case alone. Please protect her despite her carelessness."

Phil pulled the phone out of his pocket and dialed Kathryn's number. After five rings, it went to her voicemail. Why wasn't she picking up? Phil pressed the pedal to the floor, not caring if the police caught him for speeding. He had to get to her. Hopefully, Drew and Barney were not with her now. He dialed her number again and after five more rings, it went to voicemail again.

"God, please!" His phone rang. Pops again. "Hello!"

"Son? You okay?"

"Not really, Pops. I've got a situation over here with one of my renters. Do you need something now, or can I call you back?"

"I believe your renter is going to have to wait. We need to talk."

The tone in his voice was more serious than usual, and Phil applied the brakes and pulled over onto the side of

Whiddon Avenue. "Okay."

"In the paper today, there was an article about your uncle."

Phil squeezed his eyes shut. Not now. "Pops, I already told you I'm not going to defend him."

"I know you told me that. That's not why I'm calling you. Will ya listen, you bonehead? The article mentioned that they dismissed the Assistant District Attorney assigned to the case for fraternizing with one of Louie's relatives. She was spotted in Cedar Key for an undetermined reason with an unidentified male, who later turned out to be Louie's nephew. Phil, speak the truth to me. Have you been with the A.D.A.?"

Phil opened his eyes and squeezed the back of his neck. His worst nightmare had just happened. If it was in the newspapers, then his cousins were about to find out who Kathryn was and that he knew her. Their lives were in danger.

"Phil?"

"Pops, listen to me. I met the Assistant D.A. down here Friday night. She came here to find the weapon because witnesses said it was here, and her investigators hadn't been able to find it."

"A bulldog of an attorney. I like that."

"You have no idea." Kathryn's sparkling ebony eyes found their way to Phil's memory, and his chest warmed with longing to see her again. And to see her safe and unharmed.

"But why did she want to meet with you?"

"No, you don't understand. She didn't schedule a meeting with me. We met each other for the first time by pure coincidence."

"Are you sure about that?"

Phil ran his fingers through his hair. Was he sure? It was possible that Kathryn knew all along who he was and that she came down and located him on purpose. Phil shook the thought out of his head. Kathryn wouldn't do something so calculated. She couldn't pull off a charade like that for this long.

"Yes, Pops, I am. Anyway, she told me what she was looking for, but I didn't know she was prosecuting Uncle Louie until she let his name slip. That's when I called you to find out if he was guilty or innocent."

"Forget his guilt or innocence for a minute. If your cousins find out she's there, you know what'll happen."

"They already know she's been here. They just don't know I know her. I told them to go home. I said I'd found out she was off the case. I feel terrible because they took the case that could've made her career away from her all because of me."

"Is she with you now?"

"No, sir. She won't answer her phone either. I'm scared she's gone back to look for the gun without me."

"So she hasn't located it yet?"

"No, but we're almost positive we know where it's at."

"Go to her, son. Call me later, and let me know how things go. Do you have your gun?"

"Yes, sir."

"Be prepared to use it."

CHAPTER 18

Kathryn couldn't reach her phone in her pocket before it went to voicemail. She had to get to Phil. She'd actually found the gun. He wasn't going to believe this. She pulled out of the driveway and headed east on 7th Street. Should she go to Phil's house or just go back to the rental? She'd go to Phil's first.

Kathryn's phone rang again, and she dug it out of her pocket. She unlocked the screen. "Hello."

"Where have you been?"

"I'm sorry! I couldn't get to my phone. I'm on my way to your house."

"Why? I was meeting you back at the rental."

"Because I—I mean…what's wrong?" She sat at the stop sign, which was barely visible amongst the cactuses and shaggy palms.

"Why did you leave Airport Road? You know you shouldn't be out by yourself right now. Drew and Barney could be anywhere, and the way they looked at you earlier, I—"

"Phil, listen to me! I found the gun!"

"What? How?"

"I came—came back to the tree house because I—"

"You did *what?*"

"Don't treat me like I'm your child, Phil!" Her shoulders and neck pinched up into a knot. Four days with this man and already he was trying to dominate her. This is why she stayed clear of relationships with men.

"I'm not. I'm sorry. It's just...it's not safe."

She relaxed her shoulders and waved a car through the intersection that waited for her to move. "I know. But did you hear me? I found the gun."

He sighed and then groaned like an unidentifiable beast. "I heard you. Where are you now?"

"I'm on my way back to Airport Road since you weren't home."

"Okay. Hurry! I'll meet you there."

Kathryn pressed the gas pedal to the floor. "Okay."

"Where was the gun, by the way?"

"You're not going to believe it. It was in the well in the backyard at the tree house."

"The well? How did you find it?"

"I started thinking about the fact that there had to be a clue somewhere. Something I'd missed. So I went back over there, and I looked at everything. The one thing I'd missed was the guest book on the end table. I looked through it and sure enough, the last entry was from someone claiming to be on a honeymoon. They left hints about the well."

"I can't believe this."

"I know." A giggle escaped Kathryn's lips.

"So you think it wasn't Drew or Barney that hid the gun?"

"No, but I think one of them is responsible for using it."

"Were you able to get it without smudging fingerprints?"

"Yes."

"Good. Who signed the guest book?"

"Uh, someone named Mario and Angelista."

"That's my grandparents."

"Your grandparents hid the gun?"

"No, they're dead. Someone I'm related to used their names."

* * *

Phil stopped at the 7th Street stop sign and jumped when Drew tapped on his window with his scarred knuckles. He pressed the button and rolled down the window with a sigh. The air was still and muggy, as if a storm brewed out at sea. "What are you doing here? You following me?"

"Maybe. You trying to go somewhere you wouldn't want me to know about?"

"What I do is none of your business, Drew. Whatcha want?"

He twirled a lit cigarette between his forefinger and middle finger of his right hand. "I need a minute of your time."

Phil tapped on his steering wheel. "Well, I'm kind of in a hurry to meet someone. I got behind in my schedule earlier moving the furniture." His eyes watered, and he tried to hide his panic and guilt-by-association from Drew.

"This is island life, Cuz. You're sure not takin' it easy like Jimmy Buffet sings about."

Phil let out a nervous chuckle, trying to remain calm and to hide his worry about Kathryn. "I wish I could. Sometimes it's as hectic as the courtroom." A shadow blocked the stream of sunlight shining into his SUV, and he turned to find Barney standing at the passenger door. "What's going on here?"

"Nothing, man." Drew jerked open his door and yanked him out of the vehicle by his left arm into the street.

Barney rushed around the front of the vehicle and grabbed Phil's right arm.

Phil tried to break free, but his cousins had a death grip on him. "Drew, unhand me. I've got to go—and my SUV is rolling."

Drew released Phil, but Barney squeezed his arm tighter. Drew reached in and jammed the SUV into park, removing the keys, and slamming the door.

"Barney! Let go of my arm!" Phil yanked his arm out of Barney's grasp. Something was up, and there wasn't a lot Phil could do about it. Two against one, he'd learned as a kid, was no good. He turned around to face his thick-necked cousins.

"The only place you're going is with us." Drew pointed to his car.

Phil's eyebrows knotted at the bridge of his nose. "Where?"

"Don't worry about it."

"Tell me where, and I'll drive and meet you there." Phil reached for his car door handle, but Barney blocked his way, and grabbed his arm again.

"No, you're riding with us. I'll even ride in the backseat with you to keep you company."

Phil swallowed down a giant dry lump in his throat. This wasn't going as he'd planned, and he had no way to warn Kathryn that his cousins had the advantage in this game they were playing. "Whatever you say, Barney. Just let me move my car out of the road." Phil wiped the sweat from his stubbly upper lip and tried to calm his nerves by reminding himself that he wasn't in this battle alone.

"I'll get it." Barney jingled the keys in the air and pulled the Range Rover into the parking lot of a kayak rental shop then rejoined Phil and Drew.

Drew led the way to his Mercedes. Barney shoved Phil in that direction and then shoved him into the backseat. The cigarette smoke inside the car mixed with his cousin's cheap cologne churned his stomach. And so did the realization that he was about to go for a ride he'd never forget.

* * *

Kathryn stopped at the last stop sign before the rental. There to her left was Phil's SUV parked at a kayak rental place. She yanked the steering wheel in the direction of the shop and slammed her car into park when she made it to the parking lot.

A fair-skinned blonde woman in a mint-green jumper with white sneakers and a straw hat passed her on a bicycle. Kathryn pressed the button to lower her car window, but nothing happened. She pushed it a few more times, but the window refused to acquiesce. "I should've had them take a look at this when I had the oil changed the other day." She opened her door, climbed out, and ran over to the SUV. The doors were locked, and there was no sign of Phil.

"Excuse me," she yelled to the woman before she got too far away. "Did you happen to see the driver of this vehicle?"

The woman circled back around, stopped pedaling, and rested a foot on the pavement for balance. She slipped off her sunglasses and smiled. "You mean Phil Tag? Yeah, I saw him a few minutes ago on my way up the street."

Kathryn chewed on her thumbnail. "What was he doing?"

The woman studied Kathryn for a moment with a raised eyebrow, as if measuring her motives. "Uh, he was with two guys."

"Did they leave together?"

"Yes, and something must've been going on because I waved at him, but he didn't wave back. Normally, he's friendly. Even when he's busy. He's a nice guy. Cute. Kinda keeps to himself though."

Well, that was more information than Kathryn needed right now. "Okay, thank you." Fear shot through her. Drew and Barney had taken him. But where could they have gone? She jumped back into her car and headed toward Phil's house in case they were there.

She arrived within a minute, but they weren't there. She walked around to the back to check on Phil's boat. It was tied to his dock. She left his house and went back to the rental on Airport Road. They weren't there either. He'd disappeared.

Kathryn slid out of the car defeated and went inside to Sadie, who was unharmed, as were her case files. She placed the gun underneath the kitchen sink to hide it in case Drew and Barney returned.

So they hadn't been here. Where were they then? Discouragement and worry ate away at her like saltwater on a piece of metal. She should've never left Phil's side. She'd had no way of knowing he'd been in as much danger as she'd been in, but still she shouldn't have left him.

She threw herself down onto the sofa and patted her lap for Sadie to join her. It was time to call D.A. Schwartz and risk disbarment for interfering in an investigation she wasn't assigned to. She waited for him to answer, aimlessly brushing Sadie's fur with her hand.

"Hello."

"Hello, Mr. Schwartz."

"Kathryn, how is your time off going?"

"Well…I haven't had much of a vacation. I've been dodging two of Louie Ezzo's nephews the whole time."

"You should have come on back to Georgia then."

She twirled the ends of her hair. "I know, but you told me to stay. Besides, something kept haunting me about this case, and I couldn't leave. I've got some news for you."

"Okay, what have you got?"

"First of all, and most importantly, I found the weapon."

"You what? Why were you looking for it?"

"Because I knew it was here. That doesn't matter right now. What matters is that I found it."

"Have you got it in your possession now?"

She could feel the excitement in the D.A.'s voice, like the charge of energy in the air after a summer storm. Without the gun, it would be next to impossible to convict Louie Ezzo or anyone else of the crimes. "Yes, sir."

"Okay, and you're coming home?"

"I was planning to, but now I don't know."

"Why?"

She rubbed away the pounding behind her eyes. "Well, Phil, Phillip Tagliaferro, Louie's nephew, has been kidnapped by his two cousins."

"What?"

"I don't know for sure, but I suspect that's what's happened."

"Why do you suspect that?"

"He was on his way to meet me at the rental unit I'm staying in, which he owns. I just talked to him on the phone a few minutes ago. He should be here, but I found his SUV abandoned, and a woman said she saw him leave with two men and that he didn't seem like himself. His cousins are very intimidating! They want him to defend Ezzo. I'm sure they've taken him."

"Does he know you found the gun?"

"Yes."

"And you don't suspect that he duped you?"

"No, sir, I don't."

"Do you think they could force him to go?"

"Phil seemed to think so. And he wouldn't have gone with them willingly, not without telling me. I have no idea where to look."

"Okay, normally I'd tell you to get yourself home, but I don't want you traveling alone. Stay put where you're at for right now. Let me make a few phone calls and see if I can get a detective to escort you home."

"Thank you. But what about Phil?"

"Can you give me a description of all three of the men?"

"Sure."

"Okay, tell me what they look like and anything you know about their vehicles, and I'll contact local law enforcement. We'll see if we can track them down."

Kathryn gave D.A. Schwartz a thorough description of the Ezzo men and Phil and then allowed herself to weep until no tears remained.

CHAPTER 19

Drew turned off Whiddon Avenue then onto Gulf Blvd. and finally onto Airport Road. Phil's heart plummeted to his stomach. They'd figured it out, and now they were taking him to Kathryn, where they'd no doubt kill them both. How could his life end this way? He'd stepped away from the unscrupulous dealings of his family, had a career he could be proud of, and had finally found a woman he wanted to spend more time with, and it was going to end before it could even start? He gritted his teeth and clinched his jaw.

The shadows of the mid-afternoon sun flickered through the palms and mangroves, and Phil's hopes began to dwindle. Drew and Barney rambled on about something, but all Phil could think about was how disgraceful he'd look to Pops and to the rest of the family. They'd look at him like a prodigal son returned by force. They'd never respect him, as if they ever had, and he'd be forced to represent every crook known to the family.

Of course, Pops had sounded like he'd shifted his support in Phil's favor when he told him to protect Kathryn. He'd taken his word about her trustworthiness. Or was that a trap? Was that Pops' way of finding out what Kathryn knew?

It didn't matter. He couldn't waste his thoughts or energy worrying about Pops right now.

They passed the driveway to his rental, and his heart skipped a beat at the sight of Kathryn's Honda parked beneath a stately Live oak. She was there and was probably frantic by now. They weren't going after her? Then where were they going? Drew pulled right into the airport, and Phil's heart plummeted again. "What are you doing, Drew?"

"What do you think I'm doing? I'm taking you to talk to Uncle Louie."

Phil reached for the door handle, but Barney had a gun shoved against his ribs before he could get the door open. He released the handle. "I'm not going! I told you I'd call him."

"Yeah, you've been saying that for days. We're gonna make sure you see him."

As much as Phil didn't want to fly to Georgia or see Louie, this would distract his cousins from Kathryn long enough for her to get the gun to authorities. He had to get word to her that she'd be safe to move forward with the two thugs out of Cedar Key. But what about the guys from the grocery store? Maybe it would be best if Kathryn stayed put until he returned.

Drew got out of the car and opened Phil's door for him. He tossed the keys to Barney.

Phil looked back and forth from Drew to Barney. "What's going on, Cuz?"

"Barney is staying here to watch out for the D.A. You're going with me." Drew yanked Phil's arm and dragged him toward a waiting twin-engine plane, black and white with blue and gold stripes down the side.

"I told you, she's not on the case anymore. Why do

you have to keep looking for her?"

"What's it to ya?"

"It's nothing. I just think you guys are wasting your time here. Go back to New York and be with your *precious* family!"

Barney rushed up behind Phil and yanked him by his hair. He punched him in the stomach and grabbed his jaw. "You listen here, Cuz. The next time I hear you make a comment like that about our family, I'm going to make sure you take a long dirt nap. Capisce?"

Phil yanked away from him. "Capisce." He turned to Drew. "Let's get this over with."

In the Beechcraft Baron six-seater private plane, Phil sat on the left side, behind and facing the pilot. Drew sat on the right side diagonal to and facing Phil, as if he needed to watch him to ensure he wouldn't escape. Where could he go at 20,000 feet?

They lifted off the ground, and Phil squeezed the armrests, his knuckles white from the force of his grip. Take off was his least favorite part about flying, and in a plane no wider than his Range Rover, his fear level had just doubled.

When they leveled off, he eased back into the leather bucket seat and stretched out his legs until they touched the seat facing him. If he had to be taken somewhere by force, this piece of luxury was the way to travel. He adjusted the air control above his head and focused his attention on the scenery outside the window since the interior of the plane contained his moose of a cousin.

As the pilot circled around Cedar Key, Phil directed his gaze to the rental house. Was Kathryn still waiting for him there? Was she panicking because she couldn't find him?

What would she do? Would she go back to Georgia without saying goodbye to him? He'd send her a text when they landed to let her know he was in her county, if he could break away from Drew long enough to do so. He'd wait for her there, if she wanted him to.

He closed his eyes and prayed. All hope couldn't be lost. God would watch out for him even in this plane, and he'd watch out for Kathryn. He rubbed his face and scratched the stubble on his jaw. "Where are we going?"

"Cobb County Airport at McCollum Field."

"You've got to be kidding me!"

"Nope. I told you I'm taking you to see Uncle Louie."

"Then why not fly out to the Paulding County airport, Drew? That's a lot closer than McCollum."

"Because I wanted to fly in to Kennesaw. That's why."

Phil slapped his legs. "This is unbelievable. Where's Barney?"

"I told you that too. He's staying back to make sure the lady D.A. doesn't pull any funny stuff." Drew twirled a cigarette between his fingers then tucked it behind his right ear. "We know you know her, Phil. Did you think we wouldn't find out?"

Phil grabbed the armrests and jerked his body forward to the edge of his seat. "Captain, land this plane! I need to get out now."

Drew laughed. "Ha, I hired him. Not you. He only takes orders from me. Don't worry though. We'll land in an hour and thirty minutes. We'll be at the jail by 4:00 p.m., and back to Cedar Key before sunset."

Phil sat back in his seat, clamped his jaw shut, and stared out the window. There was nothing he could do about his predicament now. However, when they landed, he'd give Drew a fight as he'd never given him before, one to make up for all those times of bullying as kids.

* * *

Kathryn walked Sadie around back to avoid Drew or Barney spotting her, the hum of a small plane circling in the air above their heads beckoning her to join its passengers. If only she could escape this impossible situation on a private jet and fly to somewhere peaceful and trouble-free. Cedar Key could be that kind of place, but it wouldn't be until this murder case was closed and Louie Ezzo and the cousins were behind bars for a long time.

Kathryn slipped into the house and locked the door behind her. Sadie danced around for a treat, and Kathryn laughed. No matter what the situation, Sadie always thought of her belly first. Kathryn's stomach growled as Sadie chewed on her treat, and she clasped her hand over it. Had she really not eaten since the light breakfast she'd shared with Phil?

She uncovered the steaks and pulled the salad out of the refrigerator. She might as well eat. She couldn't go searching for Phil. He'd be angry with her if she did. Surely, he was okay. Maybe he was stalling his cousins.

Kathryn heated one steak, wrapped the other one in foil, and placed it in the refrigerator. She prepared a small salad in a wooden bowl, added ranch dressing to it and then sat down at the bar. Sadie whined and begged at her feet. "You already had a treat, Sadie. Go get on your bed. I'm not in the mood for you right now."

Kathryn nibbled on a cucumber and sighed. "God, if you're listening, please protect Phil. He's been my protector while I've been here in Cedar Key, and now he needs protecting. I don't know a lot about the way you work, but from what I've seen, you really take care of him, and you've let him take care of me the last few days. I hope you'll take care of him now."

Kathryn cut a piece of steak and took a bite. Savory. Juicy. Phil knew how to pick a good steak. Phil knew a lot about a lot of things.

"God, I don't know where my life is going. I don't know if I want to be a Senior Assistant D.A. I'm pretty sure I don't want to be a judge or Supreme Court Justice. When I talked to Phil about doing dental work for underprivileged people, my heart started to tingle in a way it hasn't in a long time. If you care about what I do, will you show me if you want me to leave the legal system? I think you might care for me the same way you care for Phil...although I don't deserve it. I haven't gone to church, and I haven't done things right in my life. But I'd like a second chance."

Tears streamed down Kathryn's face. What was happening to her? Something was budding in her like the hibiscus plant outside the window. If only Phil was with her now, she'd tell him what she was feeling, and he could explain it to her.

Was this something to do with God? The pastor's sermon on Sunday about the treasures of one's heart poked at her thoughts. Phil was a treasure to Kathryn. She didn't want to lose him. "God please help him! Please return him to me."

* * *

When they landed at Cobb County Airport, Phil excused himself to the FBO's restroom, where he sent Kathryn a text.

Too much to explain in a text. Drew took me by plane to Georgia to see Uncle Louie. I should be back before nightfall. Barney is still there in Cedar Key. Stay in the house.

Kathryn sent a text back immediately.

Wish I could have stopped them from taking you. Please be careful! I'll wait for you.

She was safe, and she'd wait for him. Relief flooded Phil's heart like the tide flooding the shoreline on the bayou in the afternoon light. If she'd stay where she was, and if Barney remained clueless about her location, all would stay well until he returned.

Phil turned off his phone to save his battery and to keep the phone from roaming while inside the concrete walls of the jail.

* * *

The steel bars slammed shut behind Phil as he followed the uniform-clad female deputy down the echoing corridor to visitation room number nine where Uncle Louie waited for him. Would he be able to get out of there without committing to defend him?

Based on the evidence Kathryn had and the fact that she'd found the gun, how could Louie deny his involvement? In true Louie fashion, he'd blame his employees and his nephews. If his fingerprints were on that gun, he'd still find a way to blame someone for that. If he forced Phil to represent him, he'd have to go over the information in Kathryn's file with more scrutiny than he'd ever before used on a case. His job would be to clear Louie or risk an uncertain future.

What was it Barney had said? Something about clearing their uncle or taking an eternal dirt nap? Phil didn't want to go into the Witness Protection Program, but that might be where he was headed.

He straightened his shirt and stepped into the drab grayness, an oscillating fan blowing air across the room like a wind tunnel. The floors glistened, and the scent of bleach touched Phil's nostrils. An orange jumpsuit replaced Uncle

Louie's usual European suit, and he sat at a metal table instead of behind his oak desk. What a contrast.

Wrists handcuffed and fingers interlocked, he gave one nod. "Phillip, what news do you have for me?"

Phil slid into the chair across from Uncle Louie. "Well, Uncle, I was taken by force by Drew and brought here against my wishes. I can't say that I have much of anything for you."

"Abducted? So you don't want to represent me?"

He drummed his fingers on the table. "It's not personal. I gave up practicing law a long time ago."

"No one ever gives up practicing law. Not when there's a family member who needs you. What do you know about the case? What about the D.A.?" Louie opened his hands and then locked his fingers together again. "I hear it's a woman."

"Well—"

"I can't believe they'd let a woman prosecute me." He swung his head like a pendulum and laughed. His laugh crawled up Phil's spine. "I'm as good as free. No woman can win a case against an Ezzo."

"Uncle, I hear she's off the case now. D.A. Schwartz is prosecuting you, so it's not so open and shut as you'd like to think. They've got evidence."

Louie slammed his fists onto the table, and Phil jumped. "You'll find the loophole, nephew. Do you hear me? You'll find the weakest link and pin everything on him. I will not go away to prison at sixty-five years old. I've already been in here two months. That's enough." He pointed at him. "If you want your inheritance, get me out of here, nephew. Or else!"

"Uncle, I don't need an inheritance from you. I'm

doing fine on my own."

"Oh, you're that self-sufficient, eh? You shunning me?"

"No, Uncle Louie. I'm not shunning you. And your offer of inheritance is more than I deserve. All of that aside, I need to know how involved you are with these murders."

"Why does that matter?"

"You want me to defend you. You need to tell me the truth."

"I'm not telling you anything. You haven't said you'd defend me."

"I guess we've reached an impasse then, right? I'm not going to defend you unless I know the truth."

"Maybe if you knew the truth, you wouldn't defend me anyway."

Phil held his hands up in surrender. "I think my job is done here." He stood and headed toward the door of the chamber.

"Listen, I need to know how likely it is that I'm gonna go away to prison."

Phil turned around to face Louie. For the first time, he looked like a withered old man, defeated and frightened. His dark eyes glistened with tears, and his brow bore worry lines across it. "Uncle, right now, witnesses are saying that you did it. Unless you've got something to give me that'll help me find the information I need to clear your name, I don't really see what else I can do to help you."

* * *

Kathryn showered, dried her hair, and dressed in her black bike shorts and the blue Cedar Key T-shirt she'd bought on Saturday at the Trading Post. Who cares if she looked like a tourist? Cedar Key would forever hold a special place in her heart. She'd learned about surviving and discovered how much courage she had deep inside her more this week than in her entire life.

She went to the closet and pulled her clothes off the hangers. This would be her last night here, and she might as well go ahead and pack while she waited on Phil to return in case she had to flee in a hurry.

After she'd packed everything, she placed her bags beside the front door then packed her laptop and files into her laptop bag. She stacked her books beside the laptop bag on the bar, the unread crime novels, and giggled. Who had time for reading about crime when there was real crime unfolding right before her eyes?

She moved Sadie's bed to the foyer. Sadie cocked her head and perked her ears. "We're going home tomorrow, Sadie." Sadie whined. "I know. I don't want to go either, but we don't live here. And I have a job to get back to."

Kathryn's shoulders slumped. Why did she dread going back? It wasn't the Ezzo case alone that had her reluctant to return. It was everything. Being trapped inside a courthouse building all day every day, spending hour upon hour researching, filtering through the truth versus the lies, dealing with the heart-broken families when a criminal went free. It's a wonder she ever slept at night.

Kathryn yawned and stretched. It was only 7:00 p.m., but she couldn't keep her eyes open. The antihistamine must still be in her system, and the hot shower had relaxed her to the point that she needed a nap or she'd never make it through whatever was ahead for her and Phil later that night. She clicked the air conditioning down a few degrees and grabbed the seashell fleece blanket off the back of the sofa. A chilly room and a soft blanket were a perfect combination for a nap.

"Come on, girl. Let's take a short nap." Kathryn tossed her phone onto the coffee table and stretched out on the sofa, as thunder rumbled in the distance. Sadie sidled up next to her and tucked her nose underneath Kathryn's arm. She closed her eyes. Just a few minutes, and she'd be refreshed and ready for the evening.

CHAPTER 20

Phil raced ahead of Drew out of the jail and straight toward the taxi. If traffic held off, they'd be at the airport by 5:15 p.m. and back in Cedar Key long before sunset. Phil needed to think up a good escape plan for ditching his cousin and getting to Kathryn as soon as possible.

"How about we grab something to eat before we head back to Cedar Key?" Drew whacked Phil on the back.

Phil shook his head as he sank into the backseat. He'd rather be used as shark bait than to spend one more minute with his cousin than he had to. "I'm not hungry."

"I know you are. You probably haven't eaten a thing since lunch." Drew tapped the driver on the shoulder. "McCollum airport, please."

"Why ya being so nice to me now?"

"Because you did what I asked you to do. I know you'll make sure Uncle gets released from jail."

Phil huffed. He hated to disappoint Drew, but he couldn't guarantee Louie's freedom, especially since he wouldn't tell him anything about his involvement. "Thanks for the offer, but I just want to get back home. I've got to let the person who I was meeting know where I went."

"I can go with you and personally explain to *this person* why you ditched." Drew winked.

"Drew, there's no reason you need to go back."

"I have to get my car. You think I'd let Barney drive it back to New York? No way! Besides, I'd like to see that little honey of a D.A. You should really make good use of your time with her."

"Shut up, Drew. You're disgusting."

"You're getting mighty defensive about someone you don't know." Drew looked down his nose at Phil.

Phil balled his fists. "I met her. Okay? I doubt she's that kind of woman."

"You met her and didn't take her for a ride?"

"No, I didn't."

"If you're not interested in her then she's fair game."

Phil interlocked his fingers to avoid punching his cousin in the face. "Absolutely not. Leave her alone."

"I may have no choice if Barney's already had his way with her. I don't need his leftovers." Drew screwed up his face as if disgusted by the thought of Barney getting to Kathryn before he could.

"Drew, you had better hope he hasn't because if he has, there will be hell to pay! Now let's get back to Cedar Key."

* * *

Phil and Drew arrived via taxi at the Cobb County Airport and waited in the FBO for the pilot to finish a call. Phil sat in one of the leather guest chairs and crossed his legs, the ankle of his right leg resting on the knee of his left. After all of today's sitting and being cooped up, he couldn't wait to get back out on his skiff and take a tour around the islands of Cedar Key, hopefully with Kathryn by his side.

Drew stepped outside and lit a cigarette, and Phil pulled his phone from his pocket. He powered it on, pulled up his messaging box, and typed out a text to Kathryn.

We're at the airport getting ready to fly back. It should take less than two hours. Maybe we can catch the sunset.

He locked his phone and shoved it into his pocket. How quickly things change. Four nights ago, he was carefree, reeling in sharks on the pier, and renting out his properties to happy vacationers. Last night, he was taking care of Kathryn after her allergic reaction, and now he was miles away and trying to get back to her on what would probably be their last night together. It was good she'd found the gun, but now she had no reason to remain in Cedar Key. If he searched hard enough in the recesses of his mind, maybe he could find a reason to make her stay. He groaned. How had he let his heart become attached to a woman he couldn't see with regularity?

The pilot ended his call and shook his head. He turned around toward Phil and slipped off his sunglasses, revealing serious blue eyes. "Excuse me, Mr. —" He adjusted his shirt collar.

"Tagliaferro."

He scratched his chin and sighed. "Sir, I'm afraid we're not going to be able to fly out just yet." He shook his head again, exposing a sunburned neck beneath a head full of brown hair.

"Why?" Phil leaned forward on the edge of the seat and shoved his hands into his pockets in an effort to hide his anxiety. Why couldn't he have been dressed more professionally instead of in his running shorts and a T-shirt? Maybe if he looked better the pilot would realize the importance of his flight.

Drew returned from smoking his cigarette, the stench of smoke lingering on his clothes. "What's up? Is there a problem?"

"Yes, sir. There's a rough storm blowing over the Florida Panhandle right now, and it's hitting Cedar Key pretty hard."

"So we can't fly in?" Phil raked his fingers through his hair and pivoted in his seat.

"No, sir, but we should be clear for takeoff in an hour. Why don't you go over to the restaurant at the FBO and get a drink or something to eat? I'll call you when we're good to go."

Drew was going to get his way after all. Phil shrugged and pointed for him to lead the way.

"The restaurant is real nice, and you can watch the planes take off and land."

"Thanks." Drew nodded.

"All the planes but the one we're supposed to be on."

Drew whacked Phil on the back. "What's the problem, Cuz? I know you've got to be as hungry as I am."

"Yeah, I guess I am. I just want to get back home. You guys basically kidnapped me and didn't even let me dress decent enough to go to the jail. I felt like a bum in there today. I'm really going to look like a bum in the restaurant. Besides, I had to leave my car parked in some random parking lot and leave my client hanging. You don't understand the concept of professionalism."

"I don't? I'm very professional at what I do."

"Yeah? And what's that? Roughing people up and manipulating them to get what you want?"

"Hey, I resent that. You might want to watch the way you talk to me."

Phil followed Drew into the restaurant and let the conversation drop. Unfortunately, Drew was right about the way he treated him, and it had nothing to do with his fear of them burying him out behind the shed. He should treat Drew better because he was another human being, family. Drew had no concept of the gift God could give him, and if Phil didn't treat him better, he might not ever know.

The entire Ezzo family, mainly the men, knew nothing about the great gift of freedom they could have if they'd only surrender their lives. True, some of them went to Mass and confession on occasion, but few of them did it, he guessed, for reasons other than asking for forgiveness for the crimes they'd committed.

Phil stood next to Drew as they waited for the hostess to seat them. He pulled his phone out of his pocket. No text from Kathryn. His arms and legs tingled with apprehension over her safety, but he pushed the fear away. He couldn't do anything to help her until he returned. "Hey Cuz, have you talked to Barney since we've been up here?"

"Yeah, he went clamming again. Can you believe that?" Drew laughed.

"So he really went the other day?"

"Yeah, why?"

"I figured that was a cover up for some drug deal or something."

Drew punched him in the arm as they walked to their table overlooking the runway. "No, man. He really went clamming. He spends a lot of time on the water back home. He loves to fish. Everybody needs a life outside of work."

A jet took off, and the building vibrated as Phil tucked his legs under the white tablecloth. "Why doesn't he do something like that instead of doing what he does for Louie?"

"He's thirty years old. He's kind of too old to change his ways."

"Maybe, but one day he's going to end up in jail. Or dead."

"I don't think he cares. He just lives one day at a time. What else does he have to live for?"

The waitress came and took their order; Phil ordered the salmon, Drew, the burger. "Doesn't he want to settle down? Have a wife and kids?"

"He's got kids. He's had several girlfriends for a while, but he can't decide which one he likes the most."

Phil scratched his eyebrow and grimaced. "He's got kids?"

Drew laughed. "Yeah. Two boys and a girl. Cute little brats."

"All with the same woman?"

Drew laughed again as if Phil were the stupidest man he knew. "Nah, three women. Two of them are married now. The other was married at the time he fathered the kid."

Phil's heart sank to the pit of his stomach. Drew was clueless about how good and pure life could be, and apparently, so was Barney. There was no way he could ever do the honorable thing for these women. How sad. "What about you, Drew?"

"What about me?"

"You got any kids?"

Drew dug into his right ear with his pinky finger. "Nah. I've been too busy with business. And I'm too careful to make the mistakes Barney has made."

Phil could relate. He'd been consumed with business too for a while—so consumed that he'd lost his fiancé. "Don't you ever want to settle down? Ever get tired of this way of life? You're my age, right? 28?"

"Yeah."

The waitress came with their spinach and artichoke dip appetizer and tortilla chips. "Don't you ever think about leaving a legacy? A good legacy?"

Drew sat back and folded his arms across his chest. "What are you now? Some kind of counselor or something? Or a priest?"

"No, man. I just...I want to settle down and be a part of something bigger than myself. I want to belong to someone."

"I'm surprised you want to try again after what happened with Maria."

"Yeah, I'm surprised too, but I get lonely. I want someone to share my life with."

"So get a woman for the night. That'll cure what ails you." Drew flicked a chip at Phil.

"Drew, no. I'm looking for something more fulfilling than that. I want what Ma and Pops have. I want commitment, honesty, faithfulness, love." There was so much more to life than making money and gambling it away, more than blindly following a mob boss, more than viewing a woman as an object to satisfy a man's most primal urges.

"Your Ma and Pops have that? I thought your Pops just kept your Ma put up in that nice house so he could golf and spend time with the ladies."

"No, man. Pops may be a lot of things, but he's not a cheater." Or was he?

"You've gotten even softer than I thought, Phil. You sound like a character in one of those chick flicks."

Phil shrugged and scooped a heap of dip up with a tortilla chip. He shoved the chip into his mouth and held Drew's clear eyes with his own. "I'm all right with that."

"What gives?"

"What do you mean?"

"What makes you so relaxed and resigned to live a boring—peaceful life?"

Phil felt his insides burst with excitement. The opportunity had finally come to share with Drew about his faith. But first, he needed to apologize for his bad attitude when dealing with Drew and Barney earlier. He took a sip of water, pushed down the lump of humility that grabbed at his throat, and began to tell the story of the day that changed his life.

* * *

Kathryn bolted up off the couch, knocking Sadie to the floor. She grabbed the fleece throw to her chest, and her heart pounded in her ears. What had startled her awake? A clap of thunder and a flash of lightning outside the window answered her question. Something banged and scraped the glass patio door. Could it be Barney?

She ran to the door and peeked out into the darkness. What time was it? Where was Phil?

She shifted her weight to her right leg and crossed her arms across her chest. The banging and scraping continued, and she leaned her head to the right to try to see around the corner of the house. She flipped on the floodlights, but the rain came down so hard the lights did little to illuminate the yard.

She reached for the doorknob to check outside, but her phone vibrated on the coffee table with a reminder notification. A text from Phil awaited her. She'd missed it because she'd been sleeping.

We're at the airport getting ready to fly back. It should take less than two hours. Maybe we can catch the sunset?

Before sunset? He'd missed the sunset. According to the time he'd sent the text, he should've arrived already. Where was he? Kathryn sent him a return text.

Phil, I just got your text. I fell asleep and didn't know you sent it. Where are you?

She put the phone down and returned to the door to try to figure out the source of the noise. When she reached the door, a palm frond hit the glass. Sadie yelped, ran to her bed in the foyer, and Kathryn let out a nervous laugh. The storm was playing games with her mind. It brought little comfort knowing that she only imagined something menacing happening to her and that she would, in fact, be safe there until Phil returned.

A flash of lightning lit up the darkness through the dwindling rain and revealed a broad-shouldered silhouette. Kathryn shrieked and yanked the heavy drapes across the door. She reached through them to make sure the door was locked then ran to the front door to secure it. She jammed a chair underneath the doorknobs and returned to the sofa, scooping up her phone in the process. Sadie whimpered. "Come here, girl. It's okay." Kathryn received another text from Phil.

"We were delayed because of weather, but we're almost there. How are you?"

Kathryn shot a quick text back.

"I was doing okay, but it's storming, and I saw a man outside my door just now."

CHAPTER 21

An explosive pounding came at the door and Sadie growled. Kathryn jumped and dropped her phone on the floor where it spun out of sight underneath the sofa. Every nerve ending in her body felt raw and electrified.

"Open up! You've got something I need, little lady."

Frozen, Kathryn clasped her hands over her mouth and screamed a muffled scream into them. Everything she'd fought against this week was now standing behind that door. She'd found the weapon. Why hadn't she left Cedar Key when she'd had the chance?

The pounding at the door came again. The chair jammed under the doorknob should hold, but there was no guarantee.

"Let me in!" That voice! It was Barney, the same voice from the threatening phone call.

Kathryn dropped to the floor and searched for her phone in the dimly lit room, finally landing her hand on it beside the foot of the sofa. From her place on the floor, she rushed a text to Phil.

Are you close yet? Barney is banging on the door and trying to get in. If he breaks in, he'll kill me. Or worse.

Her phone chimed a few seconds later.

We landed a few minutes ago. Get Sadie and the gun and escape out the other door. Follow the lights to the airstrip. I'll be waiting here.

She ran to the kitchen, grabbed Sadie's leash, and connected it to her collar. Her breath caught in her throat and threatened to choke her. Sadie continued to bark and growl, the hairs on her back standing at full attention and her ears pinned back.

Kathryn flung her purse strap over her shoulder, grabbed the gun from its hiding place, picked up her laptop bag and keys, and headed toward the patio door. Barney banged on the front door again. This was Kathryn's chance to escape. She tugged on the leash and forced Sadie to follow her. Barney rang the doorbell and banged on the door until the door facing sounded like it would crack.

"Help me!" Kathryn scream-whispered, fear gripping her vocal chords. Who was she talking to? No one was around to help her. But maybe God was. "Come on Sadie," she whispered. "Be quiet." If Sadie barked once they got outside, Barney would be on her trail within seconds, and her hopes of escaping would be dead forever.

She jammed her feet into her sandals and made it to the patio door, her arms heavy-laden, and slid the lock open with a click. The rain had stopped, but the wind still tossed the trees around in the night sky. She had a choice to make right now. Would she shrink back like a coward, like a first year law student in a mock trial, or would she straighten her shoulders and boldly conquer what was out there? Would she give in, or would she win this battle?

She'd win it, or die trying.

She pulled the door open, and then halted. She whispered, "God, if you're there, please get me and Sadie to safety."

Barney banged again on the door and screamed words at Kathryn she'd only heard in the belly of the prison. Now was her chance. She darted out the door, pulling Sadie along, although the dog tried to go toward the front yard where Barney waited on the porch. Kathryn tiptoed across the pool deck and inched her way to the edge of the tree-lined property. A distant rumble of thunder sent an eerie tension to her bones. The sky flickered with heat lightning, and she bolted toward the airport.

* * *

On the flight back, Drew had said few words. He hadn't had much to say when Phil told him the story of how his life had changed. How after Maria dumped him, he took a long look at the direction of his life. That that's what caused him to quit the law practice and stop defending criminals.

But, in truth, there was more to it than that. He'd wanted his life to not only be absent of negative things but to include positive things. He'd wanted to have relationships with people that mattered. When Phil started going to church and turned his life over to God, he'd met all sorts of new people who really cared for him and who he could care for. His life changed in unimaginable ways.

Drew obviously wasn't ready to make a change like that. He had too much invested in the family business. His quiet on the way back to Cedar Key spoke volumes about what was on his mind. Phil's words had to have made an impact on him, if even just a little.

They climbed out of the plane, and Phil reached for Drew's hand. "It was good catching up with you. I'll see you around."

"Hold up. We're not done here."

"What do you mean, Drew?"

"We've still got a matter of that D.A. She's down here snooping around."

"Drew, I told you it doesn't matter. She's not on the case anymore."

"It matters. If she's looking for something, and she finds it, we could all be in a lot of trouble."

"Don't say we. I have nothing to do with this. And I recommend if you do, you'd better come clean. If you don't, you'd better tell the authorities what you know. Or else you could go away for a long time."

"Not going to happen."

Phil turned away from Drew. Even though he'd told Kathryn to meet him there at the airstrip, he'd head toward his SUV to distract Drew.

"Where you going, Cuz?"

"To get my Range Rover."

"I'll drive you."

"That's okay. I can walk. I need to stretch my legs."

"No, I'll drive you. We need to go have a visit with your friend."

Phil patted his pockets and held up his index finger. "Hold on. I left something in the plane."

"Hurry up then."

Phil climbed back into the plane. The pilot sat in his seat adjusting his controls for takeoff. "Excuse me. Can you wait here a few minutes?"

The pilot's serious eyes examined him beneath an arched eyebrow. "Why?"

"I need a ride back to Georgia, but first, I've got to get one of my friends."

He chuckled, obviously finding Phil's request ridiculous. "Have you got money? I don't fly for free, you know."

"This is an emergency. Someone's in danger. We've got evidence that's crucial to a murder investigation taking place next week, and someone here doesn't want that evidence leaving Cedar Key."

The pilot clicked a few switches on his console. He faced Phil and grinned, this time his eyes sparkling. "Sounds dangerous. I'd love to be a part of your scheme. I could use some excitement. I'll wait."

"Thanks, man. My friend, Kathryn, should be here in a second." Phil grabbed the keys out of his pocket and jumped out of the plane. He halted and turned back around to the pilot. "Oh, and, the guy that was with me before, don't let him on this plane if he gets here before I return."

"Yes, sir."

Phil jogged down the airstrip through the fence to the parking lot and jingled his keys in the air so Drew could see them. "I found them."

"Good. Now let's go."

"I'd really like to get my SUV out of the kayak rental's parking lot. Will you take me to it?"

"Yeah, whatevah. Get in."

As Phil started to climb into the car, Kathryn and Sadie burst forth from the trees and rushed straight up the road toward him. Then Kathryn froze, her eyes wide with fear, and she yanked Sadie close to her side. She'd obviously seen Drew there.

Drew was already sitting in the car and didn't see her. Phil motioned with a nod for Kathryn to head toward the plane. She jerked Sadie's leash and ran, balancing her laptop and purse. Did she have the gun with her? Hopefully, she'd not dropped it in her frantic escape from the house. Phil plopped down into Drew's car but kept his legs outside.

"What are you doing? We need to get going."

"I'm stretching my legs for a minute. We've done nothing but sit and ride ever since we left."

Drew laughed. "You're getting old, cousin."

"Hey, since I've lived here in Cedar Key, I've become a lot younger than I was before. I walk a lot. I stand for hours when I fish. So forgive me if I've gotten stiff by sitting so much today. You ought to try something other than sitting around smoking cigarettes sometime."

"How do you know I don't exercise?" Drew cranked the car.

"I don't know, but you don't look like the type."

"Shut up and get in. You're stalling the inevitable."

Phil swung his legs around, pivoting in the seat. He glanced up toward the plane. Kathryn and Sadie had made it safely inside. "Aw, man, I'm missing my phone. I must've left it in the plane too."

"Forget it. You can get another one. We've got an appointment with your lady D.A." Drew pulled the car out of park.

"I don't think so." Phil jumped out of the car and took off through the gate and across the runway toward the waiting plane.

"Stop! Phil, I'll shoot you!" Drew screamed and came after him.

Phil froze and turned around. Drew's gun glimmered in the moonlight. Phil raised his hands in the air, but took small steps backward toward the plane. "You won't shoot me." There was no way he was going to let Drew stop him from getting on that plane and getting Kathryn to safety.

"Phil! Come back here." Drew's face looked like it would explode.

Phil spun around toward the Baron and bolted the last few feet to the door. He launched himself into the plane using the footrest, jumped in, and slammed and locked the door behind him. "Go!" He shouted, his breath coming in gasps. He hadn't run that hard or fast since the Moratti clan chased him down Brooklyn Avenue after their leader went to prison for running an illegal gambling ring.

"Yes, sir!" The pilot accelerated, and they were off.

Phil plopped down into the seat next to Kathryn, sweat dripping from his face and wet circles staining the armpit areas of his shirt. Kathryn, on the other hand, was a vision of loveliness, dressed in a blue Cedar Key T-shirt and shorts. Her eyes were wide with fear, but they were beautiful and glossy just the same. Her cheeks were rosy from running to the plane in the evening's humidity, and hopefully a little bit from being with him.

CHAPTER 22

"Phil, I'm so glad you made it!" Kathryn, breathless, reached for him, and Sadie squeezed between her knees wagging her tail.

Phil's arm pressed against hers, and the heat radiated from him and soaked into her body. The most wonderful feeling in the world, to have this man beside her as they went off to make sure justice prevailed.

"Hi. How you doin'?" He shrugged his eyebrows and winked.

Kathryn laughed at the accent and the flirtation she'd grown so accustomed to, then she grabbed Phil's forearm. "How am I doin'? I'll tell you how I'm doin'. I'm freaking out! I'm scared to death. I've never been so glad to get off the ground in all my life, even though I've been on buses bigger than this plane."

Phil leaned over toward her and rested his forehead on hers. "We're going to be okay now." He withdrew his head from hers and apologetically wiped his sweat from her forehead. Kathryn's skin tingled from his touch regardless of their dangerous situation.

"Fasten your seatbelts, please," the pilot said as Drew banged on the side of the plane and tried to open the door.

Kathryn pointed out the window into the darkness where Drew ran alongside the plane. "What about your cousins? They've got to be stopped."

"We'll call the police when we land."

"Here we go," the pilot called out. The plane pushed forward and left Drew behind them on the runway, waving his hands in the air.

Kathryn gripped the armrests. "There's no time for that. They'll get away."

"I'll call the chief right now before we take off." Phil reached for his phone.

"Good luck getting him. I tried several times this week, but he was never available for me."

"He'll answer."

"And I'll text my mom and get her to call the D.A. He needs to be waiting on us at the airport. The police should be there too in case Drew and Barney manage to catch a plane in the next few minutes."

"Good idea."

They buckled their seatbelts, and the plane lifted off of the runway as several loud thuds pounded its sides. "Go, go, go! He's shooting at us!" Kathryn screeched to the pilot.

Phil leaned over Kathryn and looked out the window. Kathryn pressed her body against the seat and kept her eyes closed, and Sadie whimpered and tucked her head between Kathryn's knees. Phil dialed the police and waited. "Chief, this is Phil Tagliaferro. I'm flying out of Cedar Key right now on an emergency. I need you to get to the airport and arrest my two cousins."

He sat silent for a moment, while Kathryn texted her mom, then hollered over the roar of the plane's engines. "I don't have time to explain. We've lifted off, and I can't talk but a second more. It's Drew and Barney Ezzo. They're in a black Mercedes, and they were last seen at the airstrip. They're involved with the Louie Ezzo murder trial in Georgia—hello? Hello!" He sighed and powered down his phone. "My phone dropped the call."

"They'll get them." Kathryn patted his hand. "Thank you for thinking so fast and getting this plane."

"I wasn't thinking that fast. It's the plane we flew in on, and I just happened to think about asking the pilot to take us back right before climbing out."

"Well, good thinking. How will I get back to my things though?"

"We'll take another flight back tonight or rent a car."

"Won't a flight be too expensive? And renting a car to drive back will take too long."

"Don't worry about the details. We'll get you back."

The plane circled Cedar Key, leaving Drew and Barney behind.

"So this is your second flight today."

"Yes, ma'am, it is."

"You're exhausted, aren't you?"

"Exhausted beyond words."

"I'm sorry you're having to fly with me back home. I feel so bad that I got you mixed up in this mess."

"You didn't get me mixed up in this. I wanted to help. Besides, my cousins—my whole family—wanted me involved in this from the beginning."

"I guess you're right. It's part of your destiny." She smiled a weak smile, and Phil shook his head. "My mom called to tell me our faces were all over the news."

"My pops called me and told me the same thing."

"She was furious until I explained how we met and that you refused to represent Louie."

"Pops was almost angry enough to fly down to Cedar Key and knock my head off my shoulders."

"I'm glad he didn't." Kathryn shook her head and laughed. "How did it go with your uncle?"

Phil sighed and rubbed his bloodshot eyes. "Like I expected it would go. He wouldn't confess. Just wanted me to represent him. He thought it was funny that a woman was prosecuting him."

"But I'm not."

"You're not a woman?"

Kathryn squinted. "Very funny. Not prosecuting."

"I told him that. He agrees with Drew that you should be dealt with because you've been snooping around Cedar Key."

"Well, at least I'm safe now, and so is the gun." She patted her laptop bag. "Did you tell Louie I'd found it?"

"No way! I didn't tell Drew either. I wanted them to sweat it out."

She laughed and covered her mouth to stop the yawn that burst forth.

"You're exhausted too, aren't you?"

She slumped. "I suppose. I took a good nap though until I was woken up by the storm and then sent into shock by Barney banging on the front door."

"Has the antihistamine worn off?"

"I think so. No leftover side effects from the reaction either." She folded her arms across her stomach and squeezed her upper arms. "Thanks for rescuing me."

"I didn't rescue you. I left you alone, and you had to make it to the airport by yourself, dragging your dog and carrying the gun and your computer. A real rescuer would've told you to hide somewhere until he came to get you."

"If we'd gone with that plan, I believe you wouldn't have made it. Drew seemed pretty determined to get you out of the way."

"Yeah. He was a little miffed with me."

"About what?"

"I asked too many questions about his lifestyle, tried to encourage him to give up his way of life and turn things over to God."

Kathryn smiled. That did not surprise her at all about Phil. He was passionate about his faith. "Good for you."

"He listened, but he didn't take it to heart."

"You don't know that."

"What do you mean?"

"Take me, for example. I've been running for a long time from something I didn't know. I wasn't happy, but didn't know why. I thought it was because of my breakup with Zeke. Or my dissatisfaction with my career. Not feeling adequate enough for my dad. You name it. I'm a mess." She let out a nervous chuckle. "Since I came to Cedar Key, something else has been eating away at me."

"You mean, other than the case?"

"Yes." The blackness outside the window reminded her of the darkness in her heart as little as a week ago.

Phil folded his hands across his lap and turned to face her. "Have you figured it out?"

"Yes." She swiped away tears that stung her eyes. This time, she didn't try to hide the flow from Phil.

A repetitive alarm sounded, and the pilot promptly flipped switches and turned dials. Phil grabbed Kathryn's hand. Whether it was to comfort her or to comfort himself, it didn't matter. Nor did it help much. Their interlocked hands wouldn't prevent the plane from going down, and it wouldn't save their lives.

"Excuse me, we're experiencing some difficulties."

"What do you mean?" Phil leaned forward.

"It appears our left wing fuel tank is lighter on fuel than the right wing tank by 1.5 tons. I'm guessing whoever shot at us punctured the tank. I'm going to use the right fuel tank only for the duration of the flight."

Kathryn gasped, yanked her hand away from Phil's, and covered her mouth. "Will the plane catch on fire?"

"No. We're going to be all right, ma'am. I've got enough fuel still to get us to the airport. I'm a former aircraft carrier pilot, and I've flown in situations worse than this. We'll be okay."

Kathryn wiped her tears away and braced herself for the unfamiliar events that were about to happen. She hated unfamiliar things. She preferred the expected. The routine. The predictable.

But she was used to unfamiliar things happening in the courtroom, and she was tired of being weak like she'd been for the last few days, so she'd have to suck it up and deal with this situation. This situation, if she lived through it, wouldn't go on her list of favorites, but as long as it ended with her heart still beating and with the opportunity to tell the ones she loved that she'd found her purpose in life, she'd be fine.

Phil took her hand and stroked it. "Kathryn, don't worry. The pilot is going to fly this baby to Georgia without any trouble. Tell me what you were going to tell me a few minutes ago." Phil patted her hand and turned her face toward him.

She sniffed and wiped her tears away. "I don't know if it even matters now. If we don't make it, it's pointless to even ponder it."

"We're going to make it. Now tell me what's been eating away at you."

She squeezed her eyes shut. "I've—I've tried for so long to please everyone in my life by doing whatever they wanted me to do." She opened her eyes and let them find a home in the comfort of Phil's eyes. "I believed I was sacrificing my happiness for others. I realize now that in doing that, I wasn't sacrificing anything. I was instead being prideful."

"How so?"

"I was trying to please others because I cared about what they thought of me. I wasn't doing things with the right motives. I was selfishly protecting my reputation."

Phil puckered his lips and considered her words. "What could you have done differently?"

"I could've followed my heart and gone the direction I knew I was made to go."

"Which is?"

"I'm not sure yet. Maybe it's a dental non-profit type thing. Maybe it's something else. But I'm pretty sure if I go any further with my legal career, it'll be to appease my father and to impress my co-workers. I'll stack more pride on top of the cupcake of pride I've already created. Just like this weapon had to be discovered, the secrets in my heart had to be unearthed."

"That's deep. Why do you think you've come to this realization now?"

"God showed me."

"He did?" Phil smiled, the skin around his eyes crinkling.

"Yes. He unearthed everything. I can't explain it, but he did. I tell you all of this because you shouldn't give up on Drew. Or even that louse Barney. You set a good example and have a way of making people think about their lives."

"I'm not sure about that, but thanks just the same."

The plane bumped against the wind and dropped, causing Kathryn and Phil to come up off their seats. Sadie whimpered and jumped up on one of the seats across from them. Kathryn bit her bottom lip to keep her scream inside and reached her foot out to rub Sadie.

"Everything is okay, folks. It's just some turbulence."

Kathryn sighed. "Another thing I realized this week and I'm realizing even more right now is that I like to be in control. When things haven't gone the way I thought they should, I've blamed others instead of taking responsibility for my actions. I thought I didn't need anyone to protect me or rescue me. I guess I learned all that from my dad. But this week, after witnessing God in your life, I've learned that we need others, and it's okay to need rescuing and protecting every once in a while. I don't have to be in control all the time."

Phil ran his fingers through his hair and squeezed the back of his neck. Then he dropped his hands to his lap and smiled. "I'm glad God used me to show you that. You're a wonderful woman. Being strong and independent isn't always a bad thing. You wouldn't have gotten this far without those strengths."

"Maybe." Sadie jumped down off the seat and squeezed between Kathryn and Phil's legs.

Phil grabbed Kathryn's hands. "No maybe. Yes. You're where you are, the good and the bad, because God gave you strengths and weaknesses that make up who you are. You'll succeed when you learn to let go of what others think and realize that you're uniquely you for a reason. When you ask God to show you why, He will."

"Well, I'm willing to give it a try. It's going to be hard to let those old habits die though. I've been living behind this façade for a while now."

"That's all God asks."

She nudged him. "What about you?"

"What about me?"

"Please tell me you've learned something this week." She raised her right eyebrow.

"I have."

"What?"

"I've learned that women aren't all bad."

"We're not?"

"Nope. You've saved your kind from being crossed off my list forever." He winked.

"Well, I'm not sure that's good for me. I mean, if women are good now, you'll be on the hunt for as many good ones as you can find."

Phil squeezed her hands and drew her close to him. "Counselor, I have to object to your summation."

"You do?"

"Yes, ma'am. There may be a million good women out there, but the one I want to get to know better is sitting right here with me right now." Phil leaned toward her and placed a tender kiss upon her lips. Then he rested his head on the headrest and closed his eyes.

Kathryn sighed. Great. He picked now to take a nap.

CHAPTER 23

At midnight, they landed, despite the nearly-empty fuel tanks and the bumping around due to turbulence. Kathryn released her hands, which she'd clasped and pressed against her stomach while they landed. Flying wasn't her favorite activity, but she'd learned this week that flexibility was a good character trait to have.

Phil opened the hatch and climbed down out of the plane onto the lot. "Second time getting out here today."

"You poor thing." Kathryn hooked Sadie up to her leash, grabbed her things, and prepared to exit the plane.

"I'll sleep well tonight. Whenever I get back home, that is."

"Sir?" The pilot joined them on the ground. "I hope you're able to put those people to justice. The man who shot at my plane needs to be punished, and he needs to pay for damages or he'll be sued."

Phil whacked the pilot on the back. "What's your name?"

"Fred."

"Fred, thank you for getting us here in one piece. It's a miracle we landed safely with a busted fuel tank." A bead of sweat dripped down the side of Phil's face, proof his nerves had been as rattled as Kathryn's.

"I guess you could call it a miracle. There's no other way to explain our safe arrival. It was my pleasure to be involved in a matter of justice."

"I guarantee you that charges will be filed against the man who shot at us. Do you have a business card so we can get in touch with you?"

Fred pulled a card out of his pocket. "Here you go. Will you need a lift back to Cedar Key tonight?"

Phil scratched his chin, now covered in a three-day-old beard. "Are you available to take us back?"

Fred stretched each arm behind his head one at a time and rolled his obviously stiff neck. "Yes. I need to get another plane first and some caffeine in me, but I'd be happy to fly you two back. I might just stay the night there in Cedar Key instead of trying to return so late though."

Phil offered his right hand to him. "Okay, great. It may be within the hour that we'll be ready to go. And don't worry about finding a place to stay. I've got some available rentals. I'll put you up for the night and treat you to breakfast in the morning."

Fred shook his hand and then saluted Phil. "Thank you. I'll be ready. Just call." He tipped his hat up at Kathryn where she waited with Sadie to climb out of the plane.

Phil motioned for Kathryn to hand him Sadie's leash, lifted Sadie out of the plane, and then reached up and grasped Kathryn by the waist. Kathryn, with laptop bag and purse in tow, landed on the pavement, flashes of light blinding her. News crews formed a line behind several police officers, detectives, the D.A., and…Mom and Dad, standing together and seeming cordial for once.

Kathryn held her hand up to shield her eyes, and Phil stepped up behind her shielding his eyes too. She held tight to Sadie's leash to ensure she didn't run off in the excitement. "Mom was right about our faces being plastered all over the news." She giggled.

D.A. Schwartz came to their side and held out his hand to Kathryn. "Glad to see you safe, young lady."

"Thank you, sir." She smiled. Until this moment, she'd forgotten how she was dressed. Here she was on television, probably national television, looking like a shabby unprofessional touristic woman. They both were dressed for a day of exploring and painting without worrying about suits and briefcases, appointments, or wins in the courtroom.

"And you must be Phil Tagliaferro?"

"Indeed, I am." Phil accepted Mr. Schwartz's outstretched hand, a smile of pride on his face.

"Thank you for getting her home safely. I was skeptical of your involvement with her at first, but now I'm grateful she met you."

Phil pressed his lips together and then grinned. "I was skeptical of her for a while too." He elbowed Kathryn and her mouth dropped open. "But it turned out to be a delight getting to know her and work with her. Completely my pleasure. We owe our safe return all to our pilot. He did an amazing job of getting us here without a crash landing."

"Good, good." Schwartz turned to Kathryn. "Do you feel like answering a few questions for the press?"

Kathryn bit her bottom lip and scrunched her face. "I'm so exhausted."

"Just a few? I've already told them that no names will be shared until formal charges are brought against the men. Also I told them your involvement with each other is not up for discussion."

Kathryn directed her gaze up to Phil's and smiled. He placed his hand on her back for support. "Thank you."

"So you'll answer a few?"

"Sure."

"And before I forget, do you have something for the detectives and me?"

Kathryn laughed and pulled the grocery sack containing the gun from her laptop bag. She'd collected it from the well with the care of a brain surgeon, wrapped it in the bag so as not to smudge any evidence, and had hidden it under the kitchen sink thinking she'd transport it back to Georgia in her car. My, how her plans had changed.

Kathryn handed Sadie off to Mom, introducing Phil to her and to Dad, and they answered a few of the reporters' questions about the ordeal. D.A. Schwartz announced the arrest of two men in Cedar Key moments before on charges of accessory to murder and the reckless endangerment of Kathryn and Phil.

Phil grabbed Kathryn and twirled her around in the night air. Now they were safe to fly back to Cedar Key and get her things. If she had her car, she'd drive home the thirty minutes, crash on to her bed, and never leave it for the next week.

"Ms. Bellamy?"

Phil stopped spinning Kathryn and set her back onto the pavement, the flashes from the press cameras capturing the whole thing.

"Yes, sir?" Why did Schwartz have to interrupt her moment of bliss? She sighed when Phil captured her hand and squeezed it.

"You're reinstated to the case. Even though your

methods were a bit unorthodox, you deserve to win this. That is, if you want to."

She circled her right elbow with her fingers. Did she want it? What did it matter if she wasn't sure if she'd want to further her career in law? Kathryn closed her eyes and asked for peace and wisdom. From God. There she stood with Phil holding her right hand and God holding her heart. This was crazy. Had a transformation really taken place in such a short time? It didn't matter if she went to trial against Louie Ezzo or not. God had a plan for her, and He would fulfill that plan.

"Kathryn?" Phil squeezed her hand again.

She opened her eyes and focused on Mom and Dad. What would Dad say if she passed on this opportunity? What would Phil think if she moved forward against his uncle and cousins? She turned to Schwartz and nodded. "I'd like that." She mustered a smile and held out her hands in surrender. "I want it."

"Then go get 'em, tiger." D.A. Schwartz whacked her on the back as if she were one of the good old boys.

Phil grabbed her again and swung her around. "Bravo, Kathryn!"

"You don't care if I prosecute your family?"

"Not at all. I want you to have this victory."

Mom, with Dad trailing behind by a few steps, scurried over to her and joined in the embrace. Her moment had finally come to shine in Perkins County against one of the most notorious families in the country, and she was actually ready for it.

"I'm proud of you, Kate," Dad said as he kissed her on the top of the head.

"And I'm proud of the two of you for being here together tonight for me. Thank you for putting your differences aside." Mom and Dad would never be friends again and they'd never reunite, but at least they'd learned to pull together when it came to her.

"You're our Katie-bug. Nothing's more important to us than you." Mom squeezed her.

Although that wasn't true of Dad since he now had a new family and couldn't place more importance on one child over another, he loved her and wanted what was best for her. If he didn't, he wouldn't have been there.

"Mr. Schwartz, if it's okay, I'd like to go back to Cedar Key and get my luggage and car before we move forward."

"Kathryn, why don't you go home and rest for the night? Your dad will take you tomorrow."

"Mom, I want to go back tonight. If I wait until tomorrow, I might not have the energy to get up off my couch." Kathryn laughed and then yawned. Plus, she wasn't ready to let Phil out of her presence.

Mom and Dad acquiesced, and Schwartz nodded, the smile on his face the biggest Kathryn had ever seen from him. In fact, she couldn't remember when she'd seen him genuinely smile at all. "The trial is set for Monday. The jury selection starts at 9:00 a.m. Just be back in time to prepare."

"Thank you. Mom, do you mind keeping Sadie for a few days? I'm going to fly back with Phil, rest tomorrow—well today technically—and come back Thursday."

"I don't mind. I'd love to have her."

After Kathryn answered a few more questions, Phil tapped her on the elbow. "We'd better get going. The pilot won't want to fly us back if it gets much later."

"Oh, okay." She hugged Mom and then Dad.

"Kate, I'm real proud of you for risking everything to solve this case."

Heat flooded her face at the unexpected compliment, such an unusual thing from Dad. "Thank you. Love you guys." She knelt down and scratched Sadie's ears. "Be a good girl." Sadie pawed at her leg. "No, you can't go with me this time." She touched Mom's arm. "You know where I keep my spare key. Sadie's food is in the pantry."

"Okay. I'll take good care of her."

Phil pulled her by the arm. The members of the press snapped final photos of them, their flashes illuminating the parking lot. Kathryn waved to everyone and followed Phil to the plane.

Fred stood outside the replacement plane, a jet complete with an actual staircase to ascend, and reached for Kathryn's hand. "Let me help you up into the plane the proper way. Last time you shoved your dog in and somersaulted to get inside."

"How did you get a new plane so quickly?" Kathryn curtsied, gave him her hand, and allowed him to assist her. It was true her last entry had not been a ladylike one.

"I've got friends in all the right places, ma'am." Fred winked.

Phil climbed the stairs after Kathryn, took the seat beside her, and pressed his arm against hers. While Fred prepared the jet for takeoff and taxied down the runway, they rested their heads against each other and both yawned.

Kathryn stretched. "Can you believe it's one in the morning?"

"Yes, I can believe it. Last night was a long, sleepless night of watching you for signs of anaphylactic shock."

"You mean Monday night. Last night was Tuesday night."

Phil shook his head. "I've been awake since Monday morning except for a brief nap during the night." He yawned.

"Well, rest your weary head against mine, and we'll sleep until we get home—I mean back to Cedar Key." Cedar Key was a place she could call home. But she couldn't think about making a change in her life until she finished what she already had in the works.

Kathryn's heart thumped wildly, and her stomach fluttered. She was going back to Cedar Key. Now that the danger was gone, maybe she could spend the day with Phil exploring the quaint city as she'd planned to do when she'd arrived on Friday night.

Phil's phone rang. He opened his eyes and rubbed them with his fists. "Is it okay if I take this call, Fred?"

"Sure, we're flying low enough."

"Thanks." Phil unlocked his phone screen. "It's my pops. Why's he calling so late?"

"You'd better answer it before the call is lost."

Phil hit the accept button. "Hello?"

Kathryn ran her fingers through her tangled hair and wiped away the smudged eyeliner from underneath her eyes. She rested her head back on the headrest and closed her eyes. Phil's voice lulled her to a place of no worries.

"Hold on, Pops." Phil nudged Kathryn with his elbow. She opened her eyes and turned to face him, the plane's engine humming outside in the night sky. "Pops says Drew and Barney have asked me to represent them, and Uncle Louie wants to talk to me."

Kathryn yawned. "Really?"

"Yes, but I want to know how you feel about it."

Kathryn pointed to her chest. "Me? How do *you* feel about it?"

"Personally, I still don't want to represent people who are guilty, but selfishly, I'd love to be present when you win the case against them."

"How do you know I'll win?"

Phil cocked his head. "Come on, Kathryn. It's you. Of course you'll win."

"Thanks for the vote of confidence. If you want to represent them, then you should do it. Maybe you'll decide to come back to the dark side." She laughed.

"Never." Phil shook his head. "Pops, sorry for the delay. Tell them I'll see them Monday morning."

* * *

Kathryn and Phil stood on the pier soaking in the afternoon sun. Other than two fishermen at the west end, they were alone. Her car was packed, but her heart wasn't willingly leaving this paradise. Paradise. Was she really calling it that even though she'd had her life threatened? Yes, she was. "I wish I could stay and see one more sunset."

"I wish you could stay too, but I think it's best that you get on the road before it gets too late. I don't like the thought of you traveling back by yourself after dark. Some of the roads are a bit too desolate, and you've already had your share of trouble this trip."

"I know. I know." She twisted the toe of her sandal into the concrete.

"I'm going to be in Perkins County this week, remember?"

Kathryn nodded.

Phil leaned over to kiss Kathryn, but before his lips

met hers, something ricocheted with a ping off the weather station, and the men on the end of the pier threw themselves to the ground.

Kathryn screamed, and Phil covered her with his body and blocked her from the source of the attack.

Her breath caught in her throat. "What was that?" Another ping sounded, this time on the pier railing, and Kathryn screamed again. "Gunfire?"

"Get down!" Phil hunkered down, dragging Kathryn with him, and they crept over to the side railing.

Kathryn gripped Phil's shirt. Someone was shooting at them from an undetermined location, and their lives could end at any moment.

"We can make it into the bathroom if we stay low and close to the railing."

"Who would shoot at us, Phil?"

"I told you my family had long arms." Phil held tight to Kathryn's arm and guided her into the men's bathroom.

Kathryn's heart fluttered in her throat, and by the looks of Phil, his heart had left its home too. "What are we going to do?"

"I'm going to call the chief." Phil pulled his phone from his pocket and held up his index finger. "Chief, hey, it's Phil Tag. I'm in the men's restroom on the pier with Assistant D.A. Kathryn Bellamy from Perkins County. Yeah. No, we're not here because we want to be. Someone is shooting at us. Yep, that's what I said. No, my gun is at the house. I need help." Phil listened for a few seconds and squeezed Kathryn's shoulder.

Kathryn didn't have much courage left. Would she ever truly be safe when she and Phil were together?

"Thanks, Chief." Phil ended the call and returned the

phone to his pocket. "The chief said for us to stay in here. He'll be here in a few minutes."

"Comforting." Kathryn leaned against the wall. She didn't care if her sarcasm showed itself.

"I'm going to pop my head out and see if whoever was shooting at us is gone."

Kathryn sprung away from the wall and grabbed Phil's arm. "Oh no you're not! You're not leaving me for one second."

"But—"

"No. No buts. You're staying right here."

"Okay, okay." Phil embraced her. "We're going to be all right."

"Knock, knock."

Kathryn jumped and covered her mouth with her hand.

"Phil, it's the chief." The door inched open.

When Phil's face broke out into a smile, Kathryn let her shoulders relax and her hand fall away from her mouth.

"Chief, I've never been so happy to see you." Phil reached out his hand to the chief. "Did you see who was shooting at us?"

"Yeah, Sam from the grocery store. He was over there on the outside patio of the vacant pub on the corner. My deputies arrested him."

Kathryn gasped and threw her hands to her chest. "Sam? But why?"

"He apparently had to finish what Phil's cousins weren't able to." The chief shook his head.

"I knew something was off with that guy when I met him at the store. He wouldn't look me in the eye and told me to mind my business. I knew he had to know something. I guess he didn't like that I said I was going to subpoena him to testify in court." Kathryn shivered.

"He was just cleaning up, Kathryn. That's the way my family works." Phil groaned. "I'm just glad he missed."

"Me too." She scowled.

The Chief lit a cigarette and shook his head. "You sure did stir up a lot of trouble by your visit here, Ms. Bellamy."

"No, I came to make sure trouble got taken care of. Had that gun not been hidden here in the first place, your sweet little town could have stayed nice and quiet."

The chief grinned. "Well, I think we've gotten all the rats flushed out now. Maybe the peace will resume around here."

Phil took Kathryn into his arms and laughed. "This is the first time I've ever said this, I'm sure, but I am glad my cousins stirred up this trouble, or I wouldn't have had the pleasure of meeting you."

"The pleasure is all mine, Tag." Kathryn wrapped her hand in the crook of Phil's arm and accompanied him out of the restroom and off the pier to her car.

CHAPTER 24

Perkins County Government Building, Courtroom Three

Kathryn stepped through the hinged gates at the divider and made it to the prosecutor's table at 9:02 a.m. She smiled and placed her briefcase on the table. Then Judge Peterson cleared his throat and stared at her over the top of his bifocals, which were pushed down to the end of his nose. His spiky gray eyebrows looked like fuzzy caterpillars...angry caterpillars. Her smile faded.

"Thank you, Ms. Bellamy, for joining us this morning. I know you're still in vacation mode, but we've got work to do today." The courtroom fell silent as his voice boomed from the microphone.

Now why did he have to announce to the whole courtroom that she'd been on vacation? Some things were meant to be kept private. Besides, it had hardly been a vacation. If only he knew that she'd had to fight for her life down in Cedar Key, maybe he wouldn't be so tough on her.

She pulled her files from her briefcase. "Please forgive my tardiness, sir. I was delayed in the hallway by a defense attorney for an upcoming trial." She shuffled her papers with trembling hands.

Judge Peterson crinkled his brow. "Well, all right."

"I have something I'd like to put on the record before we get started, if you don't mind."

He scratched his head. "All right. Make it quick."

The United States Superior Court seal hung on the wall behind the judge. The eagle spread across it symbolized everything Kathryn's life had been based upon—justice, strength, and courage—until her life-changing visit to Cedar Key. "Judge, while I was away, I received a menacing phone call and a threatening note. Someone also slashed my tires and shot at me."

Judge Peterson tapped his pencil on the bench. "Someone shot at you?"

"Yes, sir."

"I see. Is this person being prosecuted?"

"Yes, sir. He's awaiting trial."

"All right. So you think someone else tried to harm you by slashing your tires?" He studied a file in front of him and yawned.

She grumbled under her breath. "Your Honor, I don't think. I know."

"Do you know for certain that the tires were slashed?"

"Yes, I took pictures, and I asked the repair facility to keep them on hand for evidence. I could've been killed while driving with slashed tires." In comparison to being shot at, the slashed tires didn't seem to be that much of a threat, but still worthy of mentioning to the judge.

He leaned forward and studied her face with amiable eyes. Was that a hint of compassion? "I'm sorry that happened to you, Ms. Bellamy. I wasn't aware of these incidents."

She dipped her head. It was hard to believe that he hadn't heard of the incidents since they'd been in the news, but perhaps he kept away from the media reports to stay unbiased. "Thank you. We believe the incidents occurred as a result of my prosecution of Louie Ezzo, Judge. His nephews are the suspects."

The judge folded his arms across his chest. "Well, you don't know that they did it."

Kathryn raised her hands and nodded once at the man who looked like a barn owl. "Well, no, sir. But—but it stands to reason that it was one of them since the threats occurred in Cedar Key, and they were there at the same time I was. Drew Ezzo shot at the plane I was in as it was taking off on my way here to bring the gun."

The judge sat up straight, looked over the bench and directly into her eyes. "Now Ms. Bellamy, this is a court of law, and you know we depend on evidence and not speculation in establishing one's guilt. That will have to be proven in their trial. You don't know that the person who slashed your tires isn't the same person who shot at you."

She tilted her head toward the ceiling and rubbed her forehead, hoping to squeeze out the encroaching pain. Unfortunately, the judge was right. Sam could have slashed her tires. Sam could have left the threatening note and made the phone calls too. "Yes, sir."

The judge unwrapped a piece of candy and poked it into his mouth. "What about the note and phone call?" After she informed the judge of the situation, his face pinched up tight. Now he looked like a hedgehog. Now he seemed truly concerned. "I find this quite disconcerting. Did you deliver the card to a detective?"

"Yes, sir. And I—"

"Your Honor, may I speak?"

"Yes, Mr. Stewart." The judge rocked in his leather chair.

Kathryn turned to face Jamey Stewart, defense attorney for half of the county's worst criminals, who stood behind the divider. The smug look on his tanned face, white circles around his eyes from his sunglasses, told her what he wanted to say before another word came out of his mouth.

He cleared his throat, scratched his blond lamb chop sideburns and then adjusted his glasses. "While it's very unfortunate that these things happened to A.D.A. Bellamy," he scowled at her, "we have jury selection and multiple cases to get through this morning. Each of these incidents Ms. Bellamy speaks of will have their day in court, but today is not that day. Can we move on?"

Judge Peterson looked at his files, glanced around the courtroom and then directed his gaze at Kathryn. "Ms. Bellamy, I'm sure everything'll be taken care of. Let's get to jury selection."

Kathryn closed her eyes and sighed. That was all the empathy she was going to get today. And all Jamey Stewart cared about was getting to the golf course. She gathered her strength to keep from crying and released the breath she'd been unknowingly holding. "May we take a five-minute recess before we start jury selection, Judge?"

After jury selection and a brief lunch break with Phil, Kathryn returned to the courtroom for a revocation and then part one of the Ezzo trial. This was her shining moment. Her chance to prove to everyone including herself that she was good at her job. She could finally show Phil how strong she was.

"Judge, before we get to the Ezzo case, I've got a

revocation we need to address. This is on Michael Foster; case number 10-CR-98354. Mr. Foster is here in the courtroom." She pointed at Mr. Foster with her pen.

"Hey, Judge." The shackled defendant in the county's orange jumpsuit nodded.

"Hello, Michael. How's your daddy?"

"He's good. Sittin' in the back, sir." He motioned to the back of the courtroom with his head.

The judged looked up and waved. "Oh, I see him back there. Howdy, Judd."

"Hey, Judge."

Kathryn rolled her eyes at the absurd situation. Friends one moment, judge and defendant the next. Phil must think they are all podunk rednecks. "Judge, if I may? Mr. Foster has violated the terms and conditions of the Sex Offender Registry and violated the laws of the State of Georgia. We're asking the Court to revoke his First Offender status and to resentence him up to the maximum of ten years because of his original offense and because he has thumbed his nose at the Sheriff's office, at the Sex Offender Registry, and at the Court. He is not abiding by the conditions that he was placed under."

The judge sighed. "All right. Thank you, Ms. Bellamy." He looked around the courtroom. "The issue before the court is a petition for adjudication of guilt and imposition of sentence in a first offender case. The original sentence back in December of 2010 was for two counts of sexual battery. And the sentence was ten years; five on each one, consecutive. The defendant was allowed to plead under the *Alford versus North Carolina* case, in which he has to affirm that there is a substantial likelihood he would be convicted if tried before a jury in the case. And secondly, that it's in his best interest to go ahead and plead. And the Court allowed him to do so. Then he was given the privilege of pleading under the First Offender Act, and that was explained to him during the hearing as to what that meant."

"Yes, sir," Mr. Tompkins, the defense attorney agreed.

Kathryn studied the case file and nodded. "Correct, Judge." How someone could take such a sentence so lightly was beyond Kathryn's understanding. This man had literally thrown his freedom out the window.

"The issue before the Court today is whether the State has proven that the defendant has violated his probation by not registering properly under the Sex Offender Registration Act and also did he commit the offense of rape, which he is charged with in another indictment on another case. Now over the last three days of testimony, the evidence has been gleaming, I guess you could say. There have been conflicts in the evidence, and there've been some people who have testified one way and some people have testified the other. It's been downright chaotic, I think. Don't you think, Ms. Bellamy?"

She laughed. "Yes, sir. People are sworn to tell the truth, but in this case they have not always done that."

Judge Peterson smacked his lips and in a rare moment of camaraderie, he winked at her. "Right. Well, as far as the evidence on the failure to register as a sexual offender goes, there are at least three different addresses that the defendant has moved to from one time or another and not reported the change. I am going to find that the State has proven beyond a preponderance of the evidence that he failed to report."

Kathryn's heart swelled. Although this had not been her case three years ago nor had she been in the courtroom for the testimonies over the last three days, it had fallen in her lap as soon as she'd returned home from Cedar Key, and she didn't mind claiming this victory.

"I'll also find that the second allegation, which is that the defendant committed the offense of rape, has been proven. And because of that, I'm going to revoke his First Offender status. I'm going to substitute therein a plea of guilty. I'm going to adjudicate the defendant guilty of the original charges of sexual battery, two counts, and resentence him to five years on count one and five years on count two. They are to be served consecutively. I believe he would be entitled to credit for the time that he's already served on probation. It would be up to the Department of Corrections to determine that. Do you have anything you'd like to say, Mr. Foster?"

"No, sir, Judge. Just look after my daddy and mama for me."

"Will do. I hope you do a whole lot of straightening up while you're in custody. I'll remand the defendant into the custody of the Sheriff."

Mr. and Mrs. Foster stumbled to the courtroom door leaning on each other, and the deputy removed the defendant out the side door. And as simple as that, someone's son was taken away, and his parents were left to grieve what could have been. Kathryn's victory was someone else's loss, but it couldn't be helped. She wasn't responsible for Foster's disregard for the law, and she had no time to feel empathy for them either.

Kathryn straightened her suit jacket and collected her nerves. This was the big moment where she and Phil would come up against each other in this court of law. Would their budding romance be able to withstand the harsh reality of being on opposing sides of this case?

"Your honor, we are now before the court on case number 15-CR-99843-F, the State of Georgia versus Louie Alexander Ezzo. He is charged with four counts of solicitation of murder against Stephen Diggs and Tommy Jones of Perkins County, Georgia, and Bobby Esposito and Manny La Duca of Long Island, New York, that on April 25, 2014, he ordered the murder of the aforementioned victims. Today, we're addressing the Perkins County cases, and he'll face the other charges back in New York." Kathryn closed the file and stepped away from the desk.

"Initially, Your Honor, Mr. Ezzo was charged with four counts of murder, but once the murder weapon was located, a .22 caliber pistol, Mr. Ezzo's fingerprints were not on it. The fingerprints of one of his nephew's were on the weapon instead. That would be Barney Ezzo. At his trial, the State will have to prove whether or not he actually pulled the trigger or if his fingerprints were on the gun only because he hid it in the well in Cedar Key. Louie Ezzo's other nephew, Drew Ezzo, has been charged with aiding in these crimes. It's the state's recommendation that Mr. Louie Ezzo be sentenced to twenty years in the State Penitentiary without a possibility of parole and that he pay a $20,000 fine."

"All right. Proceed."

Kathryn turned to Ezzo with Phil sitting beside him then back to the judge. "Judge, Mr. Ezzo has chosen not to testify in his defense, so we will call our first witness. We'll call—"

Phil stood from the leather swivel armchair behind the defendant's table. "Excuse me, your honor. May I interject here?"

The judge looked over the top of his glasses. "Yes,

Mr. Tagliaferro. What would you like to add?"

Kathryn lowered herself into her chair. She hadn't planned on Phil interrupting her examination of her first witness, accused shooter Sam Ricci from the grocery store. She turned her chair to face him. She hadn't planned it, but this was a great opportunity for her to examine him and his cordovan leather shoes and brown plaid skinny suit, his full beard returned and his retro glasses resting on his face again. She sighed and forced herself to concentrate on the case.

"Your Honor, my client, Louie Ezzo, would like to change his plea."

Kathryn scooted to the edge of her chair and pushed her hair out of her eyes. He was changing his plea? He was going to plead guilty instead of not guilty? Her heart began to race. Her palms moistened. Her throat went dry.

"All right, Mr. Tagliaferro. Ms Bellamy?"

Kathryn swallowed hard at the dryness in her throat. She stood and faced Phil and Ezzo. "Your Honor, the State has prepared a list of witnesses to testify against Louie Ezzo. I'm ready to proceed. If he, however, would like to change his plea to guilty, I am willing to hear what he has to say."

"Mr. Tagliaferro, does your client wish to plead guilty now?"

Phil turned toward Louie and nodded. "No, he doesn't want to plead guilty, Your Honor."

Kathryn dug her fingernails into her palms. He wasn't pleading guilty? What kind of trick was he trying to play on her?

With a voice that sounded as if he'd had ten packs of cigarettes before coming to court, Ezzo responded, "I'd like to plead Nolo contendere."

The judge cleared his throat, and Kathryn placed her

hand on her hip. "Nolo? Nolo contendere? No contest?"

Ezzo nodded. "Yes, ma'am."

"You're not pleading innocent, but you're not pleading guilty either?"

"Yes, ma'am."

"Why have you chosen to change your plea, Mr. Ezzo? If you are indeed innocent, a trial may very well prove to be in your best interest." She shoved her hands into her jacket pockets and clenched her teeth. She wanted to prosecute Ezzo, not let him make a plea bargain.

"Yes, ma'am, I understand that. I've heard my attorney's description of each plea choice, and I've decided that no contest is the best choice."

Kathryn folded her arms across her chest and studied Ezzo. What had convinced him to give up the fight? His wiry black hair and small brown eyes surrounded by dark circles proved he'd fretted over this case more than he'd wanted Phil to know when he'd visited with him Tuesday.

She turned toward the judge. "Your Honor, if Mr. Ezzo wishes to plead no contest, I recommend that we accept his plea and move forward to the sentencing phase."

"All right, Ms. Bellamy."

Kathryn handed Phil a Change of Plea form, and Ezzo signed it. Phil handed it back across the aisle to Kathryn and winked. She forced herself to remain professional and wouldn't allow her feelings to show. She examined the plea form, scratched her signature to it, and sighed. "Your Honor, at this time, I tender Mr. Ezzo's Nolo contendre plea and his Waiver of Rights form."

"All right. Thank you." The judge looked over his glasses at Ezzo and further explained his rights to have a trial and the rights he was giving up by pleading no contest. He waved his hands to emphasize the seriousness of his decision. Kathryn peeked at Phil out of the corner of her eye. How could he do this to her? He might as well have jerked the rug right out from under her. He'd robbed her moment to shine. She stole another glance at him, and her fury dissipated a bit. He bobbed in his swivel chair and drummed his fingers on the armrest. A smile spread across his face. She hadn't seen him this relaxed since he'd reeled in the shark on the pier Friday evening a week ago.

Had she really only known him ten days? Why did it seem like they'd known each other their entire lives? Better yet, how had her reservations faded away about Maria's ex, leaving only a desire to be with him every day? The greater question was: how had this man changed her life simply by being himself? Through him, she'd learned to trust God and others. There was no way he'd intended to hurt her by encouraging Ezzo to ask for a plea.

"Ms. Bellamy?"

"Yes, Your Honor, excuse me."

"Is the State in agreement to accept this plea?"

"Yes, Your Honor."

"All right. I've looked over the file here. I'm not going to rehash the details of the case in the interest of time. Let me say this: I'm aware that feelings are very high on both sides in this case. Some of you, perhaps all of you, may not be happy with what I do here. But I want to remind the spectators that whatever I do, I don't want any outbursts. I don't want any expressions—physical or otherwise. And if you're not able to do that, you need to leave the room now. Otherwise, I'm going to expect you to sit there and be quiet."

Judge Peterson waited for a moment then nodded. "All right. Mr. Ezzo, I'm going to find that you freely and voluntarily waive your right to a trial by jury. On all four counts of solicitation of murder, you entered a Nolo contendre plea. I'm going to allow you to plead Nolo on the two Perkins County cases and recommend to the Long Island court that they accept your plea on the other two. I'm going to sentence you to twenty years to serve in the penitentiary without the possibility of parole."

The back right corner of the courtroom erupted in wails. The judge looked up from his file and hammered the bench with his gavel. Everyone quieted in an instant. He sank his eyes back down with a shake of his head and flipped through the pages of Ezzo's file. "I'm also going to sentence you to a $20,000 fine plus any surcharges or other fees required, completion of a drug and alcohol evaluation and any treatments required by that, and random drug screening."

"Yes, sir."

"There are a number of things in your file here, Mr. Ezzo. For a man who doesn't live here, you sure have gotten yourself into some trouble in my town. I was looking through your records—well, it doesn't matter right now. I'm going to extradite you to New York where there are these charges and others against you there. Do you have anything you'd like to say?"

"Will I get credit for the time I've served already?"

"Yes, you'll get credit for fifty-five days. I guess every day counts on a twenty-year sentence."

"Yes, sir." He nodded. "Thank you, Judge."

"All right. Well, good luck to you, Mr. Ezzo, and God bless. We'll take a few minutes for a recess."

The deputies walked to the defendant's table and escorted Ezzo through the door beside the judge's bench.

Phil gathered his things and joined Kathryn at the

prosecutor's table. "Congratulations, Counselor."

"For what?" she whispered with vehemence in her voice even though she tried to contain it. She organized her papers and returned them to the Ezzo file.

"For winning."

She turned her gaze toward Phil. "I didn't win. He pled guilty—I mean Nolo." She rolled her eyes.

"But you're responsible for putting him away, and you were spared the trial."

She shrugged.

"Are you upset with me?" He tipped her chin toward him.

Kathryn turned to look at the people in the courtroom, who stared at them. She'd already been on the news with him. It didn't matter if they saw them together now. "No, of course not. It's just that I was ready to examine the witnesses, battle it out, and prove he was involved. He took the easy way out and took the fun out of it for me. I really wanted this. I wanted you to see that I'm a good attorney, that I'm a fighter."

"Kathryn, excuse me for saying this, but your pride is creeping up again. I know you're a good attorney. You have nothing to prove to me."

Kathryn shoved her left hand onto her hip and widened her eyes. "Pride? No, I want justice," she said through gritted teeth.

Phil held his hands up in surrender. "Okay, sorry. Honestly, it seems like your fight would be more with Drew and Barney. Louie didn't do anything personally to you."

"He may have ordered those threats on me."

"He may have, but he's going away for twenty years now at least. Let it go."

She tucked her chin. Was he right? Was her pride getting in the way of her being able to see things clearly? Again. She looked up into those creamy eyes. There was nothing but tenderness in them, and they held no malice. He truly cared for her. "You're right, Phil. I'm sorry. Prosecuting your cousins is more important to me than Louie."

"That's my girl. We'll meet to talk with them after lunch today."

"It'll be my pleasure."

Judge Peterson coughed. "Ms. Bellamy, we need to get back to these pleas, or we'll be here all day. I don't think you want that, do you?"

She pulled her gaze away from Phil's and shook her head at the judge. "No, sir. I do not."

CHAPTER 25

Kathryn grabbed her phone charger out of the wall, shoved it into her briefcase, and snapped the button to close it. She had everything she needed for the long evening at home of studying the details of Drew and Barney's cases. She clicked the office door shut and checked to make sure it was locked.

When she reached the glass door that led out to the parking lot, late summer's heat hit her square in the face. She climbed into her car, longing for relaxation by the pool at Phil's rental house, the quaint streets of Cedar Key she hadn't had enough opportunity to meander through, the missed chats with the locals. Right now, she wanted nothing more than to get a double—no, triple—scoop of ice cream from the shop on the water. To hang out on the pier and watch the fishermen—Phil—reel in the big catches of the day. To watch the dolphins swim out past the yacht club. Her toes began to curl, and a giggle erupted from her.

If she left now, she could be there before sunset.

* * *

Kathryn stood on the Cedar Key pier, Sadie by her side. Pelicans and seagulls soared in the late afternoon air, pink clouds scuttled across the sky. A vise gripped her neck and back muscles after the long ride down from her home in Mitchell's Crossing, but the fluttering in her stomach counteracted the discomfort. She drew in a deep, salty breath and released it. "Hi, stranger."

Phil turned around, his fishing pole crashing on to the pier. "Kathryn!" He ran to her and scooped her up. "What are you doing here?"

She squeezed his neck and melted against him. "It occurred to me after court today that I never got to enjoy my last sunset here in Cedar Key because you rushed me out of here."

"I didn't rush you out of here." Phil crinkled his brow and placed her safely back onto the pier.

Kathryn let her hands slip to his forearms, the strong forearms of a protector. "Mm-hmm. Sure you didn't. Anyway, I decided to throw my things in the car, grab Sadie, and head on down here. You have no idea how fast I had to drive to get here before sunset."

"So you came solely for the sunset?"

"Well, in all honesty, I love the dolphins too." She squeezed his forearms.

"And?"

"The ice cream is wonderful here. Although I've yet to finish one."

"And?"

"And—" Her eyes watered from the intensity of being near him.

Phil leaned down and captured her lips with his. When he withdrew, a tear slid from his right eye.

Kathryn rubbed her lips together, savoring his kiss, and wiped his tear away with her thumb.

"What does this mean?" Phil squeezed her waist.

Sadie pawed at Phil's leg, while Kathryn chose her words carefully. She had to find the balance between letting him know she wanted to explore their relationship potential—while not sending the wrong message about her return to Cedar Key—and protecting herself from disappointment if he only wanted to be friends. But his kiss had not insinuated friendship, so maybe she was safe to let him know what lingered in her heart. "It means that I'd like to spend more time with you."

"You're not just here to get away from the courtroom, to run away from your career decisions?"

"Absolutely not. I believe I've made my decision. I took—well, I decided—" she laughed.

"What?" He cocked his head.

"I took a leave of absence so I could make my decision. I talked to Cora at the Southern Hope ranch on the way here to find out if I could come stay there for a week or so. You remember I told you about her. She's the one whose husband was the drug dealer."

"Yes, I remember."

"But I wanted to stay the week here first."

He released her and placed his hands over his heart. "You actually want to spend your time here in Cedar Key?"

She nodded and touched his hands. "I want to spend my time with you, Phil. Well, not *staying* with you obviously. You know what I mean."

He laughed. "I know what you mean, sweet Kathryn. I wouldn't have it any other way. I'm glad you came tonight."

She crinkled her nose. "Why?"

"Because my bags are packed, and I was headed to Georgia to spend time with you."

"No way!"

"Yep. The thought of not seeing you after seeing you every day for a week here and then again in Perkins County at court was more than this guy could take." Phil knelt and reached into his tackle box. He pulled out a small clay pot wrapped in cling wrap and handed it to Kathryn while he stood.

She took it from him and crinkled her nose. "What's this?"

"Something I picked up for you on my way back into town. I was going to bring it to you when I came for my visit."

Kathryn cocked her head. "What's it for? What does it represent?"

"It's a clay pot to represent 2 Corinthians 4:7 in the Bible where it talks about jars of clay."

Kathryn shook her head. "I don't know that verse. I don't really know very many verses yet."

"That's okay. You'll learn them. Basically, we're God's treasure. He's crafted us and molded us, just like a potter makes a bowl or pot. God puts his power in us so that we'll be able to share with others about him, about Jesus. We are his vessel to be used for his works. I wanted you to know that and to always remember that."

"Wow. Thank you." What more could Kathryn say? She'd never been given a gift like this before.

"It's also a representation of just how fragile we are. We have to stay in God's strength or we can easily break. Any strength we have comes from him."

"I can attest to that after this whole experience."

Phil cupped her hand that held the pot. "I planted inside of this pot a mustard seed, which is one of the smallest seeds—if not the smallest—because the Bible says that all you need is faith the size of a mustard seed. I felt like this would be a good representation of what you've been through and of where you're going."

A tear slid down her cheek. "And you were keeping this in your tackle box?" She laughed a tearful laugh.

"I put the dirt in it when I was outside gathering all my fishing gear and stuck it in there."

"I don't know how to thank you. This means so much to me."

"You mean so much to me, Kathryn."

She smiled and stroked his cheek. "So where do we go from here?"

"We go get an ice cream and then some dinner—not seafood—and we sit on the dock and talk about something other than my uncle and cousins."

"Ice cream and then dinner?"

"Yes, because the ice cream shop closes at eight. Remember?"

"Oh yeah. I like that idea." Kathryn giggled into her hand.

"I like having you here with me, Kathryn Bellamy."

The End

ABOUT THE AUTHOR

Sherri Wilson Johnson is an Inspirational Romance novelist, speaker, and a social media/marketing junkie. She lives in Georgia with her husband and her Chihuahua, Posey, and they are empty-nesters. Sherri loves spending time with family, sitting on the beach, curling up with a good book or working on her current work-in-progress. She is the author of *To Dance Once More*, *To Laugh Once More*, and *When Love Must Wait* from her *Hope of the South* series, and *Song of the Meadowlark* and *Secrets Among the Cedars* from the *Intertwined* series.

www.sherriwilsonjohnson.com

Song of the Meadowlark Sneak Peek
If you haven't read book one in this series, here's
chapter one!

CHAPTER 1

Cora Buchanan drove her '68 Camaro through town down
Columbia Avenue, the places she'd become accustomed to in her
years of living in South Carolina with Clark zooming past her. She
pointed her car toward I-26 East, her green eyes filling with salty
tears. This picturesque place had become a prison to her since
Clark had left her to fend for herself, giving her no choice but to
move in with his parents.

Merging on to the highway symbolized the launching of
her new life—slow, cautious at first, and then no looking back.

She'd waited for a year—to the day—for Clark's return. She couldn't wait any longer. Moving away from Lake Murray would leave more of a void in her than moving away from her Florida childhood home had when she'd betrayed Mom and Dad and married Clark against their will. But it had to be done.

Ben and Judy, the best in-laws anyone could ask for, seemed sure God would work out the details of her life, that their son would return to Cora. If only her faith could be that strong. She still had so many doubts. When he'd left last June, he'd taken most of her hope with him.

When Cora crossed into Georgia, Taylor Swift's latest cd blaring through her speakers, she smiled at the welcome sign boasting a giant peach. She was one state closer to seeing this thing through. The temperature held at 85 degrees, and the sunshine beaming down on her car warmed her chilled heart; the wind whipped her cares away. White, fluffy clouds painted pictures across the Georgia sky, blue like a bluebird's wings today. Hopefully, the weather would remain clear until she got to Florida because she hated driving in the rain.

Another two hours went by as Cora admired the beauty of the land—pine trees and crape myrtles, black-eyed Susans and old oak trees. Unique mailboxes dotted the edge of the road along the way—a giant emerald green fish, a miniature mail truck, and a mailbox about the size of a washing machine. An old man in overalls climbed down off his tractor to retrieve his mail from his cow shaped mailbox, scratching his belly. "Aww, he's so cute."

The green grasses and golden hay made way for the city. Cora's stomach growled, and she stopped at a sandwich shop outside of Atlanta for a roast beef sandwich, fries and water. The cold drink burned as it slid down her throat.

Cora rubbed her bleary eyes and jumped back into the car again, stopped for gas and checked her tires, then headed toward I-75 South. She squinted in the afternoon sunlight, and cars zipped by like something from a futuristic movie. "Good grief, where are they in such a hurry to get to?"

Once on I-85, Cora battled construction along the highway. The roads were extra narrow with cement barriers along the shoulder to keep cars from veering into the construction zone. "I hate this!" She gripped the steering wheel until her knuckles whitened. If she could make it through this stretch of road and get to Columbus before having a nervous breakdown, she'd stay the night there and give her body a respite.

Cora passed rolling hills and tall spindly oak trees. Call boxes were every mile or so and white crosses lined the roadway. It seemed like forever since she'd seen another vehicle.

"I didn't think 85 was this remote." It had been a while since Cora had seen a road sign, a mileage marker, or an exit. By now she should be to Columbus. A sinking feeling reached her stomach. Had she missed an exit and headed in the wrong direction? Up ahead, a sign read I-185.

"I-185? How did I get on 185? What happened to 85?" She hit the steering wheel with her hand and let out a scream. Why hadn't she brought her GPS? The late afternoon sun caused a glare on her windshield, and she rubbed her tired eyes again, scratchier than sandpaper. "I'm going to have to stop and ask for directions."

The sign up ahead read *Lewistown*, and Cora clicked on her blinker. As she pulled off the highway, looking for somewhere to get coffee and use the restroom, her car lunged forward, and her gears shuddered. She gripped the steering wheel to keep it on the road. She drove down Main Street and passed a Piggly Wiggly, a Burger Hut, Mike's Barber Shop, and there, a block up the road, a service station.

Cora made it to the station and climbed out of her car, rubbing her hands on her jeans. What type of people would she encounter here in this out-of-the-way town? The red lettering on the white sign at the top of the building announced *Millburn Service Station*. Maybe there'd be someone nice inside.

Inside the office, a young man stood behind the counter locking up the cash register and the desk drawer. The smell of gasoline, new tires, and oil filled Cora's nostrils, sending a wave of nausea to her stomach.

"Excuse me." Cora scratched the back of her neck. "My car just died. Can you help me?" She fiddled with her keys.

"We'll see. Let's go take a look at it. You new in town or just passing through?" The attendant wiped grease off his hands with a rag covered in oil and pushed open the door, leading the way outside to the parking lot.

"I'm passing through. I'm from Lake Murray, South Carolina headed for Florida." The man seemed pleasant enough and not creepy.

"You got a long way to travel. Welcome, even if it's only for a short time and under bad circumstances. My name's Bobby Millburn. I own the place." He regarded the station with a prideful grin.

"I'm Cora."

Bobby lifted the hood, looked around, and wiggled some wires. He got down on the ground and slid his body underneath the car. After a few minutes, he pushed himself out from underneath and stood, wiping his hands on his rag, then adjusted his cap.

"Do you think you can repair it?"

"From the looks of things, it's your transmission. I can repair it, but I ain't so sure if we can get the parts for ya right away." Bobby considered her with a slight frown on his grease-smeared face, his plain blue eyes teeming with obvious empathy. A pickup drove past, and the driver honked. Bobby waved his rag in the air.

"I was afraid the transmission had gone out. It's been slipping a bit lately. How long?"

"A week, probably. We don't get many cars like this in here." He took a long admiring look at the classic automobile.

"Is there anyone else around who could get me out of here by tomorrow?"

"I don't think so. I'm pert near the only repair place around these parts. I'll tell ya what, though. I'll try to find someone for ya—maybe someone a town or two away. Do ya know where you'll be staying tonight?"

"No, wasn't planning on staying. I got off the exit and came straight here."

"I could check around for ya in the mornin', and let ya know if anyone has the parts or if the repairs can be done sooner than a week."

"That'd be great. Do you know of an inexpensive place to stay?"

"Shore do. Go up this street and over two blocks. There's a bed-and-breakfast, Apple Springs Inn, on the corner. Ms. Lottie McCallister runs the place. You can get a wonderful meal and a comfortable room. She won't charge ya much neither. Tell her I sent ya."

"Thanks so much. I really appreciate your kindness."

"Would ya like me to drive ya up there?" Bobby shut the hood and clapped his hands together.

"Oh no, that'd be asking too much of you."

"But you have your luggage with ya. You can't carry all of it."

"It's on wheels."

"I don't mind." He grinned.

Cora sighed. "I am pretty tired. I've been driving all day."

"Give me a few minutes, and I'll lock up."

* * *

No more than fifteen minutes passed before Cora stood in front of the Apple Springs Bed-and-Breakfast Inn. This historic home, probably from the early 1900s, had elegant country charm with its porches, ferns, and swings. The oak trees towering above the house had to be more than a hundred years old.

Cora's nerves settled, and she relaxed her tense shoulders. Bobby helped her with her bags as they entered the inn. Cora's nose filled with the scents of potpourri and lemon polish on antique furniture.

"Can I help you?"

"Yes, ma'am, I'd like to get a room for the night."

"She's leaving her car with me for the night. I told her you'd do her right. Have a good day, Ms. Lottie."

"Thank ya, Bobby."

Ms. Lottie, barely over five feet and round like a ball of dough, gray hair gathered into a knot on top of her head, wasn't a quiet woman. Her voice demanded attention as she led Cora up creaking stairs to her room. "Supper is at six o'clock. I like my guests to be on time."

"I won't be late." Cora closed the door behind her and surveyed the room's antique furnishings. More lemon and potpourri scent wafted over her. The first door she opened revealed an ample closet. The next door, a bathroom. She let out a gasp of excitement. She wouldn't have to share a bath with the other guests. She stashed her bags in one corner of her room and opened only the suitcase with her traveling clothes and toiletries. After freshening up in the bathroom, she changed into a pair of jeans and a cotton blouse.

Cora turned on the television and flung herself onto the soft antique bed. The room resembled Grandmother's cozy guest room; vermilion walls darkened the space. She had thirty minutes until dinner. She should go help Ms. Lottie, but her legs felt cramped from riding all day, and her head pounded. And, after all, she was a guest. She'd rest up a bit before going downstairs.

This would be a good time to call Ben and Judy. What should she say to them though? Should she tell them her car had broken down or leave out that little detail? If she told them, they'd want to come get her.

Swallowing her pride and inhibitions, she plugged her cell phone into the wall to charge her dead battery and dialed her in-laws. As she'd suspected, they wanted to come get her, but she insisted she'd be fine and that she was enjoying the adventure.

Next Cora called Mom and Dad to let them know only that she'd stopped in Lewistown for the night and would be on her way soon. If she told them about her car breaking down, Dad would leave immediately to come get her.

She left her room for dinner, and it hit her. How was she going to pay for her car repairs? She had no idea how much it would cost—or how much the expenses of staying at the inn would be. Would she run out of money before she even left Lewistown?

Do you enjoy Inspirational Historical Romance? If so, then my Hope of the South series set in Florida and Georgia may be the perfect fit for your reading taste. Here's a sneak peek at book one, To Dance Once More.

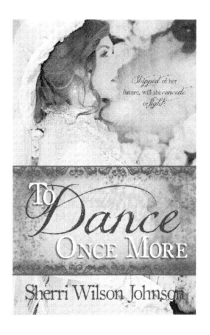

Marriage was the last thing on her mind. Now it may be her only choice.

Debutante Lydia Barrington lives a carefree, protected existence on Live Oaks Plantation in Florida. While her sisters happily prepare for their traditional roles as women and talk of courting, Lydia dreams of adventure and independence. She counts the days until she can leave home to explore the world, to leave behind the confining expectations of her family and community—and her God. Even her friendship with handsome Hamilton Scarbrough isn't enough to hold her back…until they dance, and her heart considers love.

Confused by her heart's betrayal, Lydia struggles to gain her independence. Then she overhears a private conversation about a business deal that has everything to do with her future. Now she's faced with the biggest decision of her life—to concede or to fight. Either choice will require great sacrifice…and, perhaps, countless rewards. In an attempt to escape her imminent destiny, Lydia scrambles to find a solution—at all costs. Amidst the trials that follow, as Lydia runs out of time, she learns the meaning of sacrifice, forgiveness, hope and faith. Stripped of her future, will she concede or fight?

Will she ever be able TO DANCE ONCE MORE?

Purchase on Amazon!

Made in the USA
Charleston, SC
26 October 2015